The Lure of the North

by
Harold Bindloss

The Lure of the North
by Harold Bindloss

Copyright © 2024

All Rights reserved.

No part of this publication may be reproduced, stored in a retrieval system, or transmitted in any form or by any means, electronic, mechanical, photocopying or Otherwise, without the written permission of the publisher.
The author/editor asserts the moral right to be identified as the author/editor of this work.

ISBN: 978-93-63054-96-7

Published by

DOUBLE 9 BOOKS
2/13-B, Ansari Road
Daryaganj, New Delhi – 110002
info@double9books.com
www.double9books.com
Tel. 011-40042856

This book is under public domain

ABOUT THE AUTHOR

Harold Edward Bindloss was an English novelist who published a number of adventure tales set in western Canada, as well as in England and West Africa. His writing was mostly based on his own experiences as a seaman, dock worker, farmer, and planter. Bindloss was born on April 6, 1866 in Wavertree, Liverpool, England. The eldest son of Edward Williams Bindloss, an iron dealer who employed six men at the time of the 1881 census. Bindloss has three sisters and four brothers. He spent several years at sea and in several colonies, most notably in Africa, before returning to England in 1896, his health ravaged by malaria. He appears to have started out as a clerk in a shipping office, but this did not suit his adventurous nature, and he later became a farmer in Canada, a sailor, a dock worker, and a planter. He returned to England in 1896, likely from West Africa, afflicted with malaria. Given that he spent more than a decade at sea and in the colonies, it is likely that his time overseas was divided into two parts: first as a youth, and then as a young man after 1891.

CONTENTS

Chapter I
Thirlwell Makes His Choice 7

Chapter II
Strange's Story 14

Chapter III
Agatha Makes A Promise 21

Chapter IV
Strange's Partner 27

Chapter V
A Night's Watch 32

Chapter VI
Father Lucien's Adventure 39

Chapter VII
Agatha's Resolve 45

Chapter VIII
The Burglar 51

Chapter IX
Agatha Asks Advice 57

Chapter X
Thirlwell Gets A Letter 63

Chapter XI
Stormont Finds A Clue 69

Chapter XII
On The Trail 74

Chapter XIII
The Prospectors' Return 80

Chapter XIV
Stormont Disowns A Debt 86

Chapter XV
The Grand Rapid 92

Chapter XVI
The Pit-Prop 98

Chapter XVII
Drummond Offers Help 103

Chapter XVIII
The Hand In The Water..110

Chapter XIX
A Lost Opportunity 115

Chapter XX
The Plunge 121

Chapter XXI
The Wilderness...127

Chapter XXII
Before The Wind 134

Chapter XXIII
Strange's Legacy 141

Chapter XXIV
Agatha Resumes Her Journey 148

Chapter XXV
The Broken Range 156

Chapter XXVI
The Lode...164

Chapter XXVII
THIRLWELL'S DULLNESS..171

Chapter XXVIII
Stormont Tries A Bribe..177

Chapter XXIX
GEORGE REPROACHES HIMSELF 185

Chapter XXX
A Change Of Luck 192

Chapter XXXI
Thirlwell's Reward 200

Chapter I
Thirlwell Makes His Choice

Dinner was nearly over at the big red hotel that stands high above the city of Quebec, and Thirlwell, sitting at one of the tables, abstractedly glanced about. The spacious room was filled with skilfully tempered light that glimmered on colored glasses and sparkled on silver; pillars and cornices were decorated with artistic taste. A murmur of careless talk rose from the groups of fashionably dressed women and prosperous men, and he heard a girl's soft laugh.

All this struck a note of refined luxury that was strange to Thirlwell, who had spent some years in the wilds, where the small, frost-bitten pines roll across the rocks and muskegs of North Ontario. One lived hard up there, enduring arctic cold, and the heat of the short summer, when bloodthirsty mosquitoes swarm; and ran daunting risks on the lonely prospecting trail. Now it looked as if chance had offered him an easier lot; he could apparently choose between the privations of the wilderness and civilized comfort, but while he grappled with a certain longing he knew this was not so. He had adopted the pioneers' Spartan code; one must stand by one's bargain, and do the thing one had undertaken.

For a few moments he was silent, lost in rather gloomy thought, with a frown on his brown face, and Mrs. Allott, his English relative, studied him across the table. On the whole, Jim Thirlwell had improved in Canada, and she thought he would be welcomed if he returned to England. She had been his mother's friend, and during the week or two they had now spent together, had decided that if he proved amenable she would help him to make a career. Indeed, it was largely on Thirlwell's account she had accompanied her husband on his American tour.

Jim had certain advantages. He was not clever, but his remarks were sometimes smarter than he knew. Then he had a quiet voice and manner that impressed one, even when one differed from him, as one often did. He was not handsome, and his face was rather thin, but his features were well-defined, and she liked his firm mouth and steady look. His figure was good and marked by a touch of athletic grace. Then she was, on the whole, satisfied with the way he chose and wore his clothes. His mother had held a leading place in the exclusive society of a quiet cathedral town, until her husband lost his small fortune. Mrs. Allott understood that something might have been saved had Tom Thirlwell been less scrupulous; but Tom had unconventional views about money, and Jim was like his father in many ways. Mrs. Allott, having done her best to enlighten him, hoped he would now see where his advantage lay.

"You are not very talkative, Jim," she said.

Thirlwell looked up with an apologetic smile, but his eyes rested on the girl by Mrs. Allott's side. Evelyn Grant was young and attractive, but there was something tame about her beauty that harmonized with her character. Thirlwell had not always recognized this; indeed, when they were younger, he had indulged a romantic tenderness for the girl. This, however, was long since, and the renewal of their friendship in Canada left him cold. Evelyn was gracious, and he sometimes thought she had not forgotten his youthful admiration, but she did not feel things much, and he suspected that she had acquiesced in Mrs. Allott's rather obvious plot because she was too indolent to object. For all that, he imagined that if he took a bold line she would not repulse him, and by comparison with his poverty Evelyn was rich. Then he banished the thought with an unconscious frown.

"Oh, well, I suppose it's our last evening together, and one feels melancholy about that," he said.

"But I thought you were coming to New York with us," Mrs. Allott objected.

Evelyn was talking animatedly to a young American, but looked round with languid carelessness.

"Are you really not coming, Jim?" she asked.

Then, without waiting for Thirlwell's answer, she resumed her talk, and Mrs. Allott wondered whether the girl had not overdone her part. After all, she must have known why she had been brought.

"I think not," said Thirlwell. "Very sorry, of course, but there's only a week of my holiday left and I have some business in South Ontario. Then I must go back to the bush."

"That's ridiculous, Jim," Mrs. Allott rejoined. "You know you needn't go back to the bush at all. Besides, we hoped you had decided to come to England." She paused and touched Evelyn. "Do you hear what he says? Can't you persuade him to be sensible?"

Evelyn turned and looked at Thirlwell with a careless smile. She was very composed, but Mrs. Allott thought she noted a trace of heightened color.

"Oh, no; it would be useless for me to try. Nobody could persuade Jim to do what he does not want."

"Aren't you taking something for granted?" asked Allott, who sat with the others, but had been silent. "Jim hasn't admitted that he doesn't want to come."

The girl gave Thirlwell a tranquil glance in which there was a hint of mockery.

"He has only a week left, and I imagine knows better than we do what will please him best," she replied, and turned to her companion.

"What have you to say to that?" Allott asked Thirlwell, with a twinkle.

"It looks as if Evelyn knew my character—I suppose I am obstinate. But I don't think she has stated the case correctly. It isn't that I don't want to come. Unfortunately, I can't."

The other guests were leaving the tables and Mrs. Allott, getting up, gave her husband a meaning glance.

"Then I must let Stephen talk to you. You may listen to his arguments; I have exhausted mine."

"You could not expect me to succeed where you have failed," Allott remarked, and touched Thirlwell as Mrs. Allott and Evelyn went away. "Shall we go upstairs for a smoke?"

A lift took them up, and Allott lighted a cigarette when they entered an unoccupied room. The evening was hot, and Thirlwell sat on the ledge of the open window and looked out upon the river across the climbing town. Church spires, the steep roofs of old houses, and the flat tops of modern blocks, rose in the moonlight through a thin gray haze of smoke. Lower down, a track of glittering silver ran across to the shadowy Levis ridge, along the crest of which were scattered twinkling lights. Presently Allott, who was well preserved and rather fat, turned to Thirlwell.

"I hope you won't be rash, Jim, and throw away the best chance you may ever get."

"You mean Sir James's offer of the post with the big engineering firm?"

"I mean that and other things," said Allott dryly. "Perhaps I have spoken plainly enough; you are not a fool!"

"Thanks! I don't claim much wisdom and I am sometimes rash. But perhaps we had better stick to Sir James's offer. Why does he make it now, after standing off when I needed help some years since?"

"We'll take the offer first," Allott agreed. "Sir James had not been knighted and pulled off the big business combine then. He hadn't as much influence, and perhaps wanted to see what you could do. I expect he was surprised when you got and kept the mining job in Canada. Anyhow, you're his namesake and nearest relative. My wife, you know, comes next."

"He left my father alone in his trouble," said Thirlwell grimly. "I wonder why they gave him his title. There were things done when the combine was made the shareholders didn't know, besides injustices to the staffs. You see, I had friends—"

"What has that to do with you? He offers you a good post, with a hint about favors to come."

"The post is good," Thirlwell agreed, with a thoughtful look. "In a way, I'd have been glad to take it; but I can't very well."

"Your engagement at the little wild-cat mine is an obstacle? After all, there are other engineers in Canada; I don't suppose your employers would suffer much inconvenience if you gave up the job."

"There's a year yet to go, besides an understanding that I'd stay until we got down to the deep vein."

"For very small pay? Much less than you're now offered, and with no prospects?"

"My employers are straight people and pay me as much as they can afford. They treat me well, though they're a small firm and the mine is not prospering. In fact, I expect they'll have some trouble to hold out until we reach good ore."

"The risk of their not holding out is rather a curious argument for your staying."

Thirlwell was silent for a few moments, and his face was hard when he resumed: "I know something about the combine's methods—Masters, who's still with one of the companies Sir James bought up, writes to me. I suppose one mustn't be too fastidious, but there are things the man who takes the post I'm offered will be expected to do; things I haven't done yet and mean to leave alone. You have often to throw your scruples overboard when you pay big dividends."

Allott chuckled. "The combine does not pay big dividends. It's a grievance of the shareholders'."

"Oh, well; Sir James was knighted, and I hear about another director building a hospital. One doesn't get honors for nothing. They're expensive."

"Jim," said Allott reproachfully, "you're talking like your father, and while airing one's views may be harmless, trying to live up to them doesn't always pay. Taking that line cost him much; I thought you wiser."

Thirlwell colored. "My father was an honest man. If I can live as he did, I shall be satisfied."

"Well, for some reason, Sir James is keen about bringing you back, and if you state the terms on which you'll come, I imagine he'll agree. This should make things easier, and I believe he'll be responsible if you pay your employers a fine to let you off."

Thirlwell was silent and looked out of the window. The hum of traffic came up from the dark gaps between the buildings and he heard a locomotive bell and the clash of freight-cars by the wharf. Then the hoot of a deep whistle rang across the town, and red and white flashes pierced the darkness down the river. A big liner, signaling her tug, was coming up stream, and presently her long hull was marked by lights that rose in tiers above the water. He watched her as she swung in to the wharf with her load of cheering immigrants.

It reminded him of his landing in Canada, and he looked back upon the disappointments and hardships he had borne in the country. He had soon found there was no easy road to wealth, and life had so far been an arduous struggle. He had known poverty, hunger, and stinging cold, and now his pay left little over when he had satisfied his frugal needs. All would be different if he went back to England, and he pondered over Allott's specious arguments. There was no reason he should not take the offered post if he could do so on his terms, and it was possible that his employers would release him. He was thirty years of age, had long practised self-denial, and would soon get old. Why should he not enjoy some prosperity before it was too late? Allott had said enough, but did not know this and had not finished yet.

"There's another matter, Jim," he resumed. "You can't think about marrying while you stay in the bush."

"I don't know that I want to marry. I couldn't support a wife."

"Why not, if you chose a wife with money?"

"Then she'd have to support me. Besides, I expect it would be hard to find a rich girl willing to marry a poor engineer."

Allott made a sign of impatience. "Let's be frank! The matter's delicate, and perhaps requires a lighter touch than mine, but I understand that Helen has given you a hint."

"She has," said Thirlwell, with some grimness. "I hoped you'd both let the thing go when she saw my attitude."

"We'll let it go after the next few minutes, if you like, but there is something to be said. Evelyn is an attractive girl, and has some money; besides which, Sir James would approve her marrying you. He has hinted that he'll give you a chance of making your mark in England if he is satisfied. Evelyn's relations know this, and it was significant that they agreed when Helen invited her to join us. As the girl consented, I might perhaps go farther—"

Thirlwell stopped him. "Why is Sir James anxious to help me?"

"We can only guess. Perhaps he feels you have a claim and he has neglected you. Then he may think you will do him credit and realize the ambitions he's getting too old to carry out. He has noted that you have inherited your father's character, and I've heard him remark that while Tom Thirlwell had extravagant notions, he certainly had brains. However, we were talking about Evelyn."

Thirlwell, exercising some self-control, lighted a cigarette and gave Allott a steady look.

"Then we'll finish the talk. Evelyn is a charming girl; amiable, pretty, tranquil, but there's no ground for believing she has contemplated marrying me."

"Suppose we admit that's possible?" said Allott, with a meaning smile. "I imagine, because I know you both, that if you were firm enough, you could, so to speak, carry her away. Since you own that she's charming, why don't you try?"

"If you are curious, you can take it that Sir James's gratuitous approval is an obstacle. I shall not marry to please him or let him plan my career. I mean to stand on my own feet and not be ruled by a greedy old man's caprices. Now you understand this, we'll say no more about the thing."

Allott shrugged. "Very well! I've done my best, and since you mean to take your own line, wish you success. Perhaps we had better go downstairs."

Evelyn was talking to the young American when they crossed the big hall and she smiled as they passed, but an hour later Thirlwell saw her alone. She beckoned him carelessly and indicated a place near her in a corner seat.

"So Allott has not persuaded you to come with us!" she remarked.

"No," said Thirlwell. "Very sorry, but there are matters I can't neglect."

"We shall miss you," she said, with a side glance. "I suppose you are not coming to England afterwards?"

"I'm afraid not," Thirlwell answered.

Then, to his surprise, she gave him a rather curious smile. "From the beginning I didn't think you would come."

"Ah!" said Thirlwell. "Still I don't see why—"

"That doesn't matter," she answered calmly. "After all, I dare say it's better in many ways that you should stay in Canada, and I wish you luck." She paused a moment and resumed: "I want you to feel that I do wish it. But Mrs. Allott is waiting for me. We shall, no doubt, see you before we start."

She left him puzzled but relieved. Next morning he stood on the platform of the Grand Trunk station, and Evelyn, leaning on the rails of a vestibule, smiled and waved her hand as the train rolled away.

Chapter II
Strange's Story

After Allott's departure Thirlwell went to Montreal and spent two depressing days transacting some business for his employers. Quebec was quiet and picturesque, and a cool, refreshing breeze blew up the river from the Laurentian wilds, but Montreal, shut in by the wooded mountain, sweltered in humid heat. Then the streets were being torn up to lay electric mains, and sand and cement blew about from half-finished concrete buildings. Thirlwell did not like large cities, and after the silence of the bush, the bustle of the traffic jarred.

He had, however, better grounds for feeling depressed. His employers trusted him, and actuated by loyalty as well as professional pride, he had resolved to make their rather daring venture a success. Now this looked difficult. Money was scarce, and he found credit strangely hard to get. The mining speculators he called upon received him coldly, and although he had a warmer welcome from the manufacturers of giant-powder and rock-boring machines, they demanded prompt payment for their goods. When Thirlwell stated that this was impossible they told him to come again.

It was known that there was silver in the rocks that run back into the North-West Territories, but nobody had found ore that would pay for refining. The rich strike in Ontario had not been made yet, and the prospectors who pushed into the forests with drill and dynamite were regarded as rash enthusiasts. Bankers were cautious, and declined to accept rusty mining plant and a shaft in the wilderness as good security.

On the evening before he left Montreal, Thirlwell sat in the hall of his hotel, listening to the clanging street-cars and the rattle of the Grand Trunk trains. Poisoned flies dropped upon the tables and an electric fan made an unpleasant whirring as it churned the humid air. Had his mood been normal the heat and noise would not have disturbed Thirlwell, but now they jarred.

His visit had been a failure, and his employers must develop the mine without the help of the latest machines. He doubted if they could finance the undertaking until they struck the vein. Then it looked as if he had been rash to reject Sir James's offer. He had thrown away a chance of winning prosperity and perhaps fame in England, for he knew he had some talent and he was ambitious. Instead he had chosen exhausting labor and stern self-denial in the wilds. The life had some compensations, but they were not very obvious then. It was, however, too late for regrets; he had chosen and must be content, and putting down the newspaper he was trying to read, he went to bed.

Two days later he sat in the garden of a new summer hotel on the shore of Lake Huron. A pine forest rolled down to the water past the pretty wooden building, and the air in the shade was cool and sweet with resinous smells. The lake glittered, smooth as glass, in the hot sun, but here and there a wandering breeze traced a dark-blue line across the placid surface. Along the beach the shadows of the pines floated motionless.

Thirlwell smoked and meditated on the errand that had brought him to the hotel. The clerk had told him that Miss Strange was on the beach, but he had not seen her yet and felt some curiosity about the girl whom he had arranged to meet. They had corresponded and he had brought a photograph he thought she would like to see, but on the whole he would sooner she had not asked for the interview. She might find it painful to hear the story he had to tell, and the thing would require some tact, more perhaps than he had.

In the meantime he wondered what she was like. Her letters indicated a cultivated mind, and he knew she had a post at a Toronto school; but one could not expect much from the daughter of the broken-down prospector he had met in the North. Strange had worked spasmodically at the mine, where he was employed because labor was scarce. He was not a good workman, and when he had earned a small sum generally bought provisions and went off into the bush to re-locate a silver lode he claimed to have found when he was young. He came back ragged and disappointed, and when liquor could be got indulged freely before he resumed his work.

Nobody believed his tale; Strange's lode was something of a joke. The miners called him a crank, and Thirlwell had doubted if he was quite sane, but he persisted in his search and sometimes Black Steve Driscoll went North with him. It was suspected that Driscoll made an unlawful profit by selling the Indians liquor, which perhaps accounted for his journeys with Strange. As they returned from the last expedition their canoe capsized in a rapid near the mining camp, and although Driscoll reached land exhausted, Strange's body was never found. Thirlwell knew his daughter's address, and sent her news of the accident, which led to an exchange of letters. Now he would shortly see her, give her the particulars she wanted, and then their acquaintance would end, although he liked the hotel and might stay for a few days' fishing.

His pipe went out and he was half asleep when a girl crossed the lawn. She came nearer, as if to avoid the glistening showers the nickeled sprinklers threw upon the thirsty grass, and Thirlwell watched her drowsily, noting her light, well-balanced movements and the grace of her tall figure. She wore a big white hat and a thin summer dress that he thought was very artistically made. There was something aristocratic about her, and he imagined she belonged to a party that had landed from a fine steam yacht. Then he noted with some surprise that she was coming to him.

She stopped and Thirlwell got up, imagining that she had made a mistake. Her face, like her figure, hinted at strength tempered by proud self-control. She had brown hair with a ruddy tint that caught the light, gray eyes that met his with a calm, inquiring glance, and firm red lips. Thirlwell was not a critic of female beauty, but he saw that she had dignity and charm. In the meantime, he wondered what she wanted.

"Mr. Thirlwell, I suppose?" she said.

He bowed and she resumed: "Then I must thank you for coming here to meet me. I am Agatha Strange."

It cost Thirlwell an effort to hide his surprise; indeed, he wondered with some embarrassment whether he had succeeded, for this was not the kind of girl he had expected to meet.

"It was not much out of my way, and I wanted to see the lake," he replied, as he brought a chair.

She thanked him, and sitting down was silent for a few moments while she gazed across the lawn. Some of the guests were sitting in the shadow by the water's edge, their summer clothes making blotches of bright color among the gray rocks. Out on the lake, a young man knelt in the stern of a canoe, swinging a paddle that flashed in the sun, while a girl trailed her hand in the sparkling water. As the craft passed the landing she began to sing. No breath of wind ruffled the surface now, and the dark pine-sprays were still. A drowsy quietness brooded over the tranquil scene.

"It is very beautiful," she said slowly. "Different, one imagines, from the rugged North!"

"Very different," Thirlwell agreed, and took out a photograph. "You will see that by the picture I promised to bring."

Agatha took the photograph. It showed a broad stretch of sullen water with a strip of forest on the other side. The pines were ragged and stunted and some leaned across each other, while the gloomy sky was smeared by the smoke of a forest-fire. In the foreground, angry waves broke in foaming turmoil among half-covered rocks. No soft beauty marked the river of the North, and the land it flowed through looked forbidding and desolate.

"The Shadow River," said Thirlwell. "You can see the Grand Rapid. I have marked a cross where the canoe upset."

Agatha said nothing for a few moments, and Thirlwell was relieved. He saw she felt keenly, but she was calm. In the meantime he waited; one learns to wait in the North.

"Thank you; I would like to keep the picture," she said by and by, and gave him a level glance. "I suppose you knew my father well?"

"I knew him in a way," Thirlwell answered cautiously, because he did not want to talk about Strange's habits. Perhaps the girl knew her father's weakness, and if not, it was better that she should think well of him. Yet Thirlwell imagined she understood something of his reserve.

"Ah!" she said, "you knew him in the bush, but not when he lived at home with us. I should like to tell you his story."

"Not if it is painful."

"It is painful, but I would sooner you heard it," she replied. "For one thing, you have been kind—" She paused, and when she resumed there was a faint sparkle in her eyes. "I want you to understand my father. He was my hero."

Thirlwell made a vague gesture. He had seen Strange, half drunk, reeling along the trail to the mine, but this did not lessen his sympathy for the girl. He hoped she had taken his sign to imply that he was willing to listen.

"To begin with, do you believe in the silver lode?" she asked.

"One disbelieves in nothing up yonder," Thirlwell tactfully replied. "It's a country of surprises; you don't know what you may find. Besides, there is some silver—I'm now sinking a shaft—"

Agatha smiled and he saw she had the gift of humor. The smile softened her firm lips and lighted her eyes.

"I imagine you are cautious. In fact, you are rather like the picture I made of you after reading your letters."

Thirlwell felt embarrassed and said nothing, as was his prudent rule when his thoughts were not clear.

"My father found the ore many years since, when he was employed by the Hudson's Bay Company," she resumed. "The factory was in the Territories, three or four hundred miles north of your mine, and the agent sent him out, with a dog-train and two Indians, to collect some furs. They had to make a long journey, and were coming back, short of food, when they camped one evening beside a frozen creek. The water had worn away the face of a small cliff, and the frost had recently split off a large slab. That left the strata cleanly exposed, and my father noticed that near the foot of the rock there was a different-colored band. They were making camp in the snow then, but he went back afterwards when the moon rose and the Indians were asleep, and broke off a number of bits. The stones were unusually heavy. Doesn't that mean something?"

"Silver has a high specific gravity; so has lead. Sometimes one finds them combined."

"I have a piece here," said Agatha, taking out a small packet. "My father gave it me when I was a child, and I brought it, thinking I might, perhaps, show it to you."

Thirlwell, examining the specimen, missed something of her meaning, and did not see that her decision to show him the ore was a compliment. He looked honest, and strangers often trusted him. His friends had never known him abuse their confidence.

"Yes," he said at length. "I think it's silver. Traces of lead, and perhaps copper, too; you seldom find silver pure. But won't you go on with the tale?"

"The party's food was getting short. That meant they would starve if they did not reach the factory soon, and they set off again at dawn. There was no time to prospect and deep snow covered the ground, but my father made what he called a mental photograph of the spot. It was a little hollow among the rocks, with a willow grove by the creek, and in the middle there were two or three burned pines. If you drew a line through them it pointed nearly north, and where it touched the cliff you turned east about twenty yards."

"Aren't you rash to tell me this?" Thirlwell asked.

Agatha smiled. "On the whole, I think not; but nothing I could tell would be of much use to you. My father, although he had been there, could not find the spot again."

She paused a moment and then went on: "When they reached the factory he showed the specimens to the agent, who said they were worthless and laughed at him. But it was perhaps significant that he was not sent that way again. One understands that the Hudson's Bay directors were jealous of their game preserves."

"Furs paid better than silver," Thirlwell agreed. "They didn't want miners with dynamite and noisy machines to invade the solitudes and frighten the wild animals away."

"My father, going south on a holiday, met my mother and gave up his post when they were married. She had a little money, enough to open a small store, and for her sake he started business in a new wooden town. He did not like the towns, and I know when I got older that he often longed for the wild North, but although the place grew and the business prospered, he could not spare the time and money to look for the lode. He wanted to give my brother a good education and start him well, and after a time I was sent to a university."

"That explains something," Thirlwell remarked, and then pulling himself up, added: "If you take proper appliances, a prospecting expedition costs much. But did your father often talk about the lode?"

"No; not unless it was to me."

"But why did he tell you and not your brother?"

"George was very practical; I was romantic and my father something of a dreamer. We lived happily at home, but I felt that he needed sympathy that he did not get. I think now my mother knew he longed for the North, and was afraid the longing might grow too strong and draw him back. When he did speak of the silver she smiled. I suppose when you have known the wilderness its charm is strong?"

She stopped and her face was gravely thoughtful as she looked across the shining water towards the faint blur of a pine forest on a distant point, and Thirlwell felt as if they had been suddenly united by a bond of understanding.

"Yes," he said. "It's a stern country and one has much to bear; but it calls. One fears the hardships, cold, and danger—but one goes."

Agatha looked up quietly, but he noted the gleam in her eyes.

"You *know*! Well, you can imagine what it cost my father to resist the call, but he did resist for many years. He loved my mother, but I think he hated the growing town; then there was the dream of riches that might be his. He was not greedy, and my brother did not need money. George had a talent for business and his employers soon promoted him; but I was fond of science, and it was my father's ambition that I should make independent researches and not be forced to work for pay."

She hesitated, and then went on: "Perhaps I am boring you, but I wanted you to understand what his duty must have cost. You see, you only knew him in the bush, and after he went back I noted a difference in his letters. They were sometimes strange; he seemed to be hiding things. I think he felt the disappointment keenly and lost heart."

Thirlwell saw she suspected something, and replied: "Disappointment is often numbing; but your father never lost his faith in the lode."

"Nor have I lost mine," said Agatha. "But we will not talk about that yet. He brought us up and started us well; then my mother died, and nobody had any further claim on him. His duty was done, and though he was getting old, he went back to the North. Well, I have told you part of his story, and you know the rest."

"It is a moving tale," said Thirlwell, with quiet sympathy.

He thought she felt it was necessary to defend her father, and she had done so. Indeed, he admitted that one must respect the man who had, with uncomplaining patience, for years carried on his disliked task for his wife and children's sake. Longing for the woods and the silent trail, Strange must have found it irksome to count dollar bills and weigh groceries in the store; but he had done his duty, and borne hardship and failure when at last freedom came. Still the girl must not know what he had become.

Agatha asked him a number of questions and then got up. "Thank you," she said. "I will take the photograph and would like you to keep the specimen of ore."

"I will keep it; but I wonder why you wish to give it me?"

She smiled. "I believe in the lode and would like you to believe in it, too. You are a mining engineer and can find out if there is much silver in the stone."

Then she crossed the lawn to the hotel veranda and left Thirlwell thoughtful.

Chapter III
Agatha Makes A Promise

Next morning Thirlwell wrote to his employers, stating that he meant to take another week's holiday, and smiled as he reflected that the letter would arrive too late for them to refuse. The hotel was comfortable, he had met one or two interesting people, and was told the fishing was good; besides, he thought he would not be badly needed at the mine just then. For all that, he was not quite persuaded that these were sufficient reasons for neglecting his work, and when he went through the hall with the letter in his hand he put it into his pocket instead of the box. He would think over the matter again before the mail went out. Then as he crossed the veranda Agatha came up from the beach and gave him a smile.

"You are out early," Thirlwell remarked.

"I like the morning freshness and have been on the lake."

"It looks as if you had hurt yourself," said Thirlwell, noting a small wet handkerchief twisted round her hand.

Agatha laughed. "Not seriously; I blistered my fingers trying to paddle. I have been practising since I came, but it is difficult to keep the canoe straight when you are alone."

"That's so," Thirlwell agreed. "The back-feathering stroke is hard to learn."

"For all that, I mean to learn it before I go."

"Perhaps I could teach it you. How long have you got?"

"A fortnight," she said, moving on, and when she left him Thirlwell went to the mail-box and dropped in his letter.

Afterwards he felt annoyed that he had done so, and wondered whether he had weakly given way to a romantic impulse, but next morning he went down to the beach and found the girl launching a canoe. Making her sit near the middle, he knelt in the stern and drove the canoe across the shining water with vigorous strokes. Agatha wore a white jersey and had left her hat, and he noted the color the cool wind brought to her face and how the light sparkled on her hair.

By and by they skirted a rocky island where resinous smells drifted across the water and the reflections of tall pines wavered round the canoe, until he ran the craft on a shingle point and they changed places. Agatha took the single-bladed paddle and although her hands were sore made some progress while he instructed her. After a time she stopped and let the canoe drift in the hot sunshine.

"I think you'd soon make a good *voyageur*," Thirlwell remarked. "For one thing, you're determined; I saw you wince once or twice and imagine the paddle-haft hurt."

"I must learn to use the pole yet, and mean to try it in the river by and by. You must pole, I think, when you go up a fast stream?"

"That is so, when you can't use the tracking line. But I don't see why you are anxious to learn."

"I have an object," Agatha answered with a smile.

"Then why don't you practise canoeing at Toronto?"

"The trouble is that I haven't time. You see, I teach all day."

"But you have holidays and the evenings."

"My evenings are occupied by study."

"I don't know if it's wise to over-work yourself for the advantage of your pupils," Thirlwell remarked. "At one time, I was very keen about my profession, but soon found it a mistake to tire my brain for my employer's benefit. But what do you study?"

"Science; chemistry and geology, but not in order to teach the girls."

"Well, I suppose knowledge is worth getting for its own sake. Anyhow, I thought so, but you learn when you undertake rude mining that the main thing is to be able to make a practical use of what you know. In fact, that's often better than knowing much."

"Perhaps so," Agatha agreed. "Some day I hope to make a good use of what I have learned."

"About canoeing, or geology?"

"About both," said Agatha. "Now, however, I think we'll make for the landing. Breakfast will be ready soon."

Thirlwell saw no more of her during the day, but she came down to the beach in the evening and he gave her another lesson. As they paddled home he thought she looked tired, and asked: "Where have you been since morning?"

Agatha indicated a ridge of high ground with a few pines on its summit that rose indistinctly at some distance across the shadowy forest.

"I took my lunch with me and went up there."

"But it must be a two or three hours' walk. Is there a trail?"

"A loggers' trail. It's partly grown up and broke off altogether when I got near the rocks. After that I had a rough scramble, but I like the woods and try to walk as much as possible in my holidays."

"Well, no doubt, walking is good for one. But don't the girls in Toronto prefer the street cars?"

"I don't go long walks for health's sake," Agatha answered with a smile. "But I think some people I know are waiting. Can you paddle faster?"

The canoe's bows lifted out of a wisp of foam as Thirlwell swung the paddle, and in a few minutes he helped the girl to land. After this, their acquaintance ripened fast and Agatha went fishing with him on the lake and, by disused logging trails, long distances into the shadowy bush. Thirlwell imagined she knew this excited some remark, but he saw there was an imperious vein in the girl, who did what she thought fit, without heeding conventions. Besides, no touch of sentiment marked their friendship; she accepted him as a comrade who could teach her something about lake and forest, and he was satisfied with this.

Yet he was puzzled. It was strange that an attractive girl should wish to learn something of the bush-man's skill, but she obviously meant to do so. Although it often cost her an effort to follow him, she would not let him turn back when they came to an angry rapid or a belt of tangled woods. She certainly had charm besides having pluck, because when she did not go fishing young women as well as young men gathered round her on the shady lawn. It was hard to imagine why a girl like this should practise walking long distances and combine the study of canoeing with geology.

The fortnight slipped by and on the last evening Thirlwell took Agatha out upon the lake. They were later than usual and as they stole across the glassy water the pines on a western headland cut black and sharp against an orange glow. To the east a faint track of silver ran back into the blue distance under the moon. It was very quiet except for the splash of the paddle and ripple at the bows, but somewhere in the shadows a loon was calling. By and by the lights of the hotel faded and they were alone in the dusk.

Thirlwell put down the paddle and lighted a cigarette. He had drawn nearer the girl in the last week; a curious feeling of confidence and liking united them, but he was not her lover and knew that if he drifted into philandering she would be repelled. Perhaps this was unusual, but she was different from other girls. Thirlwell could not tell how she differed, but he was satisfied that she did and let the matter go.

"You start for the mine to-morrow, don't you?" she asked presently.

"Yes," he said; "it's my last evening on the lake. There's something melancholy about the end of a holiday, but I don't think I have felt it as much before."

Agatha gave him a calm glance and saw he had not meant her to read a sentimental meaning in his admission. It was unconscious flattery and she was pleased.

"I can understand. One values the days of liberty when they are gone! But do you feel daunted by the thought of the work and hardship that waits you in the North?"

"Not in a way. Now and then you shrink from the arctic winter, but in summer, in spite of the mosquitoes, the bush gets hold of you. Sometimes you hate the solitude; but when you leave it you long to return."

"Ah," said Agatha, "I have not seen the wilderness, but next summer I hope to make an exploring trip."

"But where?"

"To the Shadow River and on into the Territories," she answered quietly. Thirlwell looked hard at her, and she smiled. "Yes; if things go well with me, I mean to look for the silver ore."

"Now I begin to understand! This is why you wanted to learn to manage a canoe and train yourself to walking through the bush. But it's a ridiculous undertaking. Your father, who found it, could not locate the ore again."

"I may be luckier. Luck counts for something when you go prospecting, doesn't it?"

"Success in prospecting is often due to luck," Thirlwell admitted. "But it's a very rough country where no food can be got. You will need canoes, tools, and tents, and two or three good packers to carry the outfit across the divides. This would be expensive. Then I doubt if you are strong enough to bear the strain; I imagine very few women could do so without breaking down."

"You have seen how I have tried to harden myself, but I have made other preparations. It's some time since I resolved to go, and every month I put by a little money. By next summer I ought to have enough."

"I wonder whether you found it easy to save."

"I did not," said Agatha, smiling. "Sometimes it was very hard; I should not have taken this holiday only that I wanted to get used to the lakes and woods. I am grateful for all you have taught me."

A thought that pleased him took shape in Thirlwell's brain, but he used some restraint. He must not encourage the girl in what he imagined was folly.

"The chance of your finding the vein is very small, and there's another thing. You have told me your father's story, and I have met men like him in the woods, who had wasted their money and lost their health following an illusion. The lode, so to speak, haunted him and made him restless when he might have been content at home, and then drove him into the wilds when he was old. It's dangerous to give oneself up to a fixed idea, and you mustn't let the infatuation get hold of you. It will bring you disappointment and trouble."

"The warning's too late," said Agatha in a curious quiet voice. "The infatuation has got hold of me, but one must follow one's bent, and life is tame if one does nothing that is not prudent and safe. Besides, romantic dreams sometimes come true."

"Not often," said Thirlwell dryly. "But why do you really want to go?"

"The silver is mine; my father gave it me. It looked as if my brother would prosper without his help, and I think he loved me best. Perhaps this was because I believed in the vein."

Thirlwell shook his head. "I cannot think you greedy."

"Then," said Agatha with a flush of color, "if you must have the truth, I feel I must finish my father's work. His son and his best friends thought him the victim of his imagination and the lode a joke; but if I succeed, his dreams will be justified."

Thirlwell said nothing for a minute or two; he saw that she was resolute and was moved by her staunch loyalty. After all, Strange's story was not uncommon; Thirlwell had known men leave work and home to follow an elusive clue to mineral treasure in the barren solitudes. Some had come back broken in fortune and courage, and some had not come back at all. Then while he mused the harsh cry of the loon rang through the dark. It fired his blood, and unconsciously he fixed his eyes on the North, for in summer the birds of the lakes and rivers push on towards the Pole. He had done his duty and tried to persuade the girl, but after all she was stronger and finer than Strange. It was possible that she might succeed, and he could help.

"When you go I hope you will let me come," he said. "We have the tools and outfit one needs for prospecting at the mine, and I could get the packers and canoes."

"But you don't believe I shall find the lode. Why do you want to come?"

"I know the bush," Thirlwell answered with a smile. "So far I've been prudent and stuck to my job, but I've felt the pull of the lone trail like other men. In fact, I'd rather like to do something rash, for a change."

"Have you never done anything rash?"

"Only once, I think. It needed all my pluck; but the curious thing is that it's now turning out better than I hoped."

Agatha pondered and then looked up. "It would be an advantage to have somebody I could trust to look after the packers and canoes; but the journey must be made at my cost. I couldn't let another undertake my duty."

"Then I may come? It's a promise?"

"Yes," said Agatha quietly; "when I am ready I will let you know. Now, however, we must get back to the hotel."

Thirlwell dipped the paddle, the canoe lurched, and her bow rose at his next vigorous stroke. The ripples she threw off widened into a fan-shaped wake that trailed away and was lost in a glitter of moonlight. The black pines on the point rose higher, resinous smells came out of the dark, and presently a row of lights twinkled ahead. Thirlwell ran the canoe alongside the landing and when they reached the veranda Agatha gave him her hand.

"You start early, I think," she said. "I have much to thank you for and am glad we have met."

He let her go and afterwards leaned against the rails. She had made him a promise and when they next met it would be beside a river of the North. But this was twelve months ahead; he felt it was a long time to wait.

Chapter IV
Strange's Partner

The day's work was over and Thirlwell and his employer sat, smoking and talking, in their shack at the Clermont mine. Scott was young and had once been fastidious, but, like Thirlwell, he wore work-stained overalls. For a time when they first came up, both had clung to a few of the refinements of civilization, but their grasp on these had slackened, and now they frankly admitted that it was too much of an effort to change their clothes when they were tired.

The shack was built of pine logs, notched where they crossed at the corners, and the seams were caulked with clay and moss. A big stove, now empty, stood at one end, its pipe running obliquely across the room before it pierced the iron roof, so as to radiate as much heat as possible. Plans, drawing instruments, and some books on mining, occupied a shelf on the wall; guns, fishing rods, and surveying tools a corner, and a plain, uncovered table the middle of the room. Besides this, there were two or three cheap folding chairs.

The door and window were open, although the mosquitoes were numerous, and the roar of the Shadow River and a smell of wood smoke came in. When he looked out, Thirlwell could see the ragged tops of the stunted pines cut against a pale-green glow. By and by Scott knocked out his pipe and stretched his legs. There was another partner, but he only visited the mine at intervals and had left it while Thirlwell was away.

"Brinsmead has gone to Nevada and probably won't come back," Scott remarked. "He has a plausible manner, but seems to have done no better in New York than you did in Montreal; it looks as if machinery agents are very shy about giving credit to the owners of half-developed mines. Anyhow, when he heard of a field for his talents in a Western town he didn't hesitate. Now he tells me that he finds the prospect of earning some money instead of spending it a refreshing change."

"It's lucky he didn't take his capital out of the Clermont," Thirlwell replied.

Scott laughed. "He couldn't take it out. Nobody would buy his share, and my fortune's represented by a shaft in danger of flooding and some cheap and antiquated boring plant. In fact, if we don't strike pay-dirt soon, the Clermont will go broke, and I imagine that's why Brinsmead skipped. After floating one or two small mines successfully, he has some reputation to lose, while I'm, of course, not an engineer or a business man." He paused and looked hard at Thirlwell. "I'd like you to stay and see me through, but wouldn't blame you if you quit."

"My reputation is not worth much and can be risked. Besides, I imagine we'll get down to the deep vein before the funds run out."

"I hope so! You're not a quitter, and we'll hold on while we can, but I think we'll talk about something else. Well, I've examined the specimen of ore you brought back. It looks like high-grade stuff and certainly carries enough metal to pay for smelting."

"What do you think about Strange's tale?"

Scott knitted his brows. "I did think the man a drunken crank and the lode an illusion that had grown on him by degrees until he really believed in the ore. When you get the tanking habit such things happen. One specimen certainly doesn't prove very much; but since Strange gave it to his daughter a long time before we knew him, I'm willing to revise my judgment."

"Miss Strange is persuaded that he did find the lode. She tells me he led a very industrious and sober life at home."

"It's rather curious you met the girl," Scott observed.

"I don't think so. When we found her address among the truck Strange had left with the foreman, it was the proper thing for me to tell her he was drowned. This led to another letter or two, and when I said I was going to Montreal she asked me to meet her."

"Is she like Strange?"

"Not at all," Thirlwell declared. "In fact, although her letters ought to have prepared me, I got something of a surprise. She was not the kind of girl I had expected to meet. I understand she teaches at a Toronto school."

"She must have some talent to get a post there," Scott remarked when he had asked the name of the school. Then he paused and vaguely indicated the North. "Well, it's a romantic story! Nobody knows yet what there is in the rocks up yonder, but we have heard of other prospectors striking pay-dirt and making nothing of their discovery. Rumors about mysterious lodes are common in a mineral belt, and while they're often imaginative, my notion is that now and then there's some fact behind the fiction. Fur-traders in Alaska heard such tales long before the Klondyke strike."

He stopped, for there were steps outside, and Thirlwell, leaning forward, saw a man come up the trail. The fellow had a dark, sullen face and wore an old gray shirt and ragged overalls. He walked with a slight limp, in consequence of getting his foot frost-bitten on a winter journey, but he was an expert trapper and had penetrated far into the wilds. When skins were scarce he worked at the mine, but generally left his employment after a drunken bout.

"I wonder whether Driscoll believes in Strange's lode," Scott resumed as the man went by. "He knew him better than anybody else. They went North together once or twice, and had been away some time when Strange was drowned coming back."

"Strange wouldn't tell Black Steve where he thought the lode was," Thirlwell objected. "I understand they only kept together until they had portaged their outfit across the divide."

"Strange would leave a trail a trapper could follow. Then I don't see why Steve stops here instead of locating on better hunting ground. It looks as if he didn't want to leave the Shadow."

"I don't see how stopping here would help him to find the lode," said Thirlwell, who went to the door.

It was getting dark and except for the turmoil of the river the bush was very still. The green behind the pines had faded, and they rose against the sky indistinctly in smears of shadowy blue. They had neither height nor beauty, but straggled back, battered and stunted by the winds, among the rocks until they faded from sight. There was not much to attract a white man in the desolation of tangled bush, but as he glanced across it, looking to the North, a hint of mystery in its silence appealed to Thirlwell. He felt that the wilderness challenged him to find a clue to the treasure it hid. Then he reflected with a smile that it was taking much for granted to admit that there was treasure there, and he went back into the shack and lighted the lamp.

A week later, he went up the river bank, one evening, with a fishing rod, and stopped at dusk at the tail of the Grand Rapid. He had gone farther than he meant and was tired after scrambling across slippery rocks and among the driftwood that lay about the bank. There was, however, a shorter way back, and lighting his pipe he sat down upon the gravel and looked about.

The sun had set some time since, but the light would not quite die out until just before the dawn, and the pines across the river rose against the green sky in a dark, broken-topped wall. Near his feet the bleached skeletons of trees, ground by floods and ice, glimmered a livid white, and beyond them the rapid frothed and roared in angry turmoil. The river had shrunk now the melted snow had flowed away, and rocks one seldom saw lifted their black tops above the racing foam. Inshore of the main rush, smooth-worn ledges ran in and out among shallow pools. A short distance ahead, the bush rolled down to the water's edge in a dark mass that threw back in confused echoes the din the river made.

By and by the mosquitoes that had followed Thirlwell got more numerous and when, in spite of the smoke, they settled upon his face and neck he reeled up his line ready to start. As he did so he thought he saw something move where the forest ran down to the river. The object was indistinct, but it looked like a man walking cautiously upon a ledge between the pools, and Thirlwell wondered what the fellow was doing there. The big gray trout had stopped rising, there were no Indians about, and the miners had not left the camp.

Thirlwell waited until the man moved out from the gloom of the trees. His figure was now distinct against the foam of the rapid, and he stooped as if he were looking down into a pool. Then he moved on, and Thirlwell, noting that he would soon pass in front of a dark rock, resolved to change his place in order to watch him better. Getting up, he went down to the water's edge, but came to a tangle of white branches that the river had thrown up. As he stopped he saw the man plainly, but when he looked up after scrambling over the driftwood there was nobody about.

This was strange and excited his curiosity. The other's figure would probably be invisible against the rock, but he must have moved rapidly to get in front of it. Then Thirlwell saw that where he stood the bush was no longer behind him. He had the inshore eddies for a background and the water reflected a faint light. There was no obvious reason why the other should be alarmed and try to steal away, but it looked as if he had done so.

Thirlwell sat down among the driftwood and waited, but saw no more of the man; and then going back quietly, turned into a trail that led to the mine. The trail was rough and narrow; in places, short brush had sprung up, and there were patches of outcropping rock. It would be difficult for anybody to follow it without making some noise, but although he stopped and listened no sound came out of the gloom.

He went on, pondering the matter with some curiosity. Since the miners were in camp, he imagined the man he had seen was Driscoll, who lived alone in a log shack near the bank. But, if this were so, what was Driscoll's object for wading among the reefs, and why had he stolen away when he thought he was watched? Thirlwell could not solve the puzzle, but he could find out if the fellow were Driscoll or not, because the trail passed his shack.

He walked faster, making as little noise as possible, and by and by reached a belt of thinner forest. He passed a fallen pine, from which he knew the shack was visible in daylight, and resolved to see if Driscoll was at home. If not, Thirlwell thought it would be safe to conclude that he had seen him among the reefs. A few moments later a light flashed among the trees, flickered once or twice, and then burned steadily. Thirlwell knew it came from the window of the shack, but it was curious that Driscoll had lighted his lamp. In summer, miners and prospectors went to bed at sunset, and Driscoll read no books or newspapers. Besides, if he wanted a light, why had he not got it before? It, however, looked as if the man had not been at the rapid and when Thirlwell passed the shack he saw his dark figure at the door.

"Who's that?" he asked, and when Thirlwell answered, added: "Watch out as you go down the gulch. There's a rampike across the trail."

When Thirlwell came to the burned pine he stopped abruptly as a thought struck him. Driscoll's voice had sounded breathless; perhaps the fellow had overdone his part. It might have been wiser for him to be silent. Driscoll often went fishing and knew the river well; now the water was low he could have saved some distance by crossing the uncovered reefs instead of scrambling along the curved bank. Besides, he had had a few minutes' start. After all, he might have been at the rapid and have hurried back in order to deceive the man who had disturbed him. Moreover, he had learned who the man was.

This, however, did not take Thirlwell far and he resumed his walk, wondering what Driscoll had been doing and why he feared to be disturbed. It was plain that he had taken some trouble to put Thirlwell off the track and might have succeeded had not the hoarseness of his voice given the latter a hint. Thirlwell felt puzzled, but could find no clue, and deciding that the matter was not important presently dismissed it. For all that, he resolved to watch Driscoll, but saw nothing to excite his suspicions for the next week or two. Then the man bought all the provisions Scott would let him have and loading his canoe started for the North.

Chapter V
A Night's Watch

Winter began unusually soon and a blizzard raged about the shack one evening when Scott and Thirlwell sat near the stove. The small room smelt of hot-iron and the front of the stove glowed a dull red, but the men shivered as the bitter draughts swept in. Thirlwell watched the skin curtain he had nailed across the window bulge while the snow beat savagely against the glass, and then picked up a book. Presently Scott hung a bearskin on the back of his chair.

"It's a pretty good hide although the forequarter's cut away," he said. "Still I don't know that I wanted the thing and reckon the half-breed who sold it me got its value in cartridges and food. Now transport's difficult, I hope he and his Indian friends won't bring us any more of the damaged stock they can't sell to the Hudson's Bay."

Thirlwell nodded. The rivers were frozen and canoeing was stopped, while the bush was deep in fresh, loose snow. It would be a long and strenuous business to break a trail to the south, and in winter the mine was often cut off from the settlements. Provisions sometimes ran short, but Scott found it hard to refuse the starving Indians a share of his supplies.

"You bought a fine skin," he resumed. "I haven't seen the thing since. What have you done with it?"

"I sent it away," said Thirlwell. "Old Musquash said he'd try to make the settlements and took it out for me."

"He'll probably get through, though I don't think a white man could. But I didn't know you had friends in Canada."

Thirlwell did not reply. He had bought the skin for Agatha and now wondered what she would think about his present, or whether she might feel he ought not to have sent it. Still he doubted if the skin would arrive, because the old half-breed would meet with many dangers on the way. Thirlwell pictured him hauling his sledge up thinly frozen rivers, crossing wide lakes swept by icy gales, and plunging into tangled forests smothered in snow. The thought of it emphasized the sense of isolation one often felt at the mine, but while he mused there was a knock at the door.

"I expect it's an Indian come to beg for food," Scott remarked and the door swung open.

The flame of the lamp leaped up and then nearly flickered out as a shower of snow blew in. The stove roared and the room got horribly cold, and for a moment or two a shaggy, white figure, indistinct in the semi-darkness, struggled to close the door. Then there was a sudden calm and when the light got steady an Indian in ragged furs leaned against the table, breathing hard and holding out a note.

"From Father Lucien," said Scott, who took the folded paper. "He's had a sick man on his hands for three or four days and wants one of us to relieve him. I allow I'd sooner stop here. It's pretty fierce to-night."

"Who's sick?" Thirlwell asked.

"Black Steve. I don't know that he has much claim on us, but Father Lucien's a good sort. I guess we've got to help him out."

Thirlwell nodded. Father Lucien was a French-Canadian missionary who had studied medicine, and, for the most part, lived with his wandering flock. In summer, he went North with canoe and tent, but generally returned in winter to a shack near the mine. Scott and Thirlwell had found his society pleasant when they sat round the stove on long cold nights, for the priest had been trained in Europe and knew the great world as he knew the Canadian wilds. A scholar and something of a mystic, he was marked by a wide toleration and liberality of thought.

"Who's going? Shall we draw cuts for it?" Scott resumed.

Thirlwell hesitated. He felt tired, the shack was warm, and he heard the blizzard rage among the tossing pines; but he was curious about Driscoll and something urged him to go to the priest's help.

"I'll take first turn. You can come along to-morrow if you're wanted," he said, and putting on his fur coat and cap, went out with the Indian.

When the door shut he let his companion take the lead, for his eyes were filled with water and snow. He knew the bush, but imagined that nobody but an Indian could find the trail that night, and to lose it would mean death. For some moments the icy gale stopped his breathing, and he stumbled forward, seeing nothing, until he struck a pine, which he seized and leaned against. Looking round, with his back to the wind, he noted that the shack had vanished, although he thought it was only a few yards off. There was nothing visible, but when the Indian touched him he pulled himself together and struggled on again.

It was a little warmer when they plunged into the bush, but the snow was soft and deep, and they stumbled over fallen branches and fell into thickets. Torn-off twigs rained upon their lowered heads, shadowy trunks loomed up and vanished, and Thirlwell could not tell where he was going; but the Indian plodded on, his white figure showing faintly through the snow. At length, when Thirlwell was nearly exhausted, another sound mingled with the scream of the gale, and he knew it was the turmoil of the Grand Rapid, where the furious current did not freeze. They were getting near the end of the journey, and he braced himself for an effort to reach Driscoll's shack. By and by a ray of light pierced the snow, surprisingly close, and a few moments later he reached the shelter of a wall.

A door opened, somebody seized his arm, and he stumbled into a lighted room. Throwing off his snow-clogged coat, he sat down in a rude chair and blinked stupidly as he looked about. His head swam, the warmth made him dizzy, and the tingling of his frozen skin was horribly painful. Then he began to recover and saw that the Indian had gone and Father Lucien sat by a bunk fixed to the wall. The priest wore an old buckskin jacket with a tasseled fringe, and long, soft moccasins, and looked like an Indian until one studied his thin face. His forehead was lined, as if by thought or suffering, and his skin was darkened by wind and frost, but the Indian's glance is inscrutable and his was calm and frank. One got a hint of patience and dignity.

"Thank you for coming," he said. "I would not have sent for you on such a night only that I cannot trust myself to keep awake and neglect just now might cost Driscoll's life. One sleeps soundly after watching for three nights."

Thirlwell glanced at the figure rudely outlined by the dirty blue blanket on the bunk. Driscoll's face was turned to the wall, but Thirlwell saw that his black hair was damp.

"What's the matter with Steve?" he asked.

"Pneumonia. Two of my people who passed the shack in the daytime saw a light burning. They went in and found him unconscious, an empty whisky bottle on the floor, and the stove burned out. They made a fire and then came for me."

"That's something of a compliment," Thirlwell remarked. "If it had happened before you came, they'd probably have cleaned out the shack and left Steve to freeze. I don't know that he'd have been regretted, and if the rumors about his selling the Indians liquor are true, imagine he's your worst enemy."

"He's a sick man. Besides, have you often seen my people drunk?"

"No," said Thirlwell thoughtfully; "I believe only once. But Steve didn't deny the thing when one of the boys at the mine called him a whisky runner, and I thought it curious, because there's a heavy penalty. I suppose he can't hear what we say?"

"He's unconscious, but has fits of weak delirium. Three or four o'clock may mark the turning, and if he lives until daybreak I'll feel hopeful. But do you imagine he didn't deny your workman's charge because it was true?"

"I'd have expected him to deny it whether it was true or not. That's what puzzled me. It looked as if he was willing to be suspected."

"Driscoll," said Father Lucien, "is a strange, dark man, but he needs our help and one of us must watch."

"I'm fresh and will take the first turn," Thirlwell offered, and pulled his chair to the stove when Father Lucien, wrapping himself in a blanket, lay down on the floor.

He found watching dreary and got very cold. The pines roared about the shack and the lamp flickered in the draughts, but the wind was falling and between the gusts one could hear the river. Drift-ice churned in the rapid and broke with jarring crashes upon the rocks. Once or twice Thirlwell thought the sound disturbed Driscoll, because he moved and muttered brokenly. Thirlwell, however, could not hear what he said, and getting drowsy with the dry warmth of the stove, struggled to keep awake. He was not sure that he altogether succeeded, for now and then his head fell forward and he roused himself with a jerk, but did not think he really went to sleep. For all that, some hours had passed when he moved his chair and looked at his watch. It was quieter outside and the roar of the river had got distinct. Then Thirlwell heard a blanket thrown back and glanced at the bunk.

Driscoll had turned his head and the light touched his face, which glistened with sweat. His eyes were wide open, his lips moved as if he tried to speak, and Thirlwell thought his brain was clear, but saw next moment that Driscoll was not watching him. He had a curious, strained look and gazed at the door, as if somebody had come in. The strange thing was that he looked afraid.

"I couldn't stop her with the back-stroke," he said hoarsely. "She rolled over as she swung across the stream."

Thirlwell shivered, because it was obvious that the sick man was going over what had happened the night Strange was drowned. His manner hinted that he was trying to excuse himself for something he had done. Shrinking back in the bunk, he resumed in a stronger voice: "I couldn't stop her! The stream was running fast."

Then he was silent for a time and Thirlwell heard the river rolling through its ice-bound channel and the dreary wailing of the pines. He felt disturbed; something in Driscoll's voice and look had jarred his nerves, and it cost him an effort not to waken Father Lucien. It was not time yet and the priest needed sleep. Driscoll lay quiet with his eyes shut, but presently moved and began to mutter. Thirlwell, leaning forward, caught the words: "I never had the thing; he took it with him."

The strained voice broke, Driscoll drew a hard breath, and feebly turned his face from the light. After this Thirlwell, whose curiosity was excited, had less trouble to keep awake, and at length roused Father Lucien, as he had been told. It was nearly three o'clock in the morning, the fire had sunk, and the shack was very cold. The wind had fallen and the bush was silent; one could hear the loose snow dropping from the boughs.

Father Lucien crossed the floor and after standing for a time beside the bunk came back and sat down by the stove.

"You can put in fresh wood; it won't disturb him now," he said. "He's sleeping well. I think the danger's over."

The cord wood snapped and crackled, the front of the stove got red, and sitting in a corner out of the draughts, they began to talk in low voices.

"Driscoll was delirious; he talked strangely," Thirlwell remarked. "Is a sick man's raving all such stuff as dreams?"

"Ah," said Father Lucien, "we know little yet about the working of the disordered brain, but the imagination sometimes centers on and distorts things that have happened. Did you get a hint of intelligence in what Driscoll said?"

"I did. He said he *never had the thing*. Somebody—Strange, perhaps—*took it with him*."

"Why do you think he meant Strange?"

"Because his mind was obviously dwelling on the night Strange's canoe capsized. He said it was an accident—he could not stop her swinging across the stream—as if he were answering somebody who accused him. The disturbing thing was that although delirious he looked horribly afraid."

Father Lucien was silent and Thirlwell went on: "You have been with him for three nights. Has he talked like this before?"

"Yes," said Father Lucien, quietly. "You can be trusted. I think he is afraid."

"Ah!" said Thirlwell, looking hard at him. "Then I wonder why the canoe capsized. Were they drunk, or was there a quarrel? But perhaps you know and cannot tell!"

"I do not know. Driscoll is not of my flock. He is ill and it is my business to cure his sickness, but I can go no farther. If he has other troubles, he would refuse my help."

"That is so," Thirlwell agreed. "There's a mystery about the capsize, and I'm curious. You see, I met Strange's daughter and she believes in the lode."

Father Lucien hesitated, and then went to a shelf.

"I will show you something," he said, and gave Thirlwell a small Russian leather wallet. It was well made, but worn and stained as if it had been soaked in water. "I found this when I undressed Driscoll," he went on. "It is not a thing you would expect a rude prospector to carry. But I found something else."

He held out a piece of broken stone and Thirlwell as he took it moved abruptly. He knew something about ore and saw that the stone had come from the same vein as the specimen Agatha had given him.

"I think Strange found the silver," Father Lucien said quietly.

Thirlwell knitted his brows. He had dark suspicions, but after all they had no solid foundation, and he thought it best to copy the missionary's reserve.

"We know Driscoll's character, and may have been mistaken about one thing. Is it logical to imagine that such a man would feel afraid?"

"Fear sometimes comes without remorse," said Father Lucien.

"Superstitious fear, working on a brain disordered by liquor and illness?"

"We will not argue about the proper name. It may be superstition, or something greater. I believe that retribution follows the offense."

Thirlwell looked hard at the other. "Well, I doubt if we will ever know the truth about Strange's death."

"It is possible," Father Lucien agreed. "Perhaps it is not important whether we know or not. One thing is certain: if wrong has been done, it will be made right, if not by the way we would choose, by another. I think we may leave it there."

"We must," said Thirlwell dryly. "There is nothing else to do. In the meantime, if I can't be useful, I'm going to sleep."

Day was breaking when he wakened and Father Lucien told him that Driscoll was better, but would need careful nursing for a time.

"Then Scott must come to-night," Thirlwell replied. "I've had enough of watching Steve, and don't mind admitting that your charity is greater than mine."

When he reached the shack he told Scott nothing about what he had heard, because he thought Father Lucien would sooner he did not. The latter knew when to be silent and it would do no good to talk about the matter unless something happened to throw a light upon the mystery. On the whole, he was relieved when Driscoll, who soon recovered, set off up river with a half-breed and a loaded hand-sledge.

Chapter VI
Father Lucien's Adventure

The snow was firm and the rivers were frozen hard when Thirlwell left the mine with two *Metis* trappers to examine an outcropping reef that one of the half-breeds had told him about. He was not very hopeful, but agreed with Scott, who thought it might be worth while to look at the reef, since the specimens the *Metis* had brought showed traces of silver and lead. Then Father Lucien had gone to visit some of his people who had camped for their winter trapping far up in the bush, the shack was lonely, and the frost hindered the work at the mine.

Winter is not a good time for prospecting, but travel is often easier then, for the hand-sledges run smoothly on the snow that covers fallen trunks and underbrush and levels the hollows. The muskegs are frozen and one can make fast marches along the rivers and across the lakes. Thirlwell had no tent, but it is not a great hardship for a well-fed man, wrapped in furs, to sleep beside a big fire behind a bank of snow, and he had no misadventures as he pushed into the wilds. The ore proved to be worthless, and soon after he started back he met an Indian who said he had seen Father Lucien going south with a dog-team two days before, and had found the trail of another white man near the spot where he and his friends had camped.

The clear, cold weather broke when Thirlwell began his homeward march. The sky was low and leaden, and a biting wind blew from the south. It drove the snow-dust into the men's smarting faces and froze their breath on their furs. Their hands stiffened on the sledge-traces and their feet got numb. The cold got worse when snow began to fall and when they camped one night Thirlwell noted that they had used more food than he thought. The transport of provisions is perhaps the main difficulty of a winter journey in the bush, for men who brave the arctic cold must be generously fed. Thirlwell, however, expected to reach the mine before their stores ran out, and set off at daybreak next morning in heavy, driving snow.

At dusk he camped in a clump of dry willows by a river. The snow had stopped, but a bitter wind blew down the valley and the cold was intense. When he had eaten a meal Thirlwell sat with his back to a snow bank and a big fire in front, holding up a moccasin to the blaze. This was necessary because moccasins absorb moisture during a long day's march, and the man who puts them on while damp risks getting frozen feet.

He was lighting his pipe when the *Metis* he had sent out for wood came back with an armful of branches and said he had seen a light up the river. Thirlwell put on his half-dried moccasins and reluctantly left the camp. He had met nobody but an Indian on the trail and was curious to know who was camping in those solitudes. Besides, it was possible that he might be able to get some supplies.

As he pushed through the willows the savage wind pierced him to the bone. The dry branches rattled and the pines upon the ridge above wailed drearily. The sky was clear and the frozen river, running back, white and level, through the dusky forest, glittered in the light of a half moon. This was all that Thirlwell saw for a few minutes, and then a twinkling light in the distance fixed his attention. It flickered, got brighter, and faded, and he knew it was a fire.

After a time he and the *Metis* left the river and climbed the steep bank. The fire had vanished, but the pungent smell of burning wood came down the biting wind, and by and by trails of smoke drifted past the scattered pines. Then as they struggled through a brake of wild-fruit canes a blaze leaped up among the the rocks and he saw an indistinct figure crouching beside a fire. The figure got up awkwardly and a few moments later Father Lucien gave Thirlwell his hand. The light touched his thin frost-browned face, which was marked by lines that pain had drawn.

"It's lucky you came, but, if you don't mind, we'll sit down," he said.

"If you're alone, you had better come back to our camp," Thirlwell replied. "Where's your truck and the dogs?"

Father Lucien indicated the torn blue blanket that hung from his shoulder. "All gone except this! But it's a long story and I can't walk."

"Then you have nothing to eat?" said Thirlwell sharply.

"Half a small bannock; I ate the rest this morning. The worst was I had only melted snow to drink."

Thirlwell made a sympathetic gesture, for men who camp in the frozen woods consume large quantities of nearly boiling tea. Then he turned to the half-breed and sent him back for his companion and the sledge.

"We'll haul you down the river as soon as they come," he said. "By good luck, we camped in perhaps the only place from which we could have seen your fire."

"Ah," said Father Lucien with a quiet smile, "I do not know if it was luck alone that made you choose the spot."

They sat down in the hollow among the rocks, and the missionary shivered although the fire snapped and threw out clouds of smoke close by. Thirlwell gave him his tobacco pouch.

"In the meantime, you can eat your bannock and then take a smoke. I'm curious to learn how you lost your outfit and the dogs."

Father Lucien ate the morsel of hard cake, and afterwards looked up. "Perhaps I had better tell you before your men arrive. Well, I traveled about with my people as they moved their traps, and one night when very tired I slept in damp moccasins. The fire got low and next morning my foot was slightly frozen. We were forced to make long marches for some days, and I found the frost-bite had gone deeper than I thought. You can, no doubt, guess what happened."

Thirlwell nodded. A frozen foot sometimes galls into a sore that will not heal while the temperature is low.

"Well," said Father Lucien, "some time after we pitched camp, a man came in with a dog-team that belonged to the Hudson's Bay. He was not going farther but offered to lend me the dogs, if I would leave them with some friends of his who were trapping to the south."

"But can you drive dogs?" Thirlwell asked, knowing that skill is required to manage the snarling, fighting teams.

"Not well, but I have driven dogs, and was anxious to reach the mine before my foot got worse. I thought I might find somebody at the Indians' camp who would go on with me. For a day or two we made good progress, though I had trouble to harness the leader in the morning; he was a stubborn, bad tempered animal, and missed his master's firm control. Then, one evening, we came to a creek. The stream had kept the channel open here and there, and I thought the ice thin, but it was open, rocky country round about, and I saw a clump of pines in the distance where we could camp. It got dark as we followed the creek and clouds drifted over the moon, but I wanted to find shelter and pushed on. Once or twice the ice cracked ominously, but it held until we came to a spot where the stream got narrower between high, rocky banks.

"The leader stopped and growled, at the edge of an open crack. His instinct warned him of danger, but I knew I could not get up the rough bank with my lame foot, and drove him past. As I limped by his side with the whip, I thought I heard the current gurgle under the ice, but we went on, the dogs snuffing and treading cautiously. Then there was a soft thud and a splash, the team was jerked back and I saw that the sledge had vanished. I suppose it had broken through a snow-bridge that our weight had shaken.

"I scrambled back a yard or two and looked down into the dark gap—I could not run because of my galled foot. Part of the sledge was covered by fallen snow, but the fore end rested on something and I leaned down and seized my blanket. There was a bag of food beneath it that I tried to reach, but perhaps I shook the sledge, which began to slip down, and I saw the dogs roll among the traces as they were dragged towards the hole. The leader clawed desperately at the snow, howling as if he begged my help, and I felt that I must save him. You have heard a dog howl in fear or pain?"

"Yes," said Thirlwell, "it makes a strong appeal. But I suppose you remembered what you risked by leaving the food?"

"I cut the trace," Father Lucien went on. "Another mass of snow fell and the sledge sank out of sight. I imagine the stream swept it under the ice, for I could only see the dark water foam. All the food I had except a bannock in my pocket was lost. I forgot the team for a few moments and when I looked up they had gone."

He paused and Thirlwell made a sign of sympathy. "A nerve-shaking jar! But what became of the dogs?"

"I think they were afraid of the ice. If my camp had been made and a fire lighted, they might have come in for warmth, but I was not their master, and perhaps they took the back trail to the spot we started from. Well, as I could not follow, I limped on until I reached the pine clump, where I slept, and then dragged myself across the divide to this corner among the rocks. I knew I could go no farther and sat down to wait—"

Father Lucien's voice was calm and Thirlwell knew his courage had not failed. The man had often risked death when duty sent him out across the snowy wilds.

"Anyhow," said Thirlwell, "I'm glad I found you before it was too late. It's something I and others will long be thankful for."

Father Lucien smiled deprecatingly. "If I had starved, another would have filled my place. Men fall on the trail, but the work goes forward. Perhaps I have said too much about my danger, but I did so because of a curious thing that happened last night. I slept as well as usual for some hours, and then opened my eyes. I think, however, I was not quite awake, or else my brain was dull, because I felt no surprise although a man was in my camp. The fire had burned low and he stood back in the gloom where I could not see his face, but a dry branch broke into flame and the light fell on me. The way the man turned his head indicated that he was looking about the camp, and he must have seen that I had nothing but my blanket. But he was silent and did not come forward."

"An Indian?" Thirlwell asked.

"No," said Father Lucien. "He was white."

Thirlwell started. "A white man? It looks impossible. But why didn't you—?"

"I did not speak. You see, I had not heard him come, and imagine now that I thought I was dreaming and was afraid to wake and find my hope of help had gone. After a few moments, he stepped back very quietly into the shadow, and I called out. There was no answer and I got up. It took a little time—the blanket was round my legs and my foot hurt—and when I stumbled away from the fire he had vanished and there was no sound in the bush. Soon afterwards I fell down in the snow, and lay until the cold roused me to an effort and I crawled back to the fire. By and by I went to sleep again and did not waken until daybreak."

"Then," said Thirlwell, meaningly, "you could find no tracks."

"I could not," Father Lucien agreed. "That was not strange, because light snow was falling when I got up and the wind was fresh. Still I found this; it shows I was not dreaming."

He gave Thirlwell a wooden pipe with a nickel band round the stem.

"Ah!" said Thirlwell, who examined the frozen pipe and scraped out a little half-burned tobacco with his knife. "Fifty-cents, at a settlement store! Not the kind of things the Indians buy, and this is not the stuff they generally smoke. Besides, you would know an Indian, whether he spoke or not, by his figure and his pose."

Father Lucien said nothing, but looked at him with a quiet smile, and Thirlwell resumed: "Well, there was a man; a white man. But the thing's not to be understood. He knew you were starving and stole away! Then where did he come from? There's no white man except Driscoll between the Hudson's Bay post and the mine, and you saved Driscoll's life."

"When I last heard of him, Driscoll was trapping about Stony Creek, a long way to the east."

Thirlwell knitted his brows and lighted his pipe, which he had put near the fire to thaw, and there was silence until the *Metis* arrived with the sledge, when they took the missionary to their camp and gave him food. After he had eaten they lay down with their feet to the fire and Thirlwell said: "If the man had seen your fire and come to borrow something or find out who you were, he would have spoken. There's nobody I can think of who has not some grounds for wishing you well, but it looks as if the fellow thought you were asleep and meant to let you starve."

"It looks like that," Father Lucien agreed with a curious calm. "Perhaps we shall find out who he was some day, and if not, it does not matter."

Then he drew the blanket across his face and went to sleep.

Chapter VII
Agatha's Resolve

Agatha looked pale and tired as she sat, rather languidly, in an easy chair in Mrs. Farnam's pretty room. There was bitter frost outside, but the new wooden house, standing among the orchards of South Ontario, was warm, and furnished with a regard for comfort and artistic taste. Mrs. Farnam was proud of her house and good-humored husband, who gave way to her except about the growing of fruit. On this subject, she had told Agatha, he was extraordinarily obstinate. She had some tact and much kindly feeling, but had been a teacher and believed she had a talent for managing other people's business. In fact, she had tried to manage Agatha's, but was forced to admit without much success. Agatha, she said, was difficult.

For all that, it had given her keen satisfaction to bring the girl there when she was threatened by a nervous breakdown in consequence of over-work. Agatha had been her confidential friend when they were at school, but since Mabel married she had sometimes felt that the confidence had been rather one-sided. She had told Agatha much, but the latter had said little about her future plans.

"I don't think you're very much better yet," Mrs. Farnam said after a pause in the talk, for she was seldom silent long.

Agatha languidly looked about the room, noting the warm color of the polished floor, on which the light of the shaded lamp lay in a glistening pool, the fine skin rugs, and thick curtains. She had not an exaggerated love of comfort and her Toronto rooms were bare, but she owned that Mabel had a pretty house. Besides, she had a husband who indulged her and was always kind.

"It's very nice to be here, and I shall soon get strong," she said. "I suppose I rather overdid things, but the examination was coming and I was anxious my girls should pass well."

"From the school managers' point of view, that was a laudable aim, but I don't know that it was worth injuring your health for. You used to agree that managers often expected too much from a teacher."

"I'm afraid I had a selfish object," said Agatha, smiling. "I wanted a better post that will soon be vacant."

"Ambition sometimes deceives one. I know the post you mean and the girl who's going. It carries duties that wore her out."

"And better pay," said Agatha.

Mrs. Farnam gave her a thoughtful look. "Well, that's plausible; but I never thought you greedy. Why do you want the extra pay?"

"I have a use for it," Agatha replied with a twinkle. "I don't suppose I shall carry out my plans, and after all, they are too ridiculous to talk about. Anyhow, you would think so. You're very practical."

"People are curious," Mrs. Farnam remarked. "I'm willing to admit I'm practical, but I married and love my husband, while you look romantic and in many ways are not. You risk your health for money, and I don't think any man ever roused a tender thought in you. There's Jake, for example—"

She stopped and Agatha was silent for a few moments, although she was moved. She was tired and felt lonely and that life was hard. Instinctive longings that she had fought against awoke. She wanted somebody to shelter her and brush her troubles away. Mabel had her husband, whom she loved; but she had chosen a rocky path that she must walk alone.

"I hope Jake is getting on well in British Columbia," she said. "I suppose you hear from him?"

"He writes to us regularly and is getting on very well. Finds his work absorbing and sees a chance of promotion, but it's obvious that he's not satisfied. I don't know if you feel flattered, but he can't forget you."

Agatha stopped her. Jake was Mrs. Farnam's cousin, and had been a teacher of science until he got a post at a mine. He had helped Agatha in her studies, and she blamed herself for imagining that common interests and ambitions accounted for their friendship. In fact, it was something of a shock when, on getting his new post, Jake had asked her to marry him.

"I'm not flattered but sorry," she replied. "I liked Jake very much—one was forced to like him—but after all that doesn't go far enough. And, you see, I didn't know—"

"I believe you really didn't know. It would be ridiculous to admit this about any other girl, but, in a way, you're not quite normal. You're too absorbed in your occupation and haven't a woman's natural feelings. You took all Jake had to give and were surprised and half indignant when he asked something from you."

Agatha wondered rather drearily whether Mrs. Farnam's reproaches were not justified; but the latter went on: "Perhaps, however, your coldness is encouraging. I don't suppose you have met anybody you liked, or felt you could like, better than Jake."

"No," said Agatha, and then hesitated. Since Mabel was capable of giving her cousin a hint, she saw that frankness was needed and remembered the fortnight she had spent with Thirlwell by the lake. She had thought about him since; indeed she had done so oftener than she knew.

"I shall never marry Jake," she said. "Just now it seems unlikely that I shall marry anybody else."

Mrs. Farnam made a sign of disappointed acquiescence. "Very well! That's done with. If there's anything more to be said about your plans for the next few months, your brother will say it. I'm glad George is coming, because he's sensible and will deal with you firmly. Now I'll go and get supper."

She left Agatha thoughtful. George, whose business occasionally brought him into the neighborhood, had written to say that he was coming and would stop the night, and Agatha wondered what he wanted to talk about. He would certainly give her good advice, but they seldom saw alike and she braced herself for a struggle, although she was fond of her brother.

Supper in the bright cedar-paneled room was a cheerful function, and as she looked about and joined in the talk Agatha was conscious of a feeling that was hardly strong enough for envy or actual discontent, but had a touch of both. Mabel looked happy and modestly proud. She was obviously satisfied and in a way enjoyed all that a woman could wish for. The house was pretty; Farnam was indulgent and showed his wife a deference that Agatha liked. He owned a large orchard and had sufficient capital to cultivate it properly. George Strange was marked by a complacent, self-confident manner that his urbanity somewhat toned down. He dealt in artificial fertilizers and farming implements, and it was said that he never lost a customer and seldom made a bad debt.

In character, George was unlike his sister, because while unimaginative he generally saw where his advantage lay. For all that, he was just and often generous. He was married, and talked to Mrs. Farnam about his wife and child when he was not eating with frank enjoyment and telling humorous stories. While the others laughed and joked Agatha mused. They had commonplace aims and duties that brought them happiness; but she had been given a harder task. Still it was a task that could not be shirked; she had accepted it and must carry it out.

Some time after supper Mrs. Farnam went away, and Farnam presently made an excuse for following his wife. When they had gone George remarked: "I must pull out to-morrow, but Florence sends a message. She wants you to stop with us for two or three months."

"Florence is kind," said Agatha. "I would like to go, but you know it's impossible."

"I don't know," George rejoined in an authoritative voice. "I'm your elder brother and it's my duty to see you do what you ought. To begin with, I looked up your doctor and he told me you needed a long rest."

"It can't be got. I must go back to school when the holidays are over."

"Wait a bit! None of us is as indispensable as we sometimes think."

Agatha felt half amused and half annoyed. George often made remarks like this and imagined that they clinched his arguments. She saw that he had been meddling.

"What did you do after seeing the doctor?" she asked suspiciously.

"I went to your principal at the school. She said she would talk to the managers and had no doubt that if it was needful they would let you off for a time. Now as I can fix the thing with the doctor, there's no reason you shouldn't quit work and stop with us."

Agatha colored angrily. George meant well, but he had gone too far. She felt this worse because she was tempted to give way. She liked her brother's wife and needed a rest.

"Well," she said, "I suppose I ought to have expected something of the kind, but it's comforting to feel that your efforts are wasted. I shall be quite well in a week or two and am going back to school. For one thing, I shall need some money before very long."

George looked hard at her. "You don't say why. Still if it's money that prevents you taking the proper line, I might lend you some—" He stopped and resumed with suspicion: "But I won't give you a dollar to waste in searching for father's silver lode!"

"I am going to look for the lode," said Agatha quietly.

"I hoped you had got over that foolishness," George rejoined, throwing his cigarette on the floor, although he was generally careful about such things. "Now listen to me for a few minutes, and try to be sensible!"

"One misses much by always being sensible," Agatha remarked with a resigned smile.

"It often saves one's relations trouble. Anyhow, the blamed lode has thrown its shadow on all our lives, and I don't mean to stand off, saying nothing, and see you spoil yours."

"You escaped the shadow, because you never believed in the lode."

"I certainly didn't and don't believe in it now! For all that, I saw father's restlessness and mother's fears."

"Ah!" said Agatha, "I didn't think—"

"I allow I haven't your imagination, but I can see a thing that's obvious. Father thought he hid his feelings, but mother knew and grieved. She was afraid he would give us up and go back to the North."

"No!" said Agatha with firmness; "she was not afraid he would give us up! Father never failed in his duty."

"Then she was certainly afraid he'd die in the bush; as he did. She knew what the prospectors were up against, and though she smiled when he talked about the ore, I knew she had an anxious heart. I don't claim that the anxiety broke her down, but it made a heavy load and helped."

"Yet when she was very ill she did not ask him to promise he wouldn't go."

"She did not mind then," said George in a quiet voice. "She was dying and we had grown up. But there was nothing selfish about her acquiescence. I think she was glad to set him free, because she loved him and knew what he had borne. He was a dreamer and not a business man. She had run the store and taken care of him, and knew he would be lonely after she had gone. Besides, I sometimes feel she thought he would follow and rejoin her soon. It did not matter by what road he came."

Agatha was silent for some moments because she was surprised and moved. George had a keener imagination and saw farther than she thought. It looked as if he had known her mother best.

"You loved her well and so you understood," she said. "But the troubles she bore are done with, and now I stand alone. I have no responsibilities; my life is mine!"

George's face got red. "Well, perhaps I don't count for much, but we didn't cut loose when I married. I have a sister as well as a wife."

"I'm sorry, George," said Agatha, putting her hand on his arm. "I didn't mean to hurt."

"Very well! I'm not a sentimental fellow; let's be practical. You can't locate the ore, because it isn't there; but you may spoil your health and get soured by disappointment. Then, if you stop long, you'll lose your post and ruin your career. The blamed silver may become a fixed illusion. That's what I'm really afraid of most. In some ways, you're very like father."

"You're persuaded the silver was an illusion?"

"I am persuaded," George declared. "Men who live in the frozen woods get credulous and believe extraordinary things, and tales of wonderful lodes are common in the mining belts. Father heard something of the kind and brooded over it until he came to believe he had located the ore. He had too much imagination and wasn't practical."

"But he gave me some specimens he found and they carry rich metal."

"I allow he thought he found them; but that's a different thing."

Agatha smiled. "Perhaps your theory's plausible, but it has some weak points."

"Anyhow, if father couldn't locate the vein he claimed to have struck, I reckon there's not much chance of your doing so."

"I mean to try," said Agatha, with ominous quietness.

George saw that she was resolute, and although he was obstinate knew he was beaten. Agatha could not be moved when she looked like that.

"I can't allow that you know best, but guess I may as well quit arguing," he remarked with a resigned shrug. "You'll come along and stop with Florence before you go back to Toronto?"

"I will come for a week," Agatha agreed, and George went away to look for Farnam.

Chapter VIII
The Burglar

George went away next morning and a few days afterwards Farnam walked home with his wife and Agatha from a visit to a neighbor's homestead. When they reached the edge of Farnam's orchard they stopped and looked about. An extensive clearing had been cut out of the forest, the evening was clear and cold, and the pines threw long blue shadows on the snow. The young fruit trees ran back in orderly rows, and a frozen creek that crossed the orchard was picked out in delicate shades of gray. Farnam told Agatha that he found the creek useful for irrigation, because he had known the apples to shrivel on the trees in a dry summer.

At the edge of the bush a group of men were at work. The thud of their axes jarred on the quietness, and the rattle of a chain rang musically through the shadows as a teamster threw the links across a log. His horses stood close by, with a thin cloud of steam rising from their bodies.

"Lumber worth sawing is getting scarce, and we'll float the best logs down to the mill when the thaw comes," Farnam said to Agatha. "In the meantime, we want them off the ground before we clean up the pieces the boys have slashed. One gets at this kind of work in winter when nothing much can be done, and I must be ready to break new soil for planting in the spring."

"You are spending a good deal of money," Mrs. Farnam interrupted. "You haven't been paid for the last shipments to England yet."

"Mabel's cautious," Farnam remarked to Agatha. "She's a pretty good business woman, but doesn't understand that the more you spend on your job the more you get. Anyhow, you ought to get more, but I admit you're sometimes badly stung." Then he turned to his wife. "I must go up and see the shippers in Montreal; in fact, now you have Agatha with you, I think I'll start to-morrow."

"Very well," said Mrs. Farnam. "I hate to be left alone, particularly when the nights are long." She indicated the teamster. "I see you have hired another man; that's a fresh extravagance. How long have you had him?"

"A week or two; thought I told you when he came. He's a pretty good worker."

"You didn't tell me; I imagine you didn't want me to know! He's certainly not what the boys call a looker and his face doesn't inspire me with much confidence. Besides, he's lame."

Agatha glanced at the man, who came towards them, walking with a slight limp beside his horses as they hauled the log across the snow. He had a sullen air and did not look up as he passed.

"He is not handsome," she agreed, and asked: "Where do the men live?"

"We have fixed up this lot in the packing shed; my regular hands leave me in winter," Farnam replied, indicating a wooden building at some distance from the house. "However, we'll go home. There are some accounts I must examine before I start for Montreal."

They went on, and when after supper Mrs. Farnam grumbled at being left without a man in the house, Farnam took out an automatic pistol and explained how it was used.

"I don't know why I bought the thing, unless it was to satisfy Mabel," he said to Agatha. "It's curious, but while she could handle mutinous pupils and bluff the managers, she quakes if a door rattles on a windy night. One's rather safer in our homestead than a Montreal hotel; but Mabel has lived in the cities and the Wild West tradition dies hard. As a matter of fact, there never was a Wild West in Canada." He opened the pistol. "You put the cartridge shells in like this—"

"You can show Agatha how it works; I won't touch the thing," Mrs. Farnam declared. "She's something of a sport, but I'm a womanly woman, except when I teach school."

Farnam laughed. "On the whole, it might be better to leave the cartridges out. If somebody did break in, all you need do would be to pretend you were asleep. Everybody in the neighborhood knows where my office is and an intelligent burglar begins at the safe. There's no money in mine now."

After a little good-humored banter, Agatha took the pistol and Farnam went to his office at the other end of the house. Next day he started for Montreal, and at night Mrs. Farnam made Agatha come with her while she examined the fastenings of the doors and windows. The house was low and the roof of the veranda in front reached nearly to the second floor. Nothing disturbing happened, and on the next night Agatha sat up after Mrs. Farnam had gone to bed, reading the letters Strange had written her from the North.

There were not many, and some were marked by a careless style that obscured the meaning. This puzzled Agatha, who remembered that her father had generally talked with lucid clearness. Still they helped her to picture the life he had led in the wilds, and she read them often, trying to follow on a map his wanderings in search of the lode. They told her more about the country than the books she read, and she had read a number, because the subject had a fascination. All she could learn would be of use when she came to carry out her plans.

When she tied up the letters and looked at the clock it was later than she thought. The room felt cold and she shivered, but sat still for a few moments, musing. The house was quiet and she imagined Mrs. Farnam was asleep; but it was snowing, for she heard the flakes beat upon the window. Looking round the comfortable room, she thought of the men who braved the rigors of winter in the frozen wilds. Thirlwell, for example, was bearing such cold as was never felt in South Ontario.

She started, for there was a noise overhead, as if a door had been gently opened, but next moment pulled herself together. Mabel had not gone to sleep as she had thought, and picking up an electric torch, she put out the lamp. When she was half way up the stairs she heard somebody moving about, but it was not like Mabel's step. The movements seemed cautious, and there was something awkward about them. Agatha, who wore felt-soled slippers, stopped and listened, while her heart beat fast. She heard nothing now, but felt alarmed, and wondered what she ought to do. A call would probably bring an answer that would banish her fears; but suppose it was not Mabel she had heard? There was, however, another way of finding out, and with something of an effort she went upstairs.

Mrs. Farnam's room was on the landing, and Agatha turned the handle cautiously. The door would not open, and it was obvious that Mabel had locked herself in. Then the latch slipped back with a jar that sounded horribly loud, and she waited, trembling and trying to keep calm. Since Mabel had not heard the noise, it was plain that she was asleep and somebody else was in the house. Still Mabel, if awakened, would not be of much help, and remembering that the pistol was in her room, Agatha went down the passage.

The passage was very cold, a curtain swayed in an icy draught, and she found the door of her room open. Stopping for a moment, she thought there was somebody inside. This, however, might be a trick of her imagination, and although she wanted to steal away, she knew that if she did so she would lose her self-respect and the confidence she would need for her journey to the North. She must brave real dangers in the wilds and live among rude men. Besides, the pistol was on a table near the door.

Somebody moved as she went in, for there was a rustle and a board cracked, but her hand touched the pistol and she turned on the powerful electric torch. As the beam of light swept across the room she saw that the drawer of a small writing-table had been pulled out. Then the beam passed on and touched a man kneeling beside her open trunk. The clothes she had not unpacked were scattered on the floor, as if the man had been looking for something, and a lantern stood near his hand. She thought he had just put it out, since she noted a smell of oil.

Now she had found the intruder, she was less afraid than angry that he had pulled about her clothes with his coarse, dirty hands. She knew him, for he was the teamster she had seen in the orchard. The beam that picked him out, however, left the rest of the room in gloom, and it was hard to hold the torch steady.

"Light your lantern, but don't move from where you are," she said. "I have a pistol."

He did as he was told, using an old-fashioned sulphur match that smelt disagreeably but made no noise. The light spread and showed her standing with the pistol in her hand, but when she risked a glance about, nothing seemed to have been disturbed except the writing-table and her trunk.

"Now you may get up, but don't be rash," she said quietly and was glad to feel she could control her voice.

He got up and waited, watching her sullenly.

"What have you taken?" she asked.

"Nothing! There was nothing worth taking!"

Agatha forced a mocking smile. "Worn clothes won't sell for much and I have no jewelry." Then she raised the pistol. "Don't move! I mean you to keep still."

He stood motionless, with a kind of dull resignation, although she thought she had noted a curious shrinking when she spoke, as if something in her voice had disturbed him.

"I don't know what to do with you," she resumed. "No doubt you knew Mr. Farnam is away, but the pistol magazine is full. To begin with, you had better empty your pockets. Pull them inside out!"

He obeyed and dropped a pipe, a tobacco tin, and two or three silver coins.

"Those are mine; I've corralled nothing of yours."

"So it seems!" Agatha rejoined. "For all that, you can leave the things there. How did you get in?"

"Over the veranda roof. You hadn't fixed the shutter in the middle."

Agatha pondered for a few moments. The fellow did not look afraid, but seemed to recognize that the advantage was with her. This was lucky, because she could not keep it up long and wanted to get rid of him.

"Well," she said, "I think you had better go out by the window you opened. Walk down the passage in front of me and don't try to turn round."

He did so until he reached the window, which opened to the side. The hinges were in good order and made no noise when he pushed back the frame.

"Get out," said Agatha. "I'll shoot if you stop."

He climbed quietly over the ledge, his lantern flickered and went out, and next moment Agatha saw nothing but the driving snow. Then she closed the window and fastened the shutter in frantic haste, and afterwards leaned against the wall, trembling and breathing hard. Still the man had gone and she thought he would not come back. Pulling herself together she returned to her room.

Although she had driven the man away, she locked the door, and when she had lighted the lamp sat down to recover her calm. There was no use in wakening Mrs. Farnam, and by and by she began to look about. The papers in the writing-table had been thrown upon the floor; her trunk was empty and the clothes it had held were scattered. The man had obviously been searching for something, and this was curious, because one would not expect to find jewelry in a writing-table, and a bureau with three or four drawers had not been opened. Then she noticed her father's letters lying in a bundle on the table, and put them back in the trunk from which she had recently taken them. After this, she re-packed her clothes, and sitting down again tried to remember all that had happened.

There was something puzzling about the adventure. To begin with, she could not see why the man had come to her room and what he expected to get. A clever thief would have gone to Farnam's office. Then she thought he was not a coward; he had given way because he was cool enough to see that he was in her power and resistance would lead to his getting shot. Yet he had seemed to shrink when he heard her voice. She reflected with faint amusement that her voice was not harsh, and she had studied its control as part of her training when she began to teach. The little tricks of tone and gesture one used to overawe young girls would not frighten a man. For all that, when she first spoke there was a hint of fear in his furtive eyes.

Agatha let this go, and pondered her own feelings and the part she had played. She had, of course, been frightened, but had preserved her judgment and seen that she could control the situation so long as she kept cool. The man had not a pistol, and she could have fired three or four shots before he could seize her; but he might have tried to seize her had she not shown that she was ready to shoot. It looked as if she had the nerve and confidence to face a crisis, which was satisfactory, since she would need these qualities when she traveled through the wilds. She had, however, long trained herself for this object; in fact, as far as possible, she made her life a preparation for the adventurous journey. Then she remembered her brother's warning and wondered whether it was justified. There was, perhaps, a danger of her dwelling too much upon the lode. She must not let it possess her mind and make her deaf to other claims. One ought to keep a proper balance. In the meantime, she was tired, and feeling limp with the reaction from the strain. She got up and shortly afterwards went to bed.

Chapter IX
Agatha Asks Advice

Agatha said nothing next morning about her adventure, although she heard that the lame man had left the packing shed when his companions were asleep and had not come back. Next day Farnam returned and in the evening, when Mrs. Farnam was busy, she found an opportunity of talking to him alone. He looked thoughtful when he heard her story.

"You did right not to tell Mabel; but I certainly can't understand the thing," he said. "I reckon you have your imagination under pretty good control."

"I didn't imagine I saw the man," Agatha rejoined with a smile.

Farnam nodded. "We'll take that for granted. I wanted a teamster and hired the fellow when he asked for the job. He worked well, but I don't know where he came from or where he's gone, and it would scare Mabel if we put the police on his trail. Besides, I guess he lit out by the train in the morning that catches the west-bound express."

"Since he knew you were away, why did he wait instead of coming as soon as you left?"

"He probably reckoned there was a risk of his being heard on a calm, frosty night; I understand it was blowing fresh and snowing when he came. The snow would cover his tracks. But I'm puzzled. It's strange that he took nothing and left my s7afe alone!"

"Do you think he knew where the safe is?"

"Sure," said Farnam. "The boys come to my office for their pay." He paused and added thoughtfully: "Looks as if the fellow had an object for searching your room!"

"I wonder whether he knew I was a school teacher," Agatha remarked. "If he did know, it complicates the thing, because teachers are not often rich. Besides, how did he learn which was my room?"

"That wouldn't be hard," Farnam replied. "The boys get talking, evenings, with Mabel's kitchen help and I guess she tells them all about the house and our habits. The girl's a powerful talker."

He lighted his pipe and then resumed: "Well, my notion is he expected to find something in your room; something that he thought worth more than money."

"But I have nothing valuable," Agatha objected, with a laugh. "Now I remember, I made him empty his pockets and he left two half-dollars! It wasn't a very big fine, and I can send the dollar to some charity."

"I can't see an explanation, and we'll have to let it go; but the man will find trouble waiting if he comes back. Let me know right away if anybody gets after you like that again."

Agatha said she would do so, and hearing Mrs. Farnam's step in the passage, they began to talk about something else.

A week later, Agatha went to visit George, and then feeling braced by the holiday, resumed her duties in Toronto. Soon afterwards, she sat in her room one evening in a thoughtful mood. The house was on the outskirts of the city and she heard cheerful voices and the jingle of sleigh-bells on the road. The moon was nearly full and riding parties were going out for a drive across the glittering snow, while where the wind had swept it clear ice yachts were, no doubt, skimming about the lake. Agatha envied the happy people who could enjoy such sports, and it had cost her something to admit that they were not for her. A ticket for a concert to which she had thought of going was stuck in a picture frame, but she was not in the humor for music, and putting down the book she held, leaned back languidly in her chair.

The room was small, plainly furnished, and shadowy, for the lamp had a deep shade that confined the light to a narrow circle. Three or four books lay upon the table and a map of the North-West Territories occupied the end in front of Agatha. It was not a very good map and the natural features of the country were sketchily indicated, for belts of the northern wilderness had not been thoroughly surveyed, but she had opened it for half an hour's relaxation. After that, she must get to work.

She was not very strong yet, but had undertaken extra duties that necessitated private study. Now she felt tired after lecturing a class of absent-minded girls, and closing her eyes, abandoned herself to moody thought. George's warning was bearing fruit. Agatha was young, but knew one soon got jaded and youth slipped away. There was a risk of her spending in unrewarded efforts the years that ought to be happiest, and then finding herself old and soured. Still, when she came to think of it, she had recognized this and felt a vague dissatisfaction with her lot before George had talked to her. In fact, the dissatisfaction had begun soon after she wandered through the bush and paddled about the lake with Thirlwell.

For all that, she was not going to give up the resolve she had made long ago. She owed her father much, and must carry out the task he had unconsciously left her. She meant to search the country he had traveled for the silver vein; and then, if she was persuaded it could not be found, she would have paid her debt and be free to lead the life that others led. In the meantime, she was, so to speak, set apart, like a nun, from common joys and sorrows by a vow that must be kept. Perhaps this was an exaggeration, but it was partly true.

Banishing her thoughts, she put away the map and opened her book, but soon afterwards a servant brought in a card and stated that a man wished to see her. On the card was printed *John Stormont* and the number of a post-office box at Winnipeg.

"I don't know Mr. Stormont," Agatha remarked. "But if he wants to see me, you may show him in."

A few moments later a man entered the room. He was young and neatly dressed, and smiled urbanely as he bowed.

"Miss Strange, I suppose? If you are not much occupied, I hope you can give me a few minutes."

Agatha, feeling curious, indicated a chair and studied him when he sat down. His voice was rather harsh, his glance was quick, and his alert manner implied self-confidence. There was, however, nothing else to be remarked about him, and she thought him a common type of young business man.

"I am not engaged just now," she replied.

"Thank you," said Stormont. "Perhaps I'd better state that I'm pretty well known in Winnipeg, where I do business in real estate and sometimes undertake the development of mineral claims. I've recently put over two or three big transactions in that line."

"But Manitoba is a farming country."

"Certainly; the prairie belt. The eastern strip, running along the edge of the Territories from Lake of the Woods, is different. There the rocks break out among the pine forests and in the last few years prospectors have found valuable minerals. Some are being worked, and I expect we will soon hear of fresh discoveries. I understand you are the daughter of Gordon Strange, who found a silver lode in North Ontario."

"I am his daughter; but I believe the lode was not in Ontario."

"Then it was in the neighboring Territories. I expect your father often talked to you about his find."

"He did," said Agatha. "Still I don't see—"

Stormont smiled. "You wonder where I am leading you? Well, it's part of my occupation to investigate mining propositions, and where the owners want to sell, to find a buyer. Sometimes I lend them money to improve the claim. In fact, I imagine you would find me useful in many ways."

"I cannot sell the lode before I know where it is."

"That's obvious," Stormont agreed. "The difficulty, however, might be overcome, and that's where I could help. But, to begin with, am I to understand your father altogether failed to relocate the claim? Although he filed no record, he may have found a clue."

Agatha gave him a keen glance. He had said nothing to excite much suspicion, but she felt that he was going too fast and asking too many questions.

"I did not see him after he went back to the North. I suppose you know he lost his life on his last journey?"

Stormont made a sympathetic gesture. "I heard so. But, no doubt, he wrote to you and told you about his prospecting."

"Yes," said Agatha, with some reserve. "He sent me letters."

"Then I expect he told you where he went. It's possible that a study of the letters would give an experienced prospector a useful hint."

Agatha pondered. She had, with the help of her map, followed Strange's journeys, and his letters showed where the silver was not to be found, which eliminated large belts of country. Then if Stormont knew much about mining and was accustomed to negotiate the sale of claims, his curiosity implied that her father's belief in the lode was well grounded. This was encouraging, but the man was a stranger and she felt a vague distrust.

"The person who finds a vein of ore and files his record is registered as its owner when he has complied with the legal formalities," she said.

"That is so," Stormont agreed with a smile. "You feel that if you parted with the letters, you would run some risk of losing the claim? Well, one must trust one's agent to some extent, and I'll make you two propositions. You can give me all the information you have about the ore, and, if I think it worth while, I will bear the cost of prospecting and development, and give you a large share of the profits when the mine is worked. Or I'll pay you a fixed sum for the letters and any clues you can supply."

"After you have read the letters?"

"Certainly. You can't expect me to make a plunge of this kind in the dark. Anyhow, if you decide on the first plan, you will be a partner and have some control. It's plain that you will benefit by my experience."

For a few moments Agatha was tempted to agree. She needed help and could not begin the search for some time, while a man who knew all about mining could undertake it with a better chance of success. Still she saw that much depended on the man's honesty, and she had no grounds for trusting Stormont.

"Can you give me two or three weeks?" she asked. "I want to consult my friends."

"The delay might upset my plans. For one thing, it would be necessary to get as much work as possible done before the thaw comes. Prospecting is difficult in winter, but it's considerably easier traveling when the rivers are frozen, and first of all we want to find the spot. I daresay you could give me some landmarks that would help us."

Agatha hesitated. Strange had often described the neighborhood where he had found the ore, and she saw that what she knew about it might be important. Stormont's explanation of his anxiety to begin the search was plausible; but it was possible he wanted to prevent her asking advice.

"I must wait until I know what my friends think," she insisted.

"Although the loss of time may spoil our chance of locating the ore?"

"Yes," said Agatha firmly. "I must run the risk."

Stormont got up. "Very well! I don't know if we'll be able to do anything when you make your decision, but you can write to me. In the meantime, I think you ought to promise that you won't negotiate with anybody else."

"I will promise this," said Agatha and knitted her brows when he went out.

She was half afraid she had been too prudent and let a good offer go by; but although it might bring her trouble and disappointment, she would sooner look for the ore herself. She had sometimes shrunk from the task, but after all it was her duty. Then she could not ask George for advice. He had never believed in the lode and would, no doubt, tell her she was lucky to get an offer, and had better make the best bargain she could. Farnam knew nothing about mining; he was absorbed in his orchard, and Mabel now and then declared that his judgment was only worth trusting about fruit trees.

Agatha paused and admitted that she had from the beginning meant to ask Thirlwell. She could trust him; he was honest, but this was not all. When he talked about important things he had a quiet, decided manner that she liked. He would not be daunted by obstacles, and if her resolution wavered, he would not let her shirk. She did not think him clever, but he would somehow carry out what he undertook. It was curious that after a fortnight of his society she knew him so well; but she did know he was trustworthy and there was nothing more to be said.

Since a letter might not reach him for some time, she had better write at once, and she got some paper and began. It was easy to write to Thirlwell, and she told him about the lame man who had broken into the house, before she came to Stormont's offer. Indeed, when she stopped she was surprised to see how much she had said. After fastening the envelope she got up and went to the window, where she drew the thick curtain behind her and looked out.

The moon was higher up the sky and the roofs glittered in the silver light. Half the street lay in shadow, a belt of grayish blue, but the rest sparkled where the sleigh-shoes had run. A sleigh came up with a load of girls and young men in blanket-coats and furs. They seemed to be talking and laughing, but Agatha no longer envied them; the depression she had felt had gone. Then as the sleigh went past with a chime of bells she tried to follow her letter on its journey to the North.

After it left the railroad it would lie in a pack on a half-breed's shoulders, or perhaps in a skin bag on a hand-sledge, in front of which men with snowshoes marched. It would travel up winding rivers between dark walls of ragged pines, across frozen lakes, and among the rocks on high divides. Then the tired men would stop at a cluster of shacks beside a shaft and an ore-dump in the wilds, and she wondered what Thirlwell would think when he opened the envelope; whether he would be pleased or not.

But this was indulging idle sentiment that she had meant to avoid, and she went back to the table and opened her books. Thirlwell's answer would not arrive for some weeks, and if she went north, summer would come before she could start. In the meantime, she had her pupils to teach. The subject for the next morning's lesson was difficult and needed careful study.

Chapter X
Thirlwell Gets A Letter

A dreary wind wailed about the shack, and now and then the iron roof cracked as it shrank and wrenched its fastenings in the bitter cold. The room was not warm, although the front of the stove glowed a bright red, and after supper Thirlwell pulled his chair between it and the wall. He had been out for some hours with snowshoe and rifle, but had seen nothing to shoot. The white desolation was empty of life, and silent except for the wind among the pine-tops.

"I'd meant to look into the Snake Creek muskegs, but the cold drove me back," he said. "In summer one's bitten by sand-flies and mosquitoes; in winter one runs some risk of freezing to death. I wonder now and then whether mining's worth the hardship and why we stop here."

"Unprofitable mining isn't logically worth much hardship," Scott remarked. "But don't you mean you wonder why you came back?"

"No," said Thirlwell, with a touch of embarrassment; "that was pretty obvious. I was offered a good post in England, but it meant I'd be dependent on a man I don't like. A rough life with liberty is better than luxurious servitude."

"The latter has some advantages," Scott rejoined. "To-night, for example, you could enjoy a good dinner instead of moldy beans and rancid pork, put on clean clothes, and go to a concert or theater. Then you'd get up next morning in a warm room, with a bath and hot water at hand, instead of freezing by a stove that had burned low. Anyhow, admitting that you're obstinate and hate to go where others want, I've a notion that you felt you had to see me out when you refused that post."

"Oh, well," said Thirlwell awkwardly. "In a sense, I was bound—"

"By your scruples? But we'll let it go," Scott rejoined. "I expect we're all to some extent the slaves of an idea. I'd pull out to-morrow if I didn't feel I had to make my mining venture good before I quit. All the same, it looks as if I'd save my money by stopping now."

He looked up, for there was a knock at the door and a man who had gone down to the settlements came in. His skin cap was pulled down to meet the collar of his coat, leaving only his eyes and nose exposed, and fine frost-dried snow stuck to the shaggy furs.

"It's surely fierce to-night," he said. "Thought we couldn't make it when we met the wind on Loon Lake, but there was no shelter on the beach and our tea had run out. I brought a letter for Mr. Thirlwell along."

"Nothing else?" Scott asked.

The man said there was nothing, and when he went away Scott smiled.

"Well, that's a relief! I had expected a reminder that we hadn't paid our last bill for tools. But I guess you want to read your letter."

Thirlwell felt a thrill of satisfaction as he recognized the hand, for it was some time since Agatha had written to him. He got thoughtful as he read the letter, and when he had finished put it down and lighted his pipe.

"I'd like you to listen to this and tell me what you think," he said.

Scott make a sign of agreement, and when Thirlwell had read Agatha's account of her meeting with the burglar and Stormont, he remarked: "It's a nice frank letter, and Miss Strange has some talent for dramatic narrative."

"That's not what I meant," said Thirlwell, with an impatient frown. "What d'you think about Stormont's visit?"

"On the whole, I imagine Miss Strange ran less risk of being robbed when she met the burglar."

"So I think. But why did the fellow go?"

Scott looked thoughtful. "Though Stormont's said to be a rogue, he's certainly not a fool. You seem to take it for granted that Strange never found the lode, but I'm not sure. Anyhow, it looks as if Stormont didn't agree with you."

"But how did he hear about the lode?"

"It's not very plain, but I have a suspicion. There's a curious thing; I don't see much difference between Stormont's object and the burglar's. Both seemed to want the letters Strange wrote to the girl."

"Now I come to think of it, perhaps there wasn't much difference. The fellow stole nothing, although he broke open the writing-table and Miss Strange's trunk. She says he disturbed nothing else. But the matter gets no clearer."

Scott smiled. "My explanation is that Stormont tried to buy the letters after he found they couldn't be stolen."

"But he'd have to trust the man he hired to break into the house; and this would put him in the fellow's power."

"I reckon the man told him about the lode; Miss Strange states that he was lame," Scott remarked in a meaning tone. "Where has Black Steve been since he left this neighborhood?"

Thirlwell started. "It's possible you have got near the truth. Nobody knows as much as Driscoll about Strange's prospecting. But I must answer the letter. What am I to say?"

"If you tell her to have nothing to do with Stormont, it ought to be enough in the meantime," Scott replied. "You could send down your answer when, the next Hudson's Bay breeds come along."

They were silent for a few minutes, and then Scott resumed: "I understand Miss Strange means to look for the vein next summer and you are going. Why is that, since you don't believe her father's tale?"

"She's resolved to go and I can help. When she's persuaded the ore can't be found she'll be content to give the notion up. I don't want the thing to occupy her thoughts until it becomes a kind of mania, as it did with Strange."

"I imagine she's an attractive girl."

"She is attractive; but that has nothing to do with it," Thirlwell replied with a frown. "I'm not in love with Miss Strange. To begin with, I can't support a wife, and marriage hasn't much charm for me. Then I think she's clever enough to make her mark, and will stick to her occupation until she does, if she gets rid of this foolish notion of looking for the ore."

"I see," said Scott, with some dryness. "You feel sorry for the girl and want to save her from getting like Strange? Well, it's a chivalrous object; but there's a thing you don't seem to have thought of yet. Prospecting a big belt of country is a long job, and if you're away much of the summer, how are you going to keep your engagement with me?"

"I have thought of it," Thirlwell replied. "It's awkward—"

Scott smiled at his embarrassment. "Well, I'll let you go. In fact, I don't mind taking a stake in the expedition, in the way of food and tools."

"Miss Strange wouldn't agree."

"Very well. Suppose you locate the ore, she'll need advice and further help. Now I know something about mining; I've paid pretty high for what I've learned. I understand Miss Strange hasn't much money, and we might save her some expensive mistakes. You see, I haven't much hope of getting down to pay-dirt here."

Thirlwell pondered. He liked and trusted Scott, and the thought of being able to offer Agatha the help she might need was attractive; but he meant to be honest and exercised some self-control.

"It would pay you better to leave the thing alone. I feel pretty sure the ore's a freak of Strange's imagination."

"It's possible," Scott agreed. "Go and see."

Thirlwell knocked out and filled his pipe; and then remarked with some diffidence: "You stated that you didn't think you had enough capital to keep the Clermont going long."

"I haven't enough," Scott said, smiling. "But I have some rich relations who might finance me if I could show them a sure snap. I'd like to do so, anyhow, because, after spending most all my money, I feel I've got to make good."

"I can understand this. Why did you come up here in the beginning?"

"It's rather a long story and I reckon it starts with a canoe trip I made in the North one fall. I had then begun a business in which family influence could give me a lift. Well, it was Indian summer; mosquitoes dying off, lakes and rivers all asleep in the pale sunshine. As we paddled and portaged through the woods I felt I'd got into another world. Wanted to stop forever and began to hate the cities; the feeling wasn't new, but I hadn't got it really strong till then. Sometimes at night, when the loons were calling on the lake and my packers were asleep, I'd lie by the fire and speculate what civilization was worth and if a man might not do better to cut loose and live by his gun and traps. Well, of course, it was a crank notion, and I wasn't all a fool. I stopped longer than I meant, but I pulled out and got to work again."

Scott paused and smoked meditatively before he resumed: "It was of no use; the city palled. Don't know that I'm a cynic or much of a philosopher, but the folks I knew seemed to have a wrong idea of values. Spent their best efforts grubbing for money and trying to take the lead in smart society. They made me tired with their hustling about things that didn't matter; I wanted the woods and the quiet the river hardly breaks."

"You went back?"

"I did," said Scott. "Felt I had to go. It was winter and the cold was fierce, but we made four hundred miles with the hand-sledge across the snow, and when I came out with some fingers frozen I was nine pounds heavier. Used to sit in my office afterwards and dream about the glittering lakes and the stiff white pines; saw them crowding round the lonely camps, when I ought to have been studying the market reports. Well, I couldn't concentrate on buying and selling things. Betting on the market and getting after other people's money seemed a pretty mean business." He paused and added with a twinkle: "That's how I felt then, and I don't know that I've changed my opinions much."

"All the same, you're anxious to make your mining pay."

"It isn't logical, but I was born a white man and had got civilized. You can't altogether get rid of what you're taught when young, and it's harder when the notions you inherit are backed by your training. Well, I saw there was a danger of my turning out a hobo if I went back North without a job. I must get some work, and when Brinsmead came with a proposition about the Clermont vein I took down my shingle and located here with him."

"But what about your relations? Did they object?"

"Not much. On the whole, I reckon they were satisfied to see me go. They had long decided I was a crank, and since I was bound to do something foolish, I'd better do it where I wouldn't disgrace them. That's about all. We're here, and I don't know that I'd go back if the road was open. Would you?"

Thirlwell pondered. It was a hard life he led, working, for the most part, in the dark underground, for when money was scarce and wages high he could not be satisfied to superintend. Scott, indeed, worked like a paid hand, and they had fought a long, and it seemed a losing, battle against forces whose strength science cannot yet properly measure. The fish-oil lamps sometimes went out in poisonous air while they examined an unsafe working face; props broke under a load they ought to have borne; and now and then the roof came down. Rock pillars crushed, massive stones fell out where one least expected, and there was always the icy water that the pump could not keep under and the frost could not stop.

Yet there was something that thrilled one in the stubborn fight, and a strange ascetic satisfaction in proving how much flesh and blood could stand. One felt stronger for bracing one's tired body against fresh fatigue, and watchfulness in the face of constant danger toned up the brain. Then, after all, the vast, silent wilderness had a seductive charm.

"This country draws, and holds what it gets," he said. "I'm satisfied to stop here, as long as I'm young."

For a time they smoked in silence, and presently went to bed, tired with exhausting labor and glad to rest in dreamless sleep until they began again in the bitter dawn.

Chapter XI
Stormont Finds A Clue

The Dufferin House was the best hotel in the small Ontario town, and about ten o'clock one evening Stormont read a newspaper in his comfortable room. His clerk had been some days in the town, looking into a proposed transaction in real estate, and Stormont left Winnipeg when a letter from him arrived. This was not because the business required his supervision, but because Watson, the clerk, had found out something that might prove to be important, although it might lead to his employer's wasting his time. Stormont seldom let what he called a fighting change go by.

He had eaten a good supper at about six o'clock, and after a talk with Watson and a young man whose acquaintance the clerk had made, had sent them off to see the town at his expense. This was not rash, because Stormont could trust his clerk. Now he waited their return, but it was not for Watson's benefit he had put a cigar-box and a bottle of strong liquor on the table. Much depended on Watson's tact and judgment, and Stormont felt relieved when he came in.

"I've got Drummond downstairs," the clerk said.

"Very good," said Stormont. "Had you much trouble?"

"I certainly had some. He wanted me to hire a sleigh and take a girl at a sweet-stuff store for a joy-ride. Suggested it when she was there, and I think she meant to go. Then he broke a lamp in the pool-room that cost us two dollars."

"Well, I hope you haven't overdone the thing."

"On the whole, I guess not," Watson replied. "It's hard to hit the proper mark, but I reckon he's just drunk enough."

"Then bring him up," said Stormont, and in a few minutes Watson came back with a young man.

The latter's skin was somewhat dark, and his coarse black hair and athletic figure hinted at a strain of Indian blood. As a matter of fact, his mother was a French-Canadian *Metis*, and he was born in a skin tent in the North. His clothes were cut in the latest fashion, and he looked self-confident; but he moved unsteadily and his face was flushed.

"Had a gay time, Mr. Drummond?" Stormont asked.

"You bet!" said the other, giving the clerk a patronizing smile. "This young fellow is surely a sport. Promised half the girls up-town he'd take them a sleigh-ride and broke a big lamp in the pool-room."

"You broke the lamp," Watson interrupted, with a glance at his employer.

"Oh, well," said Drummond, "perhaps I did. I certainly put the marker out. He allowed I couldn't hold my cue and was going to cut the cloth. Why, I'd play any man in this old town for fifty dollars!"

"And beat him!" said Stormont. "Watson told me how you play. But won't you sit down and take a smoke."

"I surely will," Drummond replied, and pulling up an easy chair, put his wet snow-boots on Stormont's bed, after which he lighted a cigar. "Now," he resumed, "if you have anything to say to me, you can go ahead."

"You're a store clerk, I think. It's a poor job making a profit for another man and Watson tells me you are enterprising. How'd you like to run a store of your own? If you could put up the stock to start with, I reckon you'd soon make good."

"I've figured on that," Drummond replied, with a cunning look, though Stormont saw he was flattered. "You want some money to begin, but I've a notion how I'm going to raise my pile."

Stormont nodded. He had appealed to the young man's raw vanity, but meant to work upon another emotion. "Watson tells me you came from Hamilton. Nice town and business was pretty good when I was there." He paused and asked sharply: "Why did you quit?"

Drummond hesitated and got confused. "Nothing much doing in my line; didn't see many chances, and Hamilton made me tired."

"Oh, well," said Stormont, who had given the other a hint that he knew something about his past history. "I reckon you didn't leave your employer your new address! Anyhow, store-clerking's a tame job, and you're a sport. You want to get out and give yourself a chance. Wasn't Hector Drummond, Hudson's Bay agent at the old Longue Sault factory, your father?"

"He was. Don't know how you know, but you've got it right."

Stormont smiled. The young man had told Watson much about himself one night when he was drunk. "I don't think it matters. You'd like to get rich and hinted that you knew how to make your pile."

"I know where there's a silver lode."

"Ah!" said Stormont, "that's interesting! But it's an expensive business to prove and develop a mineral claim, and you couldn't do much alone. I expect you know this, since you stop here clerking for a few dollars a week. You want help."

"The man who looks for that ore will want my help," Drummond rejoined.

"Well, it's my business to speculate in mines, and I'm generally willing to pay for a useful tip. But it's got to be useful. I don't like to be stung, and the woods are full of dead-beat prospectors ready to put you wise about rich pay-dirt for a dollar or two."

"My tip's all right," Drummond declared in a defiant tone. "I'll show you! When the old man was at Longue Sault he had a clerk called Strange, and sent him off somewhere one day with a sledge and dogs. Strange came back with a bagful of mineral specimens, and said he'd struck it rich, but the old man knew nothing about mining and didn't want any prospectors mussing up things round there. By and by Strange left the factory, and the old man pulled out and brought me South. Located at Owen Sound, and told me about Strange's specimens one day when he was very sick. Said he'd reckoned the fellow was a crank, but he'd kept two or three specimens and a mining man told him they carried good silver."

"Did Strange tell your father where he found the specimens?" Stormont asked carelessly.

Drummond grinned. "Since the old man sent him, I guess he knew where he went. But I've got to know what my tip is worth before I tell you."

"Certainly," said Stormont. "Suppose we take a drink?" He filled a glass and gave it Drummond, but was silent for some minutes afterwards.

The young man was not as drunk as he thought, and had obviously some caution left. The heady liquor, however, might make a difference.

"Well," he resumed, when Drummond put down his glass, "you're ambitious and enterprising. I expect you'd like to own a share in a paying mine?"

"You bet I would; I'm surely going to!"

"Then you had better let me help. It will cost you something to locate the vein, and you won't find people ready to believe your tale and put up the money," Stormont replied.

He saw by Drummond's look that he had tried to sell his secret; but the lad answered: "Cut it out! What's your offer?"

"Fifty dollars now, and five hundred when we find the lode, if it's worth working. Then a share that will depend on the cost of development and the profit."

"Shucks!" said Drummond. "I want five hundred dollars before I start."

"Then you had better try somebody else," said Stormont, smiling. "It's possible that all you can tell me isn't worth five dollars."

"I'll show you! Gimme a hundred now and 'nother drink."

"Take fifty, or I quit," said Stormont, who passed him the bottle.

Drummond drained his glass. "You're mean, but I gotter make a start. Where's the bills?"

Stormont gave him some paper money, and then turned to the clerk. "See about mailing the letters, Watson."

The clerk went out, knowing why he had been sent. His employer trusted him where he was forced, but did not want him to hear what Drummond had to say.

When Watson had gone Drummond knitted his brows, as if trying to remember something. "The vein runs out on the face of a cliff, 'bout forty paces from the first rampike pine; there's three or four rampikes, but the fire hadn't gone far into the bush."

"Not much of a clue! There are patches of burned forest all over the country," Stormont remarked.

"Don't interrupt!" said Drummond, with a frown. "It's pretty hard to remember. Give me 'nother drink. I wanter get it right."

Stormont filled his glass and he resumed in an unsteady voice: "Cliff rises from the creek in a little round hollow. There's a big rock near the top of the divide opposite—"

"Go on. How does the creek run?"

"You're hustling me," Drummond grumbled. "I wanter think. It's important. Knowing how the creek runs fixes where she is." He paused, and a vague distrust of Stormont entered his bemused brain. He had got the fifty dollars and saw, with drunken cunning, that it might be prudent to keep something back. "She runs south."

"South?" exclaimed Stormont, who knew that the natural drainage of the region is north-east to James Bay.

"Sure," said Drummond, with a sullen look. "Strange told the old man, and the old man told me."

Stormont pondered. If the creek flowed south, it drained a subsidiary basin and probably filled a lake from which a river ran north or east. The clue was worth fifty dollars because it would simplify the search for the lode.

"How does the creek lie from the factory?"

"'Bout south-west," said Drummond in a thick, drowsy voice. "There isn't a factory at Longue Sault now. Company moved the post after the old man left."

"How far is the creek from where the post was?"

"Lemme think," Drummond muttered, and his eyes half closed. "Old man reckoned Strange made it in a fortnight's march."

"From the creek, or from the place where he was sent? Or do you mean the double journey?"

"Don't know," Drummond answered dully. "Old man said fortnight. Told you all I remember."

Then he slipped down in the big chair, his head drooped forward, and he fell into a drunken sleep. Stormont got up and leaned against the table. He had borne some strain in the last few minutes, because it had been obvious that Drummond was overcome by liquor and would soon be unable to talk, while when he woke up sober he might repent his rashness. Now Stormont imagined he had told him all he knew, and it ought to be worth fifty dollars. Lighting a cigar, he waited until his clerk came back, when he indicated Drummond, who lay, snoring heavily, with his dirty boots on Stormont's bed.

"Wake the drunken fool and see him home."

Watson had some trouble to get Drummond on his feet and after Stormont shut the door there was a heavy thud. It looked as if Drummond had fallen down the stairs, but Stormont smiled. He had done with the fellow, and if Watson could get him out of the hotel, it did not matter if he reached home or not. Ringing for the bell-boy, he gave orders about being called in the morning, as he meant to leave by an early west-bound train.

Chapter XII
On The Trail

Thirlwell had been to the railroad settlement, and returning with Father Lucien, camped on the trail not far from the mine. The day had been unusually warm and at noon the pines dripped in the sun and the snow got damp. At dusk it began to freeze and a haze hung about the woods and obscured the moon, but, by contrast with the rigors of winter, Thirlwell sitting by the camp-fire, felt almost uncomfortably warm. Father Lucien had taken off his furs and sat with a blanket over his shoulders on a bundle of dry twigs. Both had hung their moccasins up to dry near the heap of snapping branches. Wreaths of aromatic smoke slowly drifted past and faded in the mist.

"One feels spring coming," said Father Lucien. "We have had a foretaste to cheer us while winter lasts. The sun is moving north, and up here, it always thrills me to watch the light drive back the dark. One could make a homily on that."

"The dark soon returns," Thirlwell remarked, "I hate the long nights."

"There are men who like the dark, in spite of the terrors it has for some."

"I wonder whether you are thinking of a particular example," Thirlwell suggested, remembering a night watch he had kept while the blizzard raged about Driscoll's shack.

"One does think of examples. Perhaps we generalize too much. It is easy to let an individual stand for a type."

"If the individual is Black Steve Driscoll, I hope he's an uncommon type."

Father Lucien made a sign of agreement. "Driscoll was in my thoughts. A strange man; dogged and sullen, with a heart that kindness cannot touch. Yet one feels he is afraid."

"He was afraid when he was ill; I wonder why. The fellow has no religious or moral code. But he drinks hard and perhaps he's superstitious."

"What is superstition?" the missionary asked with a smile. "The old atavistic fear of the dark and the mysterious dangers that threatened our savage ancestors? Or is it an instinctive knowledge that there are supernatural powers, able to punish and reward?"

"I don't know," said Thirlwell, who mused and watched the smoke drift past.

The bush was very quiet; he could hear nothing but the crackle of the fire. Now and then a blaze leaped up and pierced the shadows among the pine trunks. A few yards away, the trees got blurred and melted into the encircling gloom. In one place, however, there was an opening, and when he turned his back to the light, he saw a faint glimmer in the mist that indicated the frozen lake. Although he was used to the wilds, he felt the silence and desolation.

"It's easy to be superstitious here," he resumed. "One feels that human power is limited and loses one's confidence. I expect something of the kind accounts for Driscoll's nervous fears. In the city, he would have no time to brood; he'd spend his days in a noisy workshop and his evenings in a crowded tenement or saloon. But if he's scared of the dark and loneliness, why doesn't he pull out?"

"Human nature's stubborn. A man with a compelling object may be afraid and fight his fears."

"I'd like to know what Driscoll's object is. Since the night in his shack, when the fellow was sick, I've wondered why Strange's canoe capsized. Strange was a clever *voyageur*; so's Black Steve."

Father Lucien looked at him curiously and there was a hint of shrinking in his eyes. "I cannot tell; perhaps we shall never know! But if there was foul play, what would Driscoll gain?"

"It's hard to see," Thirlwell agreed. "I could understand it if Steve had afterwards staked a claim, but nobody has found the ore yet. There's another curious thing; I don't see what he'd gain by leaving you to starve, as I think he meant to do."

"No," said Father Lucien sharply, "that is impossible! Besides, Driscoll was trapping some distance off."

"A white man stood looking down at you and then stole away, although he saw you had no camp outfit," Thirlwell insisted.

"He may have been short of food and came to borrow. Seeing I had none, he was perhaps afraid to share any he had left with me."

Thirlwell shook his head. "I haven't met a prospector who would let a white man starve; they're a rough but generous lot. In fact, the only man I know who's capable of the thing is Driscoll."

Father Lucien did not answer and presently lay down, but Thirlwell sat for a time, thinking while he dried his moccasins. The missionary was something of an idealist, although he knew the weaknesses of human nature, but Thirlwell was practical. Somehow he had got entangled in the complications that sprang from Strange's supposititious discovery of the ore, but he did not want to break loose. Agatha Strange needed him; she had admitted that there was nobody else to whom she could look for help and advice. So far, he could find no clue to the web of mystery that surrounded the matter and had caught them both, but he meant to search.

When the moccasins were dry, he began to wonder why he was anxious to help the girl, since he was not in love with her. In a sense, it was perhaps his duty, but this did not account for his keenness. He gave it up, and after throwing some branches on the fire lay down and went to sleep.

The fire was low and gave out no light when he wakened. He felt cold and remembered with some annoyance that he had not gathered enough wood to last until morning. He had not brought his watch, partly because he had fastened a small compass on the chain, but he knew that day would not break for some hours yet. The mist was thinner, although it had not gone, and looking up he guessed the moon's height by the elusive glimmer in the haze. It was about four o'clock, and he imagined he had wakened when the heat of his body had sunk to its lowest; but was not altogether satisfied, since he had slept undisturbed by much keener frost.

For all that, it was a nuisance to get up and look for dead branches in the dark, and he waited, reluctant to throw off his blanket, for some minutes, and then roused himself with a jerk. He imagined he heard voices out on the lake. He glanced at Father Lucien, but the latter was fast asleep. Thirlwell wondered whether he himself had gone to sleep again and dreamed, but half-consciously fixed his eyes on the opening that commanded a view of the lake. He could see it indistinctly; a smooth white plain running back into the dark. The snow caught a faint reflection although the moon was hidden, but nothing broke the even surface.

Then Thirlwell got up abruptly, for he heard a shout. It sounded as if somebody had given an order, and he felt disturbed. There was, he knew, no ground for this. The few white trappers and prospectors who now and then entered the wilds were, for the most part, good-humored, sociable men; the *Metis* and Indians were friendly. Indeed, the proper line was for him to invite the strangers to share his camp, but he hesitated. He had got suspicious since he promised to help in the search for Strange's silver, and trappers and Indians did not travel at night.

As he pondered the matter, a dark object came out of the misty background on the lake. It was indistinct, but by its height and slow movements he knew it was a man. It vanished presently where the pines cut off his view, but three others followed after an interval, two apparently hauling a loaded sledge. They crossed the stretch of ice that Thirlwell could see, and when the trees shut them out he forgot to gather wood and lighted his pipe.

The hazy figures had an unsubstantial, ghostly look; he might have imagined he had not really seen them had he not heard the leader's shout. Then it was hard to see why they were traveling in the dark, since they must leave the ice soon and the trail was rough. He thought their leader knew the country, because their coming down the lake indicated that they had taken a short but difficult line from the settlements. But one would expect a man who knew the country to make for and stop at the mine, which was not far off. Thirlwell hoped to reach it next day, and wondered whether the others meant to pass it at night. If so, it would indicate that they did not want to be seen.

When he had smoked out his pipe he gathered some wood, and then, as Father Lucien had not wakened, thought he would look for the others' trail and see which way they had gone. They were traveling north, but two routes the Indians used started from the head of the lake. He found the marks of the sledge-runners, and then noted with a thrill of excitement that there was something curious about one of the men's tracks. The steps were uneven; one impression was sharper than the other.

Imagining that the party would camp soon, Thirlwell determined to follow and presently came to a rough slope where the trail left the ice. Caution was now needed, because he could not see far and might be heard if he made much noise in pushing through the bush. The silence that brooded over the woods indicated that the others had stopped. The pines were small and tangled, but he could see where the sledge had gone and when he reached the summit a gleam of light sprang up in the valley below. Thirlwell thought the man who made the fire had chosen the spot well if he meant its light to be hidden.

The wood was thin on the slope he went down and it was difficult to keep in the gloom. The glimmering moonlight was brighter and his figure would be visible against the snow as he crossed the openings. When he was some distance from the fire he stopped and studied his line of approach.

The men were moving about on his side of the fire. Their figures were distinct, but he could not see their faces, and if he crossed the belt of rather open ground, the light would fall on him. If he could creep up on the other side, the fire would be between them and, shining in the men's faces, prevent their seeing far. The trouble was, that the wood behind the camp looked tangled and thick, and he doubted if he could get through without making a noise. Something, however, must be risked, and stealing across the opening to the next tree, he presently reached a belt of thicker wood.

He could not be seen now, but he made a circuit round the fire before he began to approach it from the other side. His progress was slow and he felt anxious, because it was possible that the men had moved round the fire while he struggled through the bush. Still he thought they had not done so, because he had seen one throwing up a snow-bank behind which they meant to sleep. They would probably cook their meal and sit down on that side in the shelter of the bank. When he left the thick bush he saw that his reasoning was good, but he had yet to get near enough and the fire was burning well. There was not much wind, but the red blaze leaped up and sank, throwing out clouds of sparks, while a trail of smoke drifted about the camp. The resinous wood, however, crackled fiercely and he hoped this would drown the noise he made.

There was nothing to hide him for some distance, and then a patch of juniper scrub and some willows ran towards the camp. If he could reach them he would be safe, and he crawled across the open space and lay behind the first juniper while he got his breath. There was nothing to indicate that the others had heard him, and a few minutes later he stopped again at the edge of a gap where a fire had run through the scrub. He could see the men, though he could not distinguish their faces. One seemed to be looking in his direction, and Thirlwell felt his heart beat but did not move. He had a background of dark bushes and it was wiser to keep still than drop into the snow.

Presently the man stooped, as if to pick up something, and Thirlwell, stealing forward, sank down among the willows. They rustled as he crept between their stems, but the fire was snapping furiously and after he had gone a few yards he thought he was near enough. Rising nearly upright, he pushed the dry branches aside. Since they broke his outline, it would be hard to see him by the unsteady light.

The flames tossed and wavered, throwing a fierce red glow about the camp. Pine-trunks and snow-bank stood out sharply from the shadow, and faded again. The light played on the men's faces for a few moments and then left them blurred and dim. Thirlwell waited until one threw on some branches and a blaze and cloud of sparks sprang up. The glare touched the fellow's face and Thirlwell thrilled with excitement as he saw it was Driscoll.

He did not know the others, but one had a rather pale color, as if he had come from the cities, and his fur-coat looked new and good. The sledge carried an unusually heavy load, and among the provision bags he noted some iron drills and a small wooden box such as giant-powder is packed in. It was a prospecting party and he had seen enough.

Creeping back into the scrub, he set off for camp. When he got there Father Lucien was asleep, and when they resumed the march next morning Thirlwell told him nothing about the other party. He thought the missionary had difficulties enough of his own without being involved in the trouble that seemed to follow all who had anything to do with Strange's silver lode.

Chapter XIII
The Prospectors' Return

It was snowing, but there was no wind and the shack was warm when, on the evening after his return, Thirlwell sat, smoking, by the stove. Now and then a mass of snow rumbled down the iron roof near the spot where the hot pipe went through, and the draughts had lost their former sting. The air in the room felt different; it was not humid yet, but one no longer noticed the harsh dryness that is caused by intense frost. The long arctic winter was coming to an end.

By and by Scott, sitting opposite Thirlwell, said thoughtfully, "Driscoll's outfit will have to hustle, if they mean to do much prospecting and get back while the ice is good. I'll give them a month, and if they're not out then, they'll have trouble."

Thirlwell made a sign of agreement. Rivers and lakes are numerous in the North, and in winter one can travel smoothly on the ice. When the latter rots and cracks, *voyageurs* and prospectors wait until the melting snow sweeps the grinding floes away and canoes can be launched. To push through tangled bush and across soft muskegs costs heavy labor.

"They were taking up a big load and couldn't march fast," he said.

"I understand you don't know Stormont?"

"I know his character—and unless he's badly slandered that's enough! I haven't met him, but I'm nearly sure it was a city man I saw in Driscoll's camp."

"Stormont's indicated," Scott replied. "I reckon Driscoll went to him because he needed capital; but he wouldn't put another fellow on the track. If we take it for granted that he did go, the mystery about Strange's letters is cleared up. It's characteristic that Stormont tried to steal them before he made Miss Strange his offer."

"In a way, it's curious that he did make an offer!"

Scott smiled. "He didn't run much risk. It would be hard to frame an agreement out of which Stormont couldn't wriggle; I've met the fellow, and Brinsmead has grounds for knowing his methods. Anyhow, it's plain that he thinks it worth while to spend some money in trying to find the lode, and on such matters his judgment is said to be pretty good. Then I imagine Black Steve knows more about Strange's prospecting trips than you suspect."

"My notion is, that nobody knows much about the lode."

"Well," said Scott, "it looks like that. Strange is dead, and I don't imagine he took Black Steve very far into his confidence; though he may have given him a hint when he was drunk. But there's another man, whom nobody seems to have thought of yet."

"Who's that?"

"The Hudson's Bay agent at the factory where Strange was employed. Strange was young then, and was probably frank and enthusiastic about his find. I daresay he gave the agent all the particulars he could recollect when he saw the fellow doubted his tale. His memory was, no doubt, pretty good, since he'd seen the lode a week or two before."

"They have pulled down the factory and I expect the agent's dead," Thirlwell replied. "If not, he must be an old man and I don't know where he is. I'm not persuaded yet that Strange did find the ore; but if it hadn't snowed, I'd have followed Stormont's trail. It would be interesting to know where he means to look."

He frowned as he lighted his pipe, because it was too late to satisfy his curiosity. The prospectors had vanished into the trackless desolation, and now deep snow had fallen the wilds would hide them well. Scott pondered for a few minutes and then resumed: "You mean to help Miss Strange put this matter over, although you don't believe in the lode?"

"Yes," said Thirlwell, "I've promised her."

"Then you're up against two hard men who have got a start, and one of them is dangerous."

"Black Steve? Well, I believe he meant to leave Father Lucien to starve, but I don't see why."

"You need help yourself," Scott rejoined dryly. "When Driscoll was ill and delirious he talked in a curious way, and when he got better may have had some recollection of being badly scared. If so, I expect he imagined he said more than he did and had, so to speak, given himself away. As a matter of fact, he said enough to be suspicious. Since he was delirious, he probably didn't know you were there, and it might be prudent not to let him know. It's possible he thought Father Lucien knew too much, and saw his opportunity of getting rid of him."

Thirlwell started. "It is possible! I'm glad I told you about my watch at the shack. I didn't at first; the things I suspected looked ridiculous."

"In future you had better tell me all you can. My opinion is, that you have undertaken a very tough job. For all that, I'm getting curious about the lode, and would rather like to have a stake in the venture, if Miss Strange agrees when she comes up."

"She won't agree unless she finds the ore. Then, of course, she'd need help and money."

"Very well," said Scott, and they talked about something else.

For some weeks they said nothing more about the silver vein. Part of the roof of the main heading in the mine came down, and they had afterwards to contend with a dangerous flow of water. Extra timbering was needed and the men risked their lives as they wedged the props under the cracking beams, while now and then they worked for a shift with buckets to help the clanging pump. Their clothes were always wet, and they were generally smeared with mud when they came up to eat and sleep. The miners grumbled, and Scott and Thirlwell felt the mental and physical strain. They were highly strung and often irritable, while when they sat by the stove when work was over they only talked about the difficulties they had struggled with all day and others that must be met in the morning.

In the meantime, the thaw began. The snow softened and got honeycombed by the drops from the trees. One sank to the knees in trampled slush among the sawn-off stumps about the shaft-head. The ice rotted, and in places where the current ran fast large floes broke off, and drove down stream until they were stopped by the thick ice in the slacks. Above the Shadow Rapids, however, there was, for a time, no break in the frozen surface, and one evening Scott and Thirlwell sat listening to the growl of the rising flood in the open channel it had made near the mine. The sound swelled and sank, and at intervals they heard rain patter on the roof.

"In a week or two the canoes will be out," Scott remarked. "There's a big head of water coming down and I guess the jamb that's backing up the stream won't stand till morning."

"Some of it's going now; that's an extra large floe," said Thirlwell as a detonating crash rang across the woods. Then there was a roar that was pierced by a high, strident note, and he knew the floe was tearing open upon a rock.

The shrill scream died away, but the turmoil of the current swelled, and knowing what would happen soon, they waited with strained attention and let their pipes go out. The mine buildings stood back from the bank and they ran no risk, but nobody can listen unmoved when the ice breaks up on a river of the North.

Presently there was a deafening concussion like the shock when a giant gun is fired. The shack trembled as if struck by a battering ram, and Thirlwell felt his nerves tingle. After the concussion came a roar that grew into an overwhelming din, and they braced themselves against the strain; one could not bear that appalling noise very long. It subsided a little into a confusion of jarring sounds that were sometimes distinguishable and sometimes drowned each other. Massy floes shocked and smashed, and tore apart upon the ledges with a noise like the ripping of woven fabric. Others, lifted out of the water, ground across those that stuck fast, and some crashed against the rocky bank, throwing huge blocks among the pines.

This lasted for a time, and then the uproar got bearable and gradually sank. There were intervals when one could hear the turmoil of the liberated flood as it rolled by in swollen fury. The intervals lengthened, and by and by Thirlwell got on his feet with a sigh of relief.

"You never get used to hearing the ice break up. It's tremendous!" he said. "This is a very stern country. Sometimes it frightens one—"

He stopped abruptly and listened. The uproar was sinking fast and in a lull he heard footsteps outside. Then the door was pushed open and a man staggered in. His fur-coat was torn and muddy, his feet came through his pulp moccasins, and the water that drained from him made a pool on the floor. Three others followed and stood, dripping, in the light, while Scott and Thirlwell gazed at them. Then the first dropped into a chair and leaned his arms on the table as if overcome by fatigue. His face was gaunt and his eyes were half shut.

"The boss is pretty well used up," said one of the others and Scott crossed the floor.

"Stormont," he said, "you look as if you had been up against it hard."

Stormont lifted his head and Thirlwell thought his eyes got like a wolf's.

"I'm starving! No food the last two days."

"Not much before!" one of the rest remarked.

"Been on mighty short rations since we hit the backtrail. Had a tough job to make it; had to leave our blankets and truck."

"We can give you a meal and a place to sleep. But where have you been?"

"Up north," another answered vaguely, and Scott, recognizing his caution, smiled as he turned to the last of the party, who stood near the door.

"You look fresher than the others, Steve. However, you're used to the country and I expect you brought your partners down."

"That's so," Driscoll growled. "Didn't think they'd make it. They're a tender-footed crowd!"

In the meantime, Thirlwell studied the fellow. Driscoll was wet and ragged; his face was thin, but inscrutably sullen. Unlike the rest, he did not look overcome by fatigue. When Scott spoke he gave him a dull glance and then fixed his eyes on the floor. Thirlwell had noted something unusual in his comrade's manner. Scott's voice had an ironical note and his look did not indicate much sympathy. In the North, a demand for food is seldom refused, but Scott obviously meant to be satisfied with supplying the party's urgent needs. With this Thirlwell agreed.

Then Scott said to Driscoll, "You had better take your friends to the bunk-house and tell the cook to make you supper. You know where to get blankets."

Stormont got up with an effort, and when he went out with the others Scott smiled.

"I'm not going back on my duty, but I don't want that outfit in my shack," he said.

Next morning after breakfast Stormont came in. He had to some extent recovered from his fatigue, but looked worn and dispirited.

"I guess I owe you some thanks," he said.

"I don't know if you do or not," Scott answered coolly. "In the bush, a starving man is, so to speak, entitled to ask for food and shelter. I couldn't refuse."

Stormont gave him a keen glance. "Well, there's another thing. It's a long trail to the railroad and I want to buy stores enough to see us out."

"Then I suppose I must let you have supplies; but you can't expect to get them as cheap as at the settlements. In fact, you'll have to pay my price."

"That needn't break the deal," Stormont replied. "I know when there's no use in kicking."

"An unsuccessful prospecting trip is an expensive undertaking," Scott said meaningly. "Then there's the disappointment. You would have got a big lift if you'd been lucky enough to find Miss Strange's silver."

"The silver is not Miss Strange's. The law gives a mineral vein to the person who stakes it off and records it first."

"That is so," Scott agreed. "Well, you don't look as if you had staked a valuable claim! I suppose you stopped too long trying to find the vein, and the ice was unsafe when you left. However, you want supplies to carry you down to the settlement, and if you'll come along to the store, we'll see what I've got."

They went out, and in the afternoon Stormont's party took the trail to the South.

Chapter XIV
Stormont Disowns A Debt

The general store was empty, and Drummond, leaning on the counter, frowned as he glanced at the clock. It was a few minutes after the time for closing and he had been busily occupied all day. Besides, he had an engagement at the pool-room and thought he would be late. If so, a man whom he knew he could beat would probably begin a game with somebody else, and he would miss an opportunity of winning two or three dollars. This was annoying, because Drummond needed the money, but he had other grounds for feeling dissatisfied.

Keeping store was monotonous and rather humiliating work that left one very little time for amusement. He could drive a fast horse as well as other young men he met up town, play a clever card game, and beat his friends at pool. His talents were obviously wasted in measuring dry-goods and weighing flour. Moreover, since meeting Stormont he had been extravagant and got into debt. There was no need to be economical when he had been promised a share in a rich mining claim.

Then he wondered with misgivings what the farmer who had gone into the back office was talking about, and hearing angry voices, felt sorry he had made some alterations in the man's order. Certain stale goods carried a commission if the salesman could work them off, but the thing needed tact and a knowledge of the customer's temper. Drummond feared he had been imprudent.

In the meantime, he looked about the store with a feeling of disgust. The long room, with its cracked, board walls and dusty floor, was uncomfortably warm, and smelt of hot iron, dry-goods, and old cheese. Drummond had neglected to regulate the draught when he filled the rusty stove, and now felt that_ one could not expect a spirited young man to spend his days in such a place. Anyhow, it was after closing time, and sitting on the counter he lighted a cigarette, letting it stick to his under lip. This was the latest fashion and gave one a sporting look. Soon after he began to smoke, the farmer came out of the office.

"You can send for the truck when you like; I've no use for goods like that," he said. "Next time you pack me a dud lot I'll cut out your account. If you and the sporting guy who's sitting on your counter thought me a sucker, I guess I've put you wise!"

He went down the steps into the street, and the lean, hard-faced storekeeper turned to Drummond with an ominous frown.

"Get off that counter! You make me tired to look at you, with your dude clothes and a cigar-root hanging out of your mouth. Throw the blamed thing away and put up the canned stuff you left about."

Drummond felt tempted to refuse, but his employer's eye was on him and he obeyed sullenly.

"When you've finished, you can clean up that row of shelves," the other resumed. "Then stack the flour and sugar bags where they're kept. Guess you reckoned to leave the truck all night where the transfer man dumped it. If you can't serve a customer, I'll see you keep the store straight!"

Drummond imagined the work would occupy him for an hour and might spoil his clothes. Besides, if he gave way, his employer might make fresh encroachments on his evenings, and he thought the fellow wanted to goad him to revolt.

"No, sir," he said. "It's closing time. I'm going to quit."

"If you quit now, you quit for good! Don't know why I've kept you, anyway!"

"I know," said Drummond, who resolved to be firm. If his employer really meant to get rid of him, he risked nothing, but if not, he might win some advantage. "You couldn't get another clerk to take my job for the wages you pay."

"Well," said the other grimly, "I'm willing to try. It's a sure thing I couldn't get a man who'd muss up the store like you. Come to me for your money and light out when you like."

He went out, banging the door, and Drummond sat down, rather limply, on a dry-goods bale. After all, it was something of a shock to find himself dismissed, but in a few minutes he gathered confidence. Stormont had given him fifty dollars and promised him a share in the silver mine, and although he had soon spent the money, he would go to Winnipeg, ask for another payment, and see what progress the fellow was making. If the vein had not yet been located, Stormont would, no doubt, find him a job. In fact, the only trouble was that when he had bought his ticket he would not have enough money left to pay his bill at the boarding-house.

Four days later, he left the town, and reaching Winnipeg one afternoon, began to inquire about Stormont in the great, domed, marble-paved waiting-room. To his surprise, the officials he questioned knew nothing about the man, and when one sent him to the inquiry office, the fashionably dressed lady clerk was ignorant. She, however, threw a directory on the counter and told him haughtily that he could look for the address.

Drummond found it, and walking along Main Street, turned up Portage Avenue. There was a block of traffic at the corner where the broad roads cross, and close by a crowd had gathered to read the bulletins on the front of a newspaper office. Stopping for a few minutes, Drummond studied the row of tall buildings, but saw that the number he wanted was farther on. There was, however, an imposing block some distance ahead, but this turned out to be a huge department store, and afterwards the buildings got smaller and plainer. It began to look as if Stormont was not as important a man as he had thought, and he was conscious of some disappointment as he went on until he stopped where private houses, workshops, and shabby stores ran out towards Deer Park. Then he found the number and entered a narrow, dingy building.

It was obvious that Stormont had studied economy when he chose his office, and Drummond stopped and hesitated on a landing opposite a door that badly needed painting. He began to think he had been rash in leaving his post in the Ontario town, but nerving himself with the reflection that he had a share in a silver vein, knocked at the door. Somebody told him to come in, and he walked into a small room.

The dirty walls were hung with plans of building lots and surveys of the forest belt in Eastern Manitoba. A glass partition ran up the middle and on one side Watson sat in front of a typewriter. He looked at Drummond with surprise, but did not get up.

"Well," he said, "why have you come to town? Have you got a week off, or have you got fired?"

"You ought to know what I've come about, but I want to see the boss," Drummond rejoined.

"That's easy, anyhow," said Watson, with a grin Drummond did not like, and indicated a door in the partition.

Drummond opened the door and saw Stormont sitting at a table covered with papers. He looked up and nodded coolly.

"Hallo!" he said. "Mr. Drummond, isn't it? Sit down for a few minutes."

Then picking up a letter, he knitted his brows. He did not think Drummond could give him much trouble, but he might become something of a nuisance unless he was dealt with firmly. Stormont had not long since come back from the North, feeling disappointed and savage, for he had spent a good deal of money on the expedition. Besides, things had gone wrong at the office while he was away and he had lost some profitable business.

"What can I do for you?" he asked by and by.

"I've left the store," said Drummond. "Thought I'd locate in Winnipeg. One has better chances in the big cities, and I reckoned you could find me a job. Anyhow, I'll need some money."

"That's a sure thing. But why did you come to me for it?"

"You gave me fifty dollars—"

"When did I give you fifty dollars?" Stormont interrupted with a look of surprise.

"The evening Watson took me to your room at the Dufferin House. Besides, you promised me a share in the mine."

Stormont smiled. "That accounts for the thing! I'm afraid you were drunker than I thought."

"You did give me the money," Drummond insisted. "Are you trying to go back on your promise?"

"Oh, well," said Stormont with an indulgent smile, "in order to satisfy you, we'll ask Watson." He knocked on the partition and turned to the clerk as the latter came in. "Mr. Drummond states that I gave him fifty dollars on the evening you brought him to the Dufferin House. Do you remember anything about it?"

"Certainly not," said Watson. "You gave him a cigar and some liquor, though I thought he'd had enough. He fell down the stairs afterwards and made trouble for me when I saw him home." Watson paused and resumed with a meaning smile: "It's pretty hard to remember what happens when you've got on a big jag!"

Drummond colored angrily, but pulled himself together. "I remember I got the money and told Mr. Stormont about the ore."

"Now I come to think of it, you did tell me a curious story about a mysterious silver lode," Stormont agreed. "Somewhere in the North, wasn't it? Anyhow, I didn't give the thing much attention. You can hear tales of that kind in any miners' saloon."

"That's so," Watson supported him. "Sometimes we hear them in this office when a crank prospector comes along. All the same, they're not business propositions."

"You promised me a share in the mine," Drummond declared, and added with dark suspicion: "I guess you found the ore."

Stormont laughed ironically. "Cut it out, Mr. Drummond! It's a sure thing I haven't found a silver lode."

"If you're going to turn me down, I'll try somebody else."

"I can't object. In fact, I dare say Watson will give you the addresses of some people who speculate on mining claims. But you mustn't be disappointed if they fire you out."

Drummond's face got red and he clenched his fist, for he had already told his tale to people who heard it with amused incredulity.

"You promised you would make me rich and I've thrown up my job! I've got about five dollars and don't know what to do!"

"Well," said Stormont coolly, "there's an employment agent a few blocks up the street and as trade's pretty good it's possible he can find you a post. That's about the only thing I can think of and I'm occupied just now—"

Drummond stopped him with a savage gesture and walked out of the room.

"We have fixed him; I guess he won't bother us again," Stormont remarked.

After leaving the office, Drummond wandered moodily along the avenue and presently came to a square, past which rows of pretty wooden houses surrounded by poplars, ran towards the river bank. The snow had gone, the afternoon was warm, and finding a bench in the sun, he sat down to think. His character was complex and his thoughts involved, for he had inherited something from ancestors of different type. A touch of Indian vanity and French expansiveness was balanced by his father's Scottish caution and the Indian's stolid calm. Sometimes he was rash and impulsive, and sometimes strangely patient, but he seldom forgot an injury.

It was obvious that he had been cheated and in the meantime could get no satisfaction for the wrong he had been done. What he knew about the silver ore was worth something while he alone had the secret, but now he had told somebody else its value had disappeared. It was, however, a comfort to reflect that he had not been altogether frank with Stormont; he had kept something back that would be a useful guide when one looked for the creek. His recollection of this was hazy, but he would think about it later.

On the whole, Drummond thought Stormont had not found the ore. A hint of anger in his ironical amusement implied that he had come back disappointed; and if he imagined he had got on the right track, he would, no doubt, have been willing to pay another fifty dollars. For all that, Watson and Stormont had plotted to win his confidence, make him drunk, and find out all he knew, and this indicated that the fellow thought the vein worth looking for. When Stormont got over his disappointment he would try again.

Drummond saw that he could embarrass Stormont by selling the secret he had been cheated of to somebody else. It was amusing to think of two parties looking for the vein; the difficulty was that he did not know anybody likely to be a buyer. But he could wait, since it looked as if he had put Stormont off the track, and by and by he might find a speculator willing to believe his tale. Sooner than let Stormont locate the vein he would give, for nothing, any antagonist of the latter's all the help he could.

Then he remembered that he had only a few dollars and must find some work soon. Supper would not be served at the cheap hotels for an hour yet and he set off to look for an employment agent. The man charged a dollar and gave him a card with an address, remarking that Drummond ought to get a job, as business was good. Drummond went back up the avenue, and presenting the card at a big store, was engaged for a week and promised a post afterwards if the department boss was satisfied.

Chapter XV
The Grand Rapid

Bright moonlight touched the river, streaking the angry water with a silver track, when Scott and Thirlwell poled against the stream in the gloom of the wooded bank. The Shadow, swollen by melted snow, rolled by in flood, swirling along the stony beach in lines of foam, and tossing about battered trunks brought down by winter storms. Farther down stream, a shimmering haze of spray indicated the Grand Rapid, and Thirlwell meant to stem the current until they were far enough from the foaming turmoil to paddle across. The gray trout were shy that evening and they had let the canoe drift farther than they thought. Presently somebody hailed them from the bank, and as they let the canoe swing round in an eddy a dark figure moved out from the gloom of the pines.

"Driscoll's voice, I think," said Scott. "Head her inshore; we'll see what he wants."

It transpired that Driscoll wanted them to take him across. He had left his small canoe some distance down stream, because he thought he might be drawn into the rapid before he could reach the other bank. Scott's canoe was larger, and with three men on board they could easily make head against the current.

"I guess we've got to take him," Scott remarked. "Give her a push and run her in behind the rock."

When the canoe grounded Driscoll got on board and picked up a pole. As there was not another, Thirlwell paddled in the stern while they pushed the craft through the slack. It was hard work and he noted how slowly the pines rolled past. By and by they reached an angry-white rush of current between an island and the bank, and as they could scarcely make progress Scott suggested putting down the poles and paddling across. Driscoll, however, grumbled that they were not far enough up stream, and getting out when they ran the canoe close to the driftwood that washed about the shingle, tracked her for some distance through the shallow water. While the fellow stumbled among the dead branches, Scott gave Thirlwell a meaning look that the latter thought he understood.

It was obvious that Driscoll was anxious to avoid being swept into the rapid and Thirlwell admitted the prudence of this, but did not think the danger great enough to account for his rather excessive caution. The Indians generally shot the rapid when the water was low, and although the river was now rolling down in flood, it was not impossible for men with steady nerves to take the canoe safely through to the tail-pool. He wondered whether Black Steve had been drinking, but on the whole did not think he had, and admitting that the fellow knew the streams and eddies best, let him have his way. At length, however, Scott threw down his pole.

"We're far enough and I want my supper," he said. "Get hold of the paddles and let her shoot across."

Driscoll grumbled half aloud, but made no determined protest, and paddling hard they headed obliquely for the opposite bank. As they forged through the glittering water the current swept them down and Thirlwell noted that it was running faster than he had thought. The river was wide and the ragged pines got indistinct as they rolled back up stream. It looked as if the canoe were standing still and the banks moving on, only that the gleaming spray-cloud got rapidly nearer. It stretched across from bank to bank, and a dull roar that rose and fell came out of the wavering mist. For the most part, the current was smooth, but here and there broken lines of foam streaked its surface, and sometimes the canoe swung round in revolving eddies.

Still the dark rocks ahead got nearer and at length Driscoll made a sign that they could stop paddling. He occupied the stern, where he could steer the craft. Thirlwell, feeling breathless after his efforts, was glad to stop, and looked about as he knelt in the middle. He had often thought it was from the river one best marked the savage austerity of the wilderness. In the bush, one's view was broken by rocks and trunks, but from the wide expanse of water one could look across the belt of forest that ran back, desolate and silent, to Hudson Bay. Here and there the hazy outline of a rocky height caught the eye, but for the most part, the landscape had no charm of varied beauty. It was monotonous, somber, and forbidding.

The canoe was now thirty or forty yards from the rough bank, and drifting fast. Driscoll obviously meant to land on a patch of shingle lower down, which was the only safe spot for some distance. At low-water one could run a canoe aground among the ledges that bordered the slack inner edge of the rapid, but when the Shadow rose in flood the current broke and boiled furiously among the rocks. One faces forward when paddling, and while Thirlwell watched the dark gaps in the pines open up and close he heard Driscoll shout. Next moment Scott leaned over the bow and plunged his arm into the water. It looked as if he had dropped his paddle and Thirlwell backed his in order to stop the craft.

The paddle floated past, too far off for Driscoll to reach, and signing to Thirlwell, he swung the canoe round, but the water was getting broken and they missed the paddle by a yard. Then they drove her ahead in a semi-circle, and a minute or two had gone when Scott, leaning over cautiously, seized the paddle-haft. In the meantime, they had drifted fast, and Thirlwell saw that that patch of shingle was now up stream.

"That's awkward," Scott remarked, and the canoe rocked as Driscoll dipped his paddle.

"Drive her! You have got to make the beach," he shouted in a hoarse voice.

There was something contagious in the man's alarm, and knowing his physical courage, Thirlwell made his best effort. The sweat ran down his face, he felt his muscles strain and his sinews crack, and the canoe's bow lifted as the paddle-blades beat the water. Driscoll leaned far forward to get a longer stroke and urged the others with breathless shouts, but the shingle they were heading for slowly slipped away.

"Try along the bank," Driscoll ordered, and Thirlwell, turning to pick up a pole, saw his face in the moonlight. It was strangely set, and he was not looking at the bank, but at the rapid. His gaze was fixed and horrified.

For some minutes they scarcely held the craft against the stream. Indeed, Thirlwell afterwards wondered why they kept it up, since it was obvious that they could not reach the landing, but imagined that Driscoll urged them. The fellow seemed resolved not to be drawn into the rapid.

"We can't make it; I've got to let up," Scott gasped at length, and Thirlwell, breathing hard, wiped his wet face as the canoe drove away.

It was galling to be beaten, and there was some danger unless the craft was handled well. Steadiness and skill were needed, but after all the risk was not greater than he had often run in the mine and on the frozen trail. The daunting thing was that Driscoll, whom they had expected to steer the canoe, looked afraid. He crouched astern, paddling in a slack, nerveless manner. There was no chance of landing now; they must run through the mad turmoil into the eddies of the tail-pool.

The roar of the flood rolled in confused echoes along the wall of pines. Angry waves broke upon the reefs near the bank, and a cloud of spray wavered and glittered above a tossing line of foam. They were drifting towards the line extraordinarily fast, and Thirlwell felt his nerves tingle as he tried to brace himself. There was ground for being daunted, but he thought he would not have felt much disturbed had Driscoll not looked afraid.

Then Scott, kneeling in the bow, turned, and after a quick glance at Driscoll said, "Keep as cool as you can, partner. Steve's badly rattled and can't be trusted."

A minute or two afterwards, they plunged over the edge of the rapid. The air got cold and the light got dim, for a wind blew against the rush of water and the spray hid the moon. Still, they could see for a distance, and Thirlwell frankly shrank as he glanced ahead. The river was broken by ridges of leaping foam that ran one behind the other with narrow gaps between. White-ringed eddies span along the bank and the tops of dark rocks rose out of the turmoil. Moreover, there were rocks in the channels, and one must strain one's eyes for the upheavals that marked sunken shoals. Driscoll knew the reefs and eddies, and while they plunged down like a toboggan Thirlwell risked a glance astern. The man's eyes were fixed on the river, but his pose was slack. It was plain that he had not recovered and they could expect no help from him. Thirlwell drew a deep breath and gripped his paddle hard.

He could never remember much about the next few minutes. Sometimes he shouted to Scott, and thought Scott called to him, as a wedge of stone suddenly split the rushing foam, and sometimes when the current boiled in fierce rebound from a hidden obstacle. The canoe plunged until the water stood up above her bows, and now and then leaped out half her length. When they dared, they checked her with a back-stroke as some danger loomed ahead, but oftener drove her faster than the current to steer her round a reef or dark, revolving pool. Yet, for the most part, she must be kept straight down stream, for if she swerved across a breaking wave its crest would curl on board and bear her down.

Thirlwell was vaguely conscious that his hand had galled and bled, but this did not matter. The trouble was, that the sweat ran into his eyes and he could not see distinctly. He felt his heart thump and his breath come hard, but braced himself against the lurching and tried not to miss a stroke. If he did so, Scott, paddling in the bow, would swing her round and next moment they would be in the water.

In the meantime, he was conscious of a curious, fierce excitement, but he had braved danger too often to indulge the feeling. It led to hot rashness, and judgment and quick but calm decision were needed now. He must concentrate all the power of his mind as well as the strength of his body on taking the canoe down to the tail-pool.

She shipped some water on the way and they could not bail. It washed about their knees as the frail craft plunged, and Thirlwell wondered anxiously how much she would carry without capsizing. The rocks and pines ashore now streamed past, blurred and indistinct, but he had seldom an opportunity for glancing at the bank. He must look ahead, and every now and then his view was shortened by a ridge of tumbling foam.

Somehow she came through, half-swamped, and swung down the savage fan-shaped rush that spread in white turmoil across the tail-pool. Paddling hard, they drove her out of the eddies that circled along the bank, and finding a slack, ran her on to a shingle beach. Then they sat down, wet and exhausted, to recover breath. Driscoll helped to pull the canoe up, but when Thirlwell presently looked about he could not see him.

"He's gone," Scott remarked dryly. "Lit out while you were taking off your boots."

Thirlwell imagined that the roar of the river had drowned the fellow's steps, but he did not want to talk, about Driscoll yet, and when he put on his boots, which had been full of water, they started for the shack. After they had changed their clothes Scott sat down and lighted his pipe.

"What do you think was the matter with Black Steve?" he asked.

"It looked as if he'd taken some liquor, but I don't know," Thirlwell answered. "He was obviously scared."

"Sure," said Scott. "But he wasn't scared of getting drowned. Steve's a better canoe hand than either of us and has physical pluck."

"Then why was he afraid?"

Scott looked thoughtful. "I imagine he was afraid of the rapid and the dark. When he hailed us to take him over, I thought it an excuse; he could have got across in his own canoe if he had braced up. My notion is he didn't want to make the trip by himself." He paused and gave Thirlwell a keen glance. "Curious, isn't it?"

"He's a curious man," said Thirlwell, who had dark suspicions that he did not want to talk about. "When we were drifting into the rapid, I got a glimpse of his face and didn't look again. Thought I'd better not; the fellow's nerve had gone. Anyhow, if he hates the rapid, why does he stop here and live near the bank?"

"Steve is primitive; I guess you don't understand him yet. He's an old trapper and one gets superstitious in the bush. For all that, he's stubborn, and if he has an object, he'll persist until he carries it out."

"But what object has he got?"

Scott made a vague gesture. "I can't tell you that. Hadn't you better get out the plates? I want some food."

Thirlwell put a frying-pan on the stove and they talked about something else.

Chapter XVI
The Pit-Prop

Driscoll was sorting pit-props, throwing them on to piles at the bottom of the shaft, when Thirlwell stopped to hook a small, flat lamp to his hat. The man sometimes worked in the mine for a few weeks when the trapping season was over, and Scott was generally willing to engage him because he was skilful with the axe and labor was scarce. He made no friends among the men, and gave Thirlwell a sour look without speaking when the latter picked up his lamp.

Thirlwell went on down the inclined gallery. Water splashed upon his slickers and trickled about his feet; the tunnel was narrow and the air was foul. Here and there a smoky light burned among the props lining the walls, and the dim illumination touched the beams that crossed the roof, but the gaps between the spots were dark. The timbers were numerous, and where one could see a short distance, ran on into the gloom in rows so closely spaced that they seemed continuous.

By and by Thirlwell found Scott looking up at a massive beam a few inches overhead. The beam was not quite level, and the prop beneath one end had bent, while a threatening crack extended across the roof.

"We may have a bad fall here," Scott remarked. "The prop's getting shaky and the pressure's pretty fierce. I reckon we'd better shore her up as quick as we can. It's lucky our lumber doesn't cost us much."

Thirlwell examined the crack and thought it dangerous. There were one or two transverse splits, which indicated a heavy mass of rock was ready to come down. None of the men were near the spot, and he knew they were occupied, but Driscoll had left a few props between the timbers, ready for use where the roof was weak. Thirlwell found one and dragged it to the spot.

"We'll put this up and then I think I'll get a fresh beam across."

Scott helped him to raise the timber. It was a few inches too long, and crossed the space between floor and roof with a small slant, but it was meant to do so, in order that when its lower end was driven forward until it stood upright it would wedge fast the beam above. Then Thirlwell brought an ax and struck the prop some heavy blows with its back while Scott steadied the top. It was almost in place, and the bent timber was getting loose, when the top slipped and shook the beam. There was an ominous crack and a few small stones broke away and fell on Scott's head.

"I've got her butted solid now," he shouted after a short breathless struggle with the timber. "Be quick! The roof's coming down!"

Thirlwell saw the danger. So long as the prop slanted, it would not support the beam, and if the beam gave way, the roof would fall and crush them before they could get from underneath. He thought he had a few moments to hammer the prop straight, and swung the ax savagely while the sweat ran down his face. He dared not look up again, but the ominous cracking went on and while he wondered what was happening, Driscoll ran past. A big stone fell beside the man as he seized another prop and with a tense effort jambed it under the beam.

"I'll take some weight off her while you shore her up," Driscoll gasped.

He had brought a heavy mallet, but before he used this he dragged the foot of the timber round, bending his body forward while his arms got stiff and hard, as if carved from wood. His sullen face was darkly flushed and the swollen veins stood out from his forehead. Thirlwell saw him for a moment as he lifted his ax, and remembering the scene afterwards, thought the fellow had looked a model of savage strength. It was obvious that he had no fear.

In the meantime, he was vaguely conscious that Driscoll had saved his life. He and Scott had stayed too long, and could not have fixed their prop before the beam gave way had not the other come to help. For that matter, they were not out of danger yet. Unless they could wedge the timber in the next few moments, the roof would come down. There was not room to swing the ax properly, his body was cramped from bending, and he could not lift his head. Stooping in the low tunnel, he nerved himself for a tense effort and struck several furious blows. The prop quivered, groaned as it felt the pressure from above, moved an inch or two, and stood upright. Then Thirlwell dropped his ax and staggered back. He felt limp and exhausted, and wanted to get away. The beam would hold the roof for some minutes and might do so for a time.

"You can let up now, Driscoll," Scott called out when they stopped a few yards off. "We'll see if the prop will stand before we do anything else."

"Guess I'll fix the other," Driscoll replied.

"Come out," Scott insisted. "You don't know if it's safe."

Driscoll glanced round for a moment. His hat had fallen off and the miner's lamp flared and smoked in the water at his feet. His hair was wet with the drops from the roof, and a thin streak of blood ran down his face from a cut a falling stone had made. But his heavy eyes had a fixed, obstinate look.

"You hired me to mind the timbers; it's my job."

Scott acquiesced with a gesture and he and Thirlwell watched. There was a risk that in wedging the extra prop the man might loosen the first; and then, if neither was able to bear the load, the rock above would fall and bury him. For all that, Driscoll looked undisturbed and did not stop until he had carefully driven the timber into its proper place. Then he turned to Scott and his glance was slow and dull.

"I want you to send two of the boys along."

"Why do you want them?"

"I've got to have some help. She won't hold up long unless we run another beam across."

"It would be prudent," Thirlwell agreed, and went down the gallery with Scott to the working face.

"What do you think of Black Steve?" Scott asked when they had sent the men and stood near a lamp. "He wasn't scared just now!"

"I'm puzzled," said Thirlwell thoughtfully. "The fellow was quite cool. If he hadn't come with the prop, I expect the roof would have buried us. But that's another thing. Why did he come?"

Scott smiled. "We were plainly in some danger, but I don't imagine Black Steve was moved by a generous impulse to save our lives. In fact, if it had promised him some advantage, I rather think he'd have seen us buried."

"You don't claim it was a sense of duty?"

"Not in a way; Steve's too primitive. On the whole, I think he explained the thing best when he said it was his job. A fellow of his kind doesn't reason like you; perhaps he did once, but lost the habit in the bush. He's, so to speak, atavistic; moved by instincts, like the Indians and animals."

"But I don't see—"

"Perhaps it isn't very obvious," Scott admitted. "For all that, the Indian's instinctive obstinacy carries him far. Steve had undertaken to look after our timbering, he's used to danger, and the risk didn't count. I expect he was moved by the feeling the bushman gets when he's up against Nature; he knows he'll be crushed if he can't make good. Anyhow, I've moralized long enough. Will you see what they're doing with that rock-borer?"

Thirlwell left him and went to the machine, which made a jarring noise. He spent some time adjusting the cutters, and afterwards stood for a few minutes thinking about what his comrade had said. Scott's argument was involved, but Thirlwell thought he saw what he meant. Driscoll's bemused mind could not grasp the thought of duty that demanded self-sacrifice, but he had animal courage and stubbornness. He would carry out what he had undertaken. Moreover, he might have animal cunning without having cultivated intelligence, and his strength and resolution made him dangerous. Thirlwell did not like Driscoll better than before, but it looked as if the fellow had saved his life, and although he might not have meant to do so, this counted for something. Going back to the shaft presently, he climbed up and sat down in the sun.

A warm wind blew across the pine woods, the sun was getting hot, and the wet grounds about the shaft-head was drying fast. The river had risen as the lakes in the wilds it came from overflowed with melted snow, and raged, level with its banks, in angry flood, rolling broken trees down stream and strewing ledges and shingle with battered branches. Its hoarse roar echoed across the bush, and Thirlwell felt that there was something daunting in the deep-toned sound. One could understand that a man like Driscoll, whose brain was dulled by liquor, might let it fill him with vague terrors when the woods were still at night.

But listening to the river presently led Thirlwell to think about Strange. There was something pathetic about the story of his life, for Agatha had made Thirlwell understand her father's long patience, gentleness, and self-sacrifice. His duty to his family had cost him much, but he had cheerfully paid. It looked as if he had done best at the task he most disliked—managing the humble store in the small wooden town. One could not think of him as having failed there. His wife and children loved him, though all but one had smiled when he talked about the lode.

His daughter, who knew him best, had inherited his confidence, and Thirlwell owned that this had some weight. She was perhaps influenced by tender sentiment, but there was nothing romantic about Driscoll and Stormont, and it looked as if they shared her belief that the lode could be found. Scott, too, thought it possible, and his judgment was often sound. Thirlwell had imagined the lode an illusion of Strange's, but his disbelief was giving way.

Then he forgot the others and thought about Agatha. In some ways she was like Strange, but she was made of finer and stronger stuff. She had his patience, but her brain was keener, and her resolution was backed by moral force. Moreover, she was a very charming girl and Thirlwell admitted that he looked forward with eagerness to their journey. She would come in summer, when the rivers and lakes were open and the woods were filled with resinous smells. The sun was hot in the North then, the days were often calm, and there was a wonderful bracing freshness when the lingering twilight glimmered behind the pines.

It would be strangely pleasant to listen to the girl's soft voice while the canoes glided smoothly across sparkling lakes, and perhaps to tell her stories of the wilds when the smoke of the camp-fire drifted by and the cry of the loon came out of the shadows. For all that, there was not much risk of his falling in love with her. He was not a sentimentalist, and she had told him that her vocation was science. Her journey was a duty, and when the duty was carried out she would concentrate on her studies, and as she had talent presently make her mark. He did not think she would find the lode, but when she was persuaded it could not be found he would no longer be useful and they would go their different ways. Well, he supposed he must acquiesce. He was a poor engineer, and such happiness as marriage could offer was not for him.

Then he glanced at his watch and got up with an impatient shrug. He had forgotten his work while he thought about the girl, and there was much to be done. For one thing, he had come up to see if the smith had tempered some boring tools; and then he must send the *Metis* river-jacks to float a raft of props down to the mine. Pulling himself together, he set about the work with characteristic energy, but as he walked through the murmuring woods he unconsciously began to sing a romantic ballad he had learned when a boy. Presently, however, he stopped and smiled. It looked as if he were getting sentimental, and one must guard against that kind of thing.

Chapter XVII
Drummond Offers Help

It was a calm evening and Thirlwell and Scott sat outside the shack, watching the river while the sunset faded across the woods. A few *Metis* freighters had gone to the settlements for supplies and mining tools, and although much depended on the condition of the portages, Scott expected them that night.

"Antoine will bring up our mail," he said. "It's some time since Miss Strange has written to you about her plans."

Thirlwell said it was nearly three months, and Scott resumed: "Well, I think if I'd had a part in the business, I'd have tried to find if the Hudson's Bay agent was alive. It's possible that he could tell you something about the location of the ore."

"I don't know that I have any part in the business," Thirlwell replied. "I promised to go with Miss Strange, but that's all."

"If she finds the lode, she'll need a mining engineer."

"She'll have no trouble in engaging one if the pay is good."

"But you wouldn't think you had first claim to the post? In fact, if you helped the girl to find the ore, you'd be satisfied to drop out and leave her alone?"

Thirlwell frowned. He had made no plans for the future and certainly did not mean to trade upon Agatha's gratitude, but he knew it would hurt him, so to speak, to drop out and let her look for other help.

"The lode isn't found yet," he rejoined.

"Anyhow, I feel that the girl or you ought to have got on the agent's track," Scott insisted. "He knew where Strange went, and saw him when he returned. It's possible that Strange confused his memory by his subsequent trips, but the agent heard his story when the matter was fresh."

Thirlwell did not answer, and Scott cut some tobacco. When he had finished he looked up the river.

"The *bateaux!* Antoine has made good time."

Two craft drew out of the shadow of the pines, slid down the swift current, and presently grounded on a gravel beach. They were of the canoe type, but larger, and their bottoms were flat, since they were rather built for carrying goods than paddling fast. There was a good water route to the rocky height of land, across which the cargo was brought on the freighters' backs from a river that joined the wagon trail to the settlements. As soon as they landed, the crews began to carry up boxes and packages, but a young man left the group and came towards the shack. He wore neat store-clothes that were not much the worse for the journey, and although his skin was somewhat dark, looked like a young business man from the cities.

"Which of you is Mr. Thirlwell?" he asked.

"I am," said Thirlwell. "Who are you?"

"Ian Drummond; the boys call me Jake. A son of Hector Drummond's of Longue Sault factory."

"Ah," said Scott, "this gets interesting! Did Hector Drummond send you?"

"No; he died nine years since."

Scott gave Thirlwell a meaning look, and turned to the young man.

"Then what do you want?"

"To begin with, I want a job."

"A job?" said Scott with some surprise. "What can you do?"

"I know nothing about mining, but I'm pretty strong," Drummond answered, giving Scott a deerskin bag. "Anyhow, Mr. Thirlwell had better read his letter before you hire me. Antoine, the *patron*, brought up your mail."

"Very well," said Scott. "The cook will give the boys supper soon and you had better go along. Come back afterwards."

When the lad had gone, Thirlwell felt pleasantly excited as he opened a letter Scott took out of the bag, for he saw it was from Agatha. She told him that Drummond had met her in Toronto and related how Stormont had victimized him. The young man stated that he wanted to see the North and would like to get work where he could watch for the prospecting party he thought Stormont would send up.

"I warned him that you may not be able to give him employment, but he is keen about going and willing to take the risk," she said. "We can, I think, trust him to some extent, and perhaps he knows enough about my father's journey to be useful; but I cannot tell if it would be prudent to offer him a reward. I am glad to feel I can leave this to you, and will, of course, agree to the line you think it proper to take."

Thirlwell read part of the letter to Scott, who said, "Miss Strange seems to have a flattering confidence in your judgment. Do you want me to hire the fellow?"

"I don't know yet. I wouldn't ask you to engage him unless he could be of use."

"You needn't hesitate on that ground, since we're two men short," Scott answered, smiling. "Well, suppose we wait until we have talked to him. I guess you know this silver-lode is getting hold of me."

"I wonder why!"

Scott laughed. "You understand machines and rocks; to some extent I understand men. Anyhow, I find them interesting, and perhaps other people's firm belief in the lode influences me."

By and by Drummond came back and Scott studied him as he advanced. He saw the lad had a strain of Indian blood, and he knew something about the half-breeds' character. They were marked by certain weaknesses, but as a rule inherited a slow tenacity from their Indian ancestors. He had known a man, shot through the body, walk four hundred miles to reach a doctor, and they made the revenging of serious injuries a duty. A *Metis* would wait the greater part of a lifetime for a chance of repaying in kind a man who had wronged him. Drummond looked somewhat dissipated and had a superficial smartness that young men without much education acquire in Canadian towns, but Scott thought him intelligent.

"Sit down," he said, indicating a short pine-stump. "You want a job. Is that all?"

"Yes," said Drummond coolly, "it's all I want *now*. If you and Mr. Thirlwell mean to look for the ore and take me along, you can give me what you think my help is worth. But I've already put Miss Strange wise."

"You seem to be pretty trustful! How did you find her?"

"My father knew where Strange, located after he left the factory, and I tried to get on the track of his folks when Stormont turned me down. Talked to packing-house drummers at a department store in Winnipeg where I was employed, and found a man who sold Strange canned goods when he ran a grocery business. The drummer had known him pretty well and told me Miss Strange was in Toronto. By and by, when trade was slack in Winnipeg, the firm sent some of the clerks to their Toronto store and I bothered the department boss until he let me go. Then I was 'most a month locating Miss Strange; couldn't find her in the directory and Toronto's a big town."

Scott noted the determination that had helped him in his search. "You knew about the lode for some time," he said. "Why did you wait so long?"

"I allowed there wasn't much use in my butting in, until I read in a newspaper that Strange was drowned. Besides, the drummer reckoned his own folks thought him a crank and there was nothing to his tale. All the same, when I got tired of keeping store I thought I'd see what I could do about the lode."

"I suppose it was because the drummer put you wise that you went to Miss Strange and not her brother? No doubt you tried to interest other people first. Still, as she promised you nothing, I don't see why you came here."

"Stormont played me for a sucker; found out all I knew and turned me down!" Drummond answered with a savage sparkle in his eyes.

Scott was silent for a few moments and then looked up. "You can begin work to-morrow and Mr. Thirlwell will pay you what you're worth. We'll make no further promise, but if you like, you can tell us anything you think important."

"Miss Strange knows," said Drummond with a curious smile. "You want to remember that I told Stormont the creek runs *south*. She does run south, for a piece, but she turns and goes down a valley to the east."

"Then it's hard to see your object for playing the crook with Stormont, though I don't suppose he'd have done the square thing if you had put him on the right track," Scott remarked. "However, that's not our business. You'll find room and some blankets in the bunk-house."

Drummond left them and Thirlwell said, thoughtfully, "It's plain that he deceived Stormont by telling him the creek flowed south. This would make the fellow think the ore was on our side of the last height of land, but if the water goes east, it must run into the James Bay basin on the other slope. That's something of a clue, but I see a risk in keeping Drummond here. Suppose he makes friends with Driscoll?"

"Driscoll doesn't make friends," Scott rejoined and added with a twinkle: "Then as you don't admit there is a lode, it's not worth while to wonder whether the lad could tell Black Steve anything useful."

"We'll let that go," Thirlwell replied, and when Scott strolled away read Agatha's letter again with keen satisfaction. It was a charming, frank letter, and he thrilled as he noted her trust in him.

Drummond went to work next morning and Thirlwell, allowing for some awkwardness at first, thought he would earn his pay, while a doubt he had felt about the prudence of engaging him was presently removed. Going to the smith's shop one afternoon, he heard angry voices and stopped to see what was going on. The smithy, which stood at the edge of the clearing round the mine, was a rude log shack without a door. It was generally rather dark, but just then a ray of sunshine struck in and the charcoal fire on the hearth glowed a dull red. The smith leaned on his hammer, watching Driscoll and Drummond, who confronted each other close by.

Driscoll was heavy and muscular, Drummond wiry and thin, but as they stood, highly strung, Thirlwell noted the athletic symmetry of both figures. Driscoll had, no doubt, acquired it by travel in the woods, and Drummond by inheritance from Indian forefathers. The older man's limbs and body had the fine proportions of a Greek statue, and since he did not move one could not see that he was lame. Their faces, although different in modeling, were somehow alike, for both had a curious, quiet watchful look. They disputed in low voices, but Thirlwell saw their mood was dangerous. He knew that noisy fury seldom marks a struggle in the North, where hunting animals and men strike in silence. There was something strangely like the stealthy alertness of the animals in their attitudes.

Waiting in the gloom among the pine-trunks, he gathered that the quarrel was about the sharpening of tools. Drummond had brought some cutters from the boring machine, and Driscoll wanted his ax ground.

"I came along first," Drummond declared. "Tom's going to fix my cutters; your ax has got to wait!" He glanced at the smith, sharply, as if reluctant to move his eyes from Driscoll. "Give the wheel a spin and let's get busy!"

"He certainly won't," said Driscoll; "I've unshipped the handle. You'll get your cutters quickest if you quit talking and wait until I'm through."

"That's not playing it like a white man. Don't know why they hired you at the mine. Your job's smuggling the Indians liquor."

"Your folks!" sneered Driscoll. "You're not white."

"Stop there!" said Drummond, with stern quietness, and Thirlwell saw him balance a cutter he held. It was a short but heavy piece of steel, curved at the point.

Driscoll's eyes glittered. "Your father was a squaw-man; your mother—"

He bent his body with the swift suppleness of an acrobat, and the cutter, flying past, rang upon the wall of the shack. Then he swung forward and the end of a pick-handle missed Drummond by an inch.

Another cutter shot from Drummond's hand and struck Driscoll's side. He stooped, and Thirlwell thought he was falling but saw that he had bent down to pick up his ax. Next moment the blade flashed in a long sweep and Drummond sprang behind the anvil, which occupied the middle of the floor. He had another cutter and held it back, with his arm bent, ready to launch it at Driscoll's head, but Thirlwell imagined he was pressed too hard to feel sure of his aim and wanted to get out of his antagonist's reach. It was plain that the situation was dangerous, but Thirlwell knew he could not stop the men by shouting, and the fight would probably be over before he reached the shack. He had, however, forgotten the smith, who pulled a glowing iron from the fire.

"You can quit now; I butt in here!" he said, holding the iron close to Driscoll's chest. Then he turned to Drummond. "Put that cutter down! I don't: want to see you killed in my smithy."

All were quite still for a moment, and then Driscoll moved, as if he meant to get round the anvil, but the smith held him back.

"Try it again and I'll surely singe your hide!" he shouted, and swung round as he heard Drummond's cautious step. "If you sling that cutter at him, I'll put you on the fire. Get out now; I'm coming to see you go!"

Drummond backed to the door, with the red iron a few inches from his face, and when he had gone the smith signed to Driscoll.

"You're not going yet! Sit down right there and take a smoke."

A few moments later Thirlwell joined Drummond, who was waiting near the smithy. "If you mean to make trouble, I'll pay you off," he said. "You're hired to work, not to fight."

"If I quit now, Steve will get after me again," Drummond grumbled.

"I think not. In fact, I'll see about that; but if you provoke the man, you'll be fired as soon as I know. It's worth while to remember that you're a long way from the settlements."

"I got him with the cutter, anyhow," Drummond rejoined, and when he went off Thirlwell entered the smithy.

He imagined what he said to Driscoll would prevent the quarrel beginning again, and presently went back to the mine, feeling satisfied. There was now not much risk of Drummond and Driscoll making friends and finding that both knew something about the lode. Thirlwell was persuaded that Driscoll did know something, more in fact than anybody else; he knew where Strange had expected to find the ore. Thirlwell had not admitted this to Scott, because he shrank from stating his suspicions, which were dark but vague. Now, however, he thought he would try to formulate them and see how they looked, since he might, after all, take Scott into his confidence.

To begin with, nobody knew why Strange's canoe capsized. Strange was clever with the paddle, and Driscoll's narrative, while plausible, left something to be accounted for. It was improbable that he had quarreled with his partner while they shot the rapid, because their minds would be occupied by the dangerous navigation. Then supposing that Driscoll had intentionally let the canoe swerve when they were threatened by a breaking wave, it was hard to see what he would gain. If he thought Strange had found the ore, it would obviously be impossible to learn anything about it after the man was drowned. The theory that Strange had already told him where the lode was, and Driscoll meant to get rid of a partner who would demand the largest share, must be rejected, since if Strange had told him, Driscoll would have gone away to register the claim. But he had not done so.

The thing was mysterious, and Thirlwell could see no light. He must wait and watch for a hint, and in the meantime resolved to talk to Scott about it. So far, he had rather avoided the subject of Strange's death, but it might be better to abandon his reserve. He did not think he could expect much help from Scott, but he was clever and Thirlwell had known him to solve some awkward puzzles.

Chapter XVIII
The Hand In The Water

Scott lying among the pine-needles after work had stopped, lighted his pipe and glanced at Thirlwell, who had been talking for some minutes.

"On the whole, it was lucky the smith had an iron hot," he said. "Black Steve's a dangerous man and we know something about the *Metis* temper. Drummond, of course, is hardly a *Metis*, but he has a drop of Indian blood that must be reckoned on. It's a remarkable virile strain."

"I was rather glad they quarreled. I'd been afraid Driscoll might learn he knew something about the lode and persuade him to join the gang. I wouldn't trust him far."

"You can trust his Indian instincts," Scott replied. "No doubt he's greedy, but he hates Stormont, and I imagine he'd sooner punish the fellow than find the silver." He paused, and looked thoughtful when he went on: "The other matter's difficult; but, like Father Lucien, I don't see what we can do. It's possible that Steve drowned his partner, or anyhow, took advantage of an accident to let him drown; but we're not detectives, and you can't move against a man without something besides suspicion to go upon. Then we were under the cracking beam when he fixed the prop that stopped the roof coming down."

"I suppose, if he's guilty, that oughtn't to count?"

"It's an awkward question," Scott replied. "However, we don't know if he is guilty, and I don't see much chance of our finding out. But there's something else. Miss Strange had the shock of hearing about her father's sudden death, and it would not be kind to harrow her again."

"Certainly not," said Thirlwell, who felt annoyed because his comrade had guessed his thoughts.

A week later, Thirlwell was walking down the tunnel when he saw one or two of the men and Driscoll shoring up the roof. Drummond was helping, but a stone fell on him and he sat down. There was no light except the flicker of the lamps in the men's hats and they did not see Thirlwell.

"Are you hurt, kid?" one asked Drummond.

"He's scared," Driscoll growled. "Let him get out; this is a man's job."

Drummond sprang to his feet, although Thirlwell noted an ugly bruise on his forehead.

"Talk about being scared!" he cried. "Why you're 'most scared to death of the rapid! What d'you reckon lives there that's going to get you in the dark?"

Driscoll stepped forward. His face looked gray, but his mouth was hard and his eyes shone with savage rage. Thirlwell thought the man's passion was dangerous, and running up, got in front of him and sent Drummond to the shaft.

"Load up that broken rock," he said. "If you leave the job and come back here, I'll fire you out."

He was disturbed by the quarrel, because he understood something of Driscoll's feelings when stung by the taunt. Then he was curious about Drummond's object for making it, and wondered how much he knew. He kept them apart and when they stopped at noon Driscoll came up to him.

"I want to quit when the week's up," he said.

"Why?" Thirlwell asked, looking hard at him.

"For one thing, I've put up most of the new timbers and guess she'll hold for a while. Then I sure don't like that *Metis* kid. Reckon I'll kill him if I stop."

"Do what you think best," said Thirlwell, who saw he must get rid of one and would sooner keep Drummond. "If you come back later, we may find you a job."

At the end of the week, Driscoll went off into the bush, and after supper Thirlwell sent for Drummond. Scott was sitting near him outside the shack when the young man came up.

"If you make any fresh trouble here, you know what's coming to you," Scott remarked. "Steve is a good miner and it won't pay us to keep you and let him go."

"I guess you won't find the boys are sorry he lit out. There's something wrong about the man."

"If that's so, it's not your business," Thirlwell rejoined. "But why did you tell him he was scared of the rapid?"

Drummond sat down on a fir-stump and grinned with frank amusement. He had finished his duty until the next shift went under ground and in the meantime his employers had no authority over him. Indeed, he felt that he had conceded something by coming when he was sent for, and he might not have done so had he not liked Thirlwell.

"Because Steve certainly *was* scared," he replied.

"How do you know this?"

"Well, I s'pose I've got to put you wise. I go fishing evenings, when the trout are on the feed just before it's dusk, and I'd seen Steve prospecting round the pools among the reefs. Struck me as kind of curious, because if he was looking for something, he'd do better in daylight."

Scott glanced at Thirlwell, who remembered having come upon Driscoll when he was apparently engaged in searching the pools. It was obvious to him, and he thought to Scott, that the fellow had chosen the twilight in order to avoid being seen.

"Did Driscoll see you?" Thirlwell asked.

"I don't know; the boys tell me he's a trapper," Drummond answered with a smile.

"I suppose that means you kept out of sight and watched? But go on with your tale."

"One evening I was sitting among the rocks. It was very calm and getting dark when I heard a rattle and a splash. I reckoned Steve was looking hard for something if he trod on a loose stone."

Thirlwell nodded. Driscoll was a skilful trapper and a trapper does not disturb loose stones. Since he had made a noise, it was obvious that he was very much occupied, and thought himself alone. In a way, it was curious that he imagined there was nobody about; but although Driscoll had studied wood-craft, Drummond had, no doubt, inherited the ability to lurk unseen in the bush. Thirlwell could picture the lad crouching in the gloom of the dark pines.

"After a piece," Drummond resumed, "I got his figure against the sky, and reckoned, because he looked short, he was wading in a pool. Felt I had to see what he was looking for, but knew I couldn't get near him along the bank. There are patches of gravel among the rocks, and the brush grows pretty thick where it gets the light at the edge of a wood."

"Willows, for the most part; they're green, and soft, just now," Scott remarked.

"You can't crawl through green brush without making some noise. If you watch your arms and shoulders, you can't watch your feet."

"How'd you know that? Gone hunting often?"

"Never owned a gun," said Drummond "Still I did know."

"It doesn't matter. Go on," said Scott, who looked at Thirlwell meaningly.

"For a while, I couldn't see what I'd better do, and then I looked at the water. It was glimmering a few yards out, but there was a dark piece where the stream runs slack beside the rocks, and I took off my jacket and my boots."

"Why didn't you take off all your clothes?" Scott asked.

Drummond looked at him with surprise. "I knew my skin would shine in the water."

"Yes, of course," said Scott. "Well, it was a risky swim. If you had been washed into the main stream you'd have gone much farther than you meant. Did you get near Driscoll?"

"Sure I did. An eddy swung me out and I reckoned I was going down the main rush, but I caught the back-swirl and after that kept very close along the bank. Got a knock from a boulder, but, just paddling enough to keep on top, I drifted down to where Steve stood. He was on a ledge now, and I could hardly see him against the pines, but his head was bent, as if he was looking into the water. Then I allowed I'd been a fool. I couldn't stop unless I crawled out almost at his feet; you can't swim against that stream. Steve doesn't like me and there were some hefty rocks around."

Drummond paused, and Thirlwell imagined the lad had run some risk. A blow from a heavy stone would have stopped his swimming, without leaving a tell-tale mark, since his body would bear many bruises when the rapid threw it out among the eddies in the tail-pool. Thirlwell could picture the scene—the dark pines standing against the pale sky, and the dim reflection from the river; the unsuspecting man bending over the ledge; and the lad drifting noiselessly down stream, with only his head above water and his rather long hair streaking his dark face.

"Well," continued Drummond, "you see how I was fixed! I couldn't pull out from the bank because the slack was narrow, and, if I kept on, I must pass Steve very close. I surely didn't like it, but saw what I'd better do. He was facing down stream, turned half away from me, and I reckoned the water was about four feet deep. I'd grab his foot and pull him in. Then I'd get away while he was floundering about, while if he was too quick and gripped me, we'd be equal in the water and he'd have no rocks to throw.

"I drifted on until I could reach him and seized his foot, but the rest didn't work out as I thought. Steve didn't slip into the water; he kept on his feet and screamed."

"I suppose you mean he shouted," Thirlwell suggested.

"No, sir—I mean *screamed*; like a jack-rabbit in a trap. The ledge slanted awkwardly; he couldn't turn to see what had got hold of him, and had hard work to keep his balance when an eddy swung me off the bank. I saw him stiffen as he braced himself, and guess he felt my grip get tighter through his boot, because he gave another scream, as if he was mad afraid. Then he got his other foot against something that steadied him and I saw I couldn't pull him off. I let go and swam under water as long as I could. When I came up Steve wasn't there, but I heard him push through the willows up the bank. He was running as if he thought he had to go for his life. Well, I got out at the next slack and went for my boots and jacket. Steve wasn't watching; I guess he'd had enough!"

"It's possible," Scott agreed dryly. "Do you think he saw you just before you dived?"

"He might have seen my hand; it would look whiter than my gray shirt. He certainly didn't see my face; I didn't mean him to."

"Well," said Scott, "it's an amusing tale, but you had better not tell it to anybody else. Now you can go along, but see you keep out of trouble in future. If I find you talking about Driscoll, or quarreling with the boys, I'll butt in."

Drummond went away, and when he vanished into the shadow of the pines Thirlwell remarked: "I don't imagine Driscoll found the thing amusing!"

"Do you think he afterwards guessed it was Drummond who got hold of him? The young idiot gave him a hint when he taunted him with being scared."

"It's likely," said Thirlwell. "If he did guess, it would account for his anger; the man was carried away by a rage. He looked as if he'd have killed the lad if there had been nobody about, and perhaps he had some excuse. He's afraid of the river, and we have seen his imagination get the better of his pluck. I'm not surprised he got a nasty jar. Try to picture it! The growing dark; the roar of the rapid that we know he hates; and the wet hand that rose from the eddy and seized his foot."

Scott nodded. "Just so! *Whose* hand do you imagine he thought it was?"

"I think we both suspect. But we agreed that suspicion was not enough."

"It is not enough," said Scott, who took his fishing rod from the pegs in the wall of the shack. "Well, shall we go down to the river? The trout ought to rise to-night."

Chapter XIX
A Lost Opportunity

The class-room was very hot and a ray of dazzling sunshine quivered upon the diagrams on the yellow wall. An electric fan hummed monotonously and buzzing flies hovered about Agatha's head. Her face and hands were damp as she stood with knitted brows beside a tall blackboard, looking at the drowsy girls whom she was teaching inorganic chemistry. One or two fixed their eyes on the symbols she had written; the rest had obviously given up the effort to understand the complicated formula. In fact, they did not seem to notice that she had stopped her lecture.

For a few moments she looked about and mused. With one or two exceptions, she liked her pupils, and had led them patiently along the uphill road to knowledge. They had made some progress, but she had lost her delight in leading. For one thing, few would go far, and when they left her the rest would turn aside from the laborious pursuit of science into pleasant human paths and forget all that she had taught while they occupied themselves with the care of husband and children. Moreover, she herself could not follow the climbing road to the heights where the light of knowledge burns brightest, as she once had hoped. When the school term was finished she must turn back and begin again, at the bottom, to direct the faltering steps of another band. But she sometimes wondered whether the beckoning light was not austere and cold.

She glanced at her dress. It was a neutral color and like a uniform. After all, she had physical charm and it was sometimes irksome to wear unbecoming clothes. Then the lofty room, with its varnished desks and benches, looked bleak; her life was passed in bare class-rooms and echoing stone corridors. This would not have mattered had she been able to follow her bent and take the line she had once marked out; but she could not. She must give up the thought of independent research and teach for a living, cramping her talents to meet her pupils' intelligence, until, in time, she sank to their level.

She roused herself with an effort and mechanically resumed her lecture, for her wandering thoughts now dwelt upon the foaming rivers and cool forests of the North. The class-rooms smelt of varnish and throbbed with the monotonous rattle of the fan; in the wilds one breathed the resinous fragrance of the pines and heard the splash of running water. For all that, she must not shirk her duty and she tried to make the meaning of the symbols on the board plainer to the languid girls.

By and by she remarked that they were more alert. Some were making notes, and one or two looked past her with frank curiosity. The door was behind the board, and Agatha had heard nobody come in, but when she looked round she saw a gray-haired gentleman standing near the lady principal. He seemed to be listening to what she said and she thought his eyes twinkled as if he understood the difficulty of rousing her pupils' interest. This was somewhat embarrassing; but the school was famous and visitors were now and then shown round.

She paused, and the stranger turned to the principal. "If you will allow me—"

The principal smiled and he came up to Agatha, holding out his hand for the chalk.

"Suppose we alter the formula this way?" he said and wiped out the letters and figures.

Agatha studied him as he wrote fresh symbols. He was plainly dressed and about sixty years of age. There was nothing else worth noting, but he obviously knew his subject and she liked his face. She saw that the girls could follow his explanation, but while suited to their understanding, it was, in one respect, not quite accurate.

"I don't know if I've made it much plainer," he said deprecatingly when he stopped.

Agatha indicated a group of letters. "It is plainer, thank you! But does the combination of the two elements take place exactly as you have shown? At a normal temperature, the metal's affinity for oxygen—"

"Ah," he said, "you know that? It looks as if you had studied the new Austrian theory. But perhaps one may make a small concession, for the sake of clearness."

"Science is exact," Agatha replied.

"It's a bold claim for us to make," he rejoined, smiling. "Our symbols are guess measures; our elements split up into two or three. But I gather that you refuse to compromise about what, in the meantime, we think is the truth?"

"I think one must adhere to it, as far as one knows."

"Well, no doubt, that is the proper line. But I've stopped your lecture and perhaps bored your pupils."

"No," said Agatha. "You have helped me over awkward ground, and I expect they would sooner listen to a stranger."

He went away with the principal, and Agatha wondered about him as she resumed her task. It was plain that he knew something about science, but this was not strange, since geologists and chemists sometimes visited the school. After she dismissed her class the principal sent for her.

"I suppose you don't know who that man is?" she asked.

Agatha admitted that she did not know and colored when the other told her. The man was a famous scientist who had recently simplified the smelting of some refractory British Columbian ores, and was now understood to be occupied with the problem of utilizing certain barren alkali belts in the West.

"Oh!" she said, "I talked to him as if he were one of the girls. In fact, I believe I was gently patronizing."

"I don't think he was much hurt."

"Then he must have been amused and that is nearly as bad. After he had gone I imagined I'd seen his portrait somewhere."

"He hasn't gone yet," the principal answered with a twinkle. "He's waiting to see you in the managers' room, and I must confess to something of a plot when I brought him in quietly to hear your lecture."

"But what does he want?" Agatha asked with excited curiosity.

"I imagine he wants to offer you a post, but he will tell you about this. You have half an hour before the next class."

Agatha went out, trying to preserve her calm. The man had made his mark by the application of science to industry and the thought that she might help him gave her a thrill. This was different work from teaching beginners; taking them so far and then going over the ground again. If she got the post, she could go on, farther perhaps than she had hoped, and when she had learned enough embark on a career of independent research. She thought she had the necessary tenacity and brains. There was an obstacle, but she would not hurry to meet it and it might be removed.

When she entered the room the man got up and indicated a chair. He asked a few questions, rather carelessly, and afterwards remarked: "Miss Southern had already told me what I most wanted to know. You may have heard about the work in which I am engaged."

"Yes," said Agatha, with a touch of color, "I know what it is now."

He smiled. "Perhaps it would have been better had I asked Miss Southern to present me, but I'm not very formal. Well, I was asked by the Provincial Government and the railroad to find the best way of developing the alkali wastes, and the subject is extraordinarily interesting. If I can solve the problem, it will make important changes in our irrigation system and enable us to cultivate wide belts of barren soil. However, I must have help and want a lady who can take the charge of my correspondence with scientific people and assist in my experiments. After talking to Miss Southern, I feel I can offer you the post."

Agatha thrilled, but used some self-control.

"But you might not need me long, and I must give up the school."

He smiled. "If you wished to resume teaching, I daresay your having helped in my investigations would be an advantage."

"Then do you expect me to help much in that way?" Agatha asked with growing excitement.

"Yes; as far as you are able. I am told that you are used to laboratory work. Would this suit you?"

Agatha's eyes sparkled. "It would realize my pet ambition."

"Very well. We had better talk about the salary. My notion is—"

Agatha thought the offer generous. She would be richer than she had been yet and there was an object for which she needed money. She felt flattered and almost overjoyed. The work she was asked to do might start her well on the road she had long wished to take.

"There is another matter," the man resumed when she declared that she was satisfied. "It will be necessary for you to come to Europe. My wife will take care of you."

"Then you are going to Europe?" Agatha said with a curious sinking of her heart.

"Yes. I must consult an eminent Frenchman and two or three Austrians. They have studied some of the problems I am up against."

"When do you start?" Agatha asked with forced quietness.

"In about three weeks, if I can get ready."

Agatha tried to brace herself. The disappointment was hard to bear, and for a few moments she engaged in a bitter struggle. If she took the post and went to Europe, she could not go North for a year, and Thirlwell might not be able to help her then. She knew that she had counted on his help, and that without it she could not penetrate far into the wilds. Indeed, it was possible that she could not start at all.

Yet, if she went North, she must refuse an alluring offer and throw away an opportunity for making her mark. Her ambition must be abandoned, and if she failed to find the silver, she would have to resume her monotonous duties at the school. She was beginning to find them strangely dreary. Then George had warned her against sacrificing her youth, and perhaps all her life, to the pursuit of a shadow. Her friends did not believe in the silver, and she doubted if she could find the vein. Failure might leave her sour and the hardships break her health; she would come back with her savings exhausted to toil and deny herself again. Yet the lode was waiting to be found somewhere in the North, and the duty she had accepted long since must come first.

"Then I'm sorry I cannot go," she said with an effort.

The man looked surprised. "The voyage is short and comfortable if one travels by a big, fast boat. I expect to work hard, but you would have some leisure and opportunities for seeing famous pictures, statues, and laboratories. Then you would meet eminent chemists and learn something from their talk. In fact, the visit ought to be of help in many ways, and, if you afterwards left my employment, make it easy for you to get another post."

Agatha struggled for calm. He had rather understated than exaggerated the reasons why she ought to go. Then Toronto and Montreal were the only cities she knew, and she was offered a chance of seeing some of the capitals of Europe, with their treasures of art, and meeting men who had made famous scientific discoveries. It would help her more than many certificates if later on she resumed her work of teaching.

"Ah," she said in a strained voice, "please don't try to show me all that I shall miss! I want to go so very much, but it's impossible. If I went, I should neglect a duty that has a stronger claim."

He bowed. "Then, although I'm sorry, there's nothing to be said. Would it be an impertinence if I asked about the duty?"

Agatha was silent for a moment or two. Her refusal had cost her much; indeed, she was afraid to think what she had lost and felt she must do something to banish the crushing sense of disappointment.

"No," she said impulsively; "I cannot resent anything you ask. I must start North soon to look for a vein of ore my father told me about, I'm forced to make the search, but it would be a long story if I told you why." She hesitated and then went on: "I wonder whether you would look at this analysis and tell me what you think—I mean if you think there is ore of that kind on the Northern slope of the Ontario watershed."

He took the paper she had long carried about and studied it for a time. Then he said: "It is not the ore a practical miner would expect to strike, but practical miners are sometimes deceived. As a rule, they know more about shafts and adits than scientific geology."

"Would *you* expect to find the ore where I have told you?"

"Well," he said thoughtfully, "the Laurentian rocks are very old, and our miners have so far dealt with newer formations. On the whole, I think it possible that ore like this has been forced up from unusual depths."

"But would the silver be easily refined?"

He smiled. "There would be no trouble about its reduction. If you can locate the vein, you will be rich."

Agatha thanked him and went out, feeling somewhat comforted. She had given up much, but she saw a ray of light in the gloom ahead. The way she had chosen was difficult, but after all it was the right way, and, if she were resolute, might lead to success. Then she remembered with a strange satisfaction that for a time she need not walk alone: Thirlwell would be her guide when she plunged into the trackless wilds and she knew that one could trust him.

Chapter XX
The Plunge

Supper was over at the Farnam homestead and Agatha enjoyed the cool of the evening on the veranda with her hosts and George. The school had closed for the holidays, and George had arrived as the meal from which they had just got up was served. Although he had not stated his object yet, Agatha knew why he had come and shrank from the vigorous protest she expected him to make. In the meantime, she had something else to think about and listened for the noise of wheels.

Farnam's hired man had driven across to the settlement in the afternoon and she wondered, rather anxiously, whether he would bring her a telegram. She had written to Thirlwell, telling him when she would be ready to begin her search for the ore, and now waited his reply. Her letter might take some time to reach him, and she must allow for his messenger's journey to the railroad from the mine; but she knew she would feel restless until the answer came.

The evening was calm, the air was fresher than in the city, and she found the quiet soothing. A field of timothy grass near the house rippled languidly, the dark heads rising stiffly upright when the faint breeze dropped. Sometimes there was a movement among the tall blades and feathery plumes of the Indian corn, and then the rustle stopped and everything was still. Beyond the zig-zag fence, the fruit trees ran back in rows that converged and melted into a blurred mass at the edge of the bush. The narrow landscape had no prominent feature. It was smooth and calm, and Agatha found it rested her eyes and brain. She wanted to be tranquil, but must shortly rouse herself when Mrs. Farnam and George began their joint attack. George had an ominously determined look, and she knew Mabel would give him her support.

"Why didn't you come and stop with us? Florence expected you," he said by and by.

Agatha saw he was feeling for an opening, and since it was hard to put him off, answered with a smile: "You are a persistent fellow, and I'm not fond of argument. I wanted to be quiet."

"You mean you were afraid I'd get after you about your crank notion of finding the old man's lode? As you haven't talked about it for some time, I'd begun to hope you had given that folly up. Are you going?"

"Some time; I may go very soon. Perhaps I shall know to-night."

"Then I'll wait," George said grimly. "If you get a message from the miner fellow, I may have some remarks to make!"

Farnam began to talk about the fruit crop, and it was half an hour later when Agatha heard a rattle of wheels. Then a rig lurched along the uneven road in a cloud of dust and soon after it vanished among the trees Farnam's hired man walked up to the veranda.

"A wire for Miss Strange! There was no mail," he said.

Agatha's nerve tingled as she opened the envelope, and then the restless feeling left her and she felt very calm. The telegram was from Thirlwell, who stated where he would meet her and that the sum she named would be enough. This was a relief, because she had insisted that the journey should be made at her cost and traveling is expensive in the wilds.

One needed tents, clothes, and prospecting tools; canoes must be bought and experienced *voyageurs* engaged, since the craft and stores would have to be carried across rugged divides. Agatha had for a long time practised stern economy, doubting if her savings would cover the expense, and now when she had met all demands she would have very few dollars left. This did not matter; the money would go round, and she felt recklessly satisfied. After a moment or two she gave the telegram to George.

"I start in three days!"

George said nothing, although his face got red, and Agatha studied him with sympathetic amusement. It was obvious that he was using some self-control while he mustered his forces for an attack. He had begun to get fat and looked rather aggressively prosperous. In fact, George was a typical business man and it was ridiculous to think he could understand.

"But what about your clothes?" Mrs. Farnam asked. "You must have a special outfit for the bush."

"They're all bought! Before I left Toronto I ordered what I would need to be got ready and properly packed. The things will be sent as soon as the people get my telegram. You see, I've been thinking about my outfit. One can't take much when it must be carried across the portages."

George frowned savagely. "You ought to know my sister, Mrs. Farnam! When she undertakes a job she leaves nothing to chance, and I guess she's had it all fixed some time since." He turned to Agatha. "I've got to relieve my feelings, if I do nothing else! Well, I suppose you understand what this adventure means? Unless you get back before the new term begins, you'll lose your post, and you take steep chances of ruining your health. You're not used to sleeping on wet ground and going without food. Then you'll have to live with half-tamed *voyageurs* and perhaps help them track the canoes. They'll upset you in the rapids and the bush will tear your clothes. I hate to think of my sister going about, draggled and ragged, with a bunch of strange men. But that, while bad enough, is certainly not the worst!"

He stopped to get his breath and then resumed: "You won't find the lode, and you'll come back feeling sick and sore. If they keep you on at the school, you won't want to teach; you'll think of nothing but saving all you can and pulling out again. You're like father, and when he took the lone trail the blamed foolishness got such a grip of him that he never broke loose. Well, you'll lose your job and the next you get; in fact, you'll come to hate any work that keeps you from the North. But a girl can't let herself down until she turns into a hobo. It's frankly unthinkable. Pull up and cut out the crazy program before it ruins you!"

"It's too late," said Agatha. "I knew what I might have to pay when I resolved to go."

"I wonder whether you do know. There's something George hasn't mentioned," Mrs. Farnam remarked. "I don't think I'm prudish, but you can't keep your adventure secret, and school managers are censorious people. Have you thought what it may mean if they hear about your traveling through the woods with a man who's not a relative and a band of wild half-breeds?"

"Yes," said Agatha, coloring, "I have thought of that."

"But it didn't count?"

"It counted for much," said Agatha, in a rather strained voice.

George clenched his fist. "If you're turned out, people will talk. I'll engage to stop the men, but the women are dangerous and I can't get after them. For my sake, drop your fool plan!"

"I can't. I know the risks, but I must go on."

"Well," said George with a gesture of helpless indignation, "I allow I'm beaten and there's not much comfort in feeling I've done my duty! I didn't expect you'd bother about my views when I began. Looks as if we gave young women a dangerous freedom."

"Women have won their freedom; you didn't give it," Mrs. Farnam rejoined, and then turned to Agatha. "After all, something depends on the man's character. You haven't told us much about Mr. Thirlwell!"

The Lure of the North

Agatha did not reply and George said grudgingly: "In a sense, the fellow's all right. I made some inquiries and must admit that I was satisfied with what I learned."

"You both take it for granted that Agatha will not locate the vein," Farnam interposed. "Since Thirlwell manages a mine, he must know something about prospecting, and if he reckons the chances are pretty good—"

"Mr. Thirlwell does not really believe I will find the ore," Agatha said with incautious frankness.

George laughed ironically and Farnam looked surprised, while his wife asked: "Then why is he going?"

Agatha felt embarrassed. "I don't know—He made me promise I would let him come. I think prospecting has a charm for miners—"

She stopped as she saw Mrs. Farnam's smile, but it was some relief to note that George did not seem to remark her hesitation.

"Well," he said, "your statement's, so to speak, the climax! The only person who knows anything about the matter thinks you won't find the vein! The blamed proposition's ridiculous from the beginning." He got up and filled his pipe with an unsteady hand. "I'm too mad to sit still. Guess I'll walk round the orchard and take a smoke."

Farnam presently went after him, and Mrs. Farnam put her hand on Agatha's arm.

"My dear, you have pluck, but you have chosen a hard road and given your friends a jar. But we are your friends; don't forget that!"

Agatha smiled gratefully, though she found it difficult. "I didn't really choose. Sometimes I was afraid; but I knew I had to go."

"Very well," said Mrs. Farnam. "We won't talk about it. Tell me about your clothes."

Next day George left the homestead and Agatha walked across the orchard with him while Farnam harnessed his team. When a rattle of wheels warned them that the rig was coming George stopped and said, "This trip will cost you something and your pay's not high. How much do you reckon to have left when you get back?"

"About ten dollars," Agatha answered with a twinkle.

"I knew you had grit. But I want you to understand! I wouldn't give you five cents to help you find the lode, but you'll go broke on ten dollars long before your next pay's due. Better take this; it may help you out."

Agatha took the envelope, but as she began to open it the rig stopped at the gate, and George put his hand on her shoulder.

"We mustn't keep Farnam; wait until I've gone," he said and kissed her. "I'm not going to wish you good luck, but if you have trouble with the school people when you get back, come along and stop with Florence. I'll interview the managers, and, if needful, find you another job."

He hurried off, and when the rattle of wheels died away Agatha opened the envelope and found a check for a hundred dollars. She felt moved, but smiled. The gift was generous, but the way he had made it was very like George.

Three days afterwards, Farnam and his wife drove her to the railroad and she felt a pang at leaving them when the cars rolled in. The excitement of starting, however, helped her over an awkward few minutes, and she found a girl on the train who wanted to talk. Besides, it was evening, and after an hour or two the colored porter lighted the lamps and told her her berth was ready. She slept well, for it was too late to give way to misgivings now, and soon after she rose next morning the train stopped at the station where she must get down.

The conductor threw her baggage out upon the line. The locomotive bell tolled, the cars went on, and Agatha's heart sank as she glanced about. It was early morning and thin mist drifted among the pines. There was no platform, but a small wooden shack with an iron roof stood beside the rails, which ran into the forest a hundred yards off. The agent, after gruffly asking for her checks, vanished into his office and banged the door. There was nobody else about, and the place was very quiet except for the murmur of running water.

A narrow clearing, strewn with ashes and dotted by blackened stumps, ran along the track, and at its end were three or four shabby frame houses. A rudely painted board on one stated that the building was the Strathcona Hotel. Agatha felt very forlorn. Except for a week or two with Thirlwell, and once with a band of merry companions at a summer camp she had not seen the rugged bush, and now it daunted her. She was not going on a pleasure excursion, from which she could return when she liked, but to push far into the lonely wilds. She had done with civilization until she came back; it could not help her when she left the railroad. She must live and struggle with savage Nature as the prospectors and half-breeds did. But this was not all; she had, perhaps, cut herself off from other things than the comfort and security that civilization offered.

Mabel Farnam's warning was, no doubt, justified. It was possible that the school managers would dismiss her and she would be unable to get another scholastic post. She might have to give up her occupation and although she disliked business earn a frugal living as a clerk. Her face got hot as she remembered Mabel's statement that her rashness had given her friends a jar; but in one sense Mabel was wrong. She had not been rash; she knew she could trust Thirlwell and the men he hired. There was nothing to fear from them. Still she had made a bold plunge that might cost her much, and now the reaction had begun she felt slack and dispirited. The plunge, however, was made; she must carry out what she had undertaken, and it was foolish to indulge her doubts. She tried to pull herself together and in a few minutes a man led a team out of the hotel stable.

He leisurely harnessed the lean horses to a very dirty wagon and then drove them across the clearing to the track, where he stopped in front of Agatha's baggage. She noted that his skin was very brown and he had coarse black hair. The overalls he wore were very ragged.

"Mees Strange?" he said. "Dat your truck?"

Agatha said it was, and jumping down he threw her bag and some rough wooden boxes into the wagon. Then he climbed back up the wheel and held out his hand.

"Montez. Allons, en route!"

Agatha got up with some trouble and when she sat down on a board that crossed the vehicle he cracked his whip and the wagon, rocking wildly, rolled away among the stumps and plunged into a narrow trail chopped out of the bush.

"Eet is long way; we mak' breakfast by and by," he said. "Thirlwell wait at portage. We arrive to-night, *si tout va bien*."

Agatha said nothing, but felt somewhat comforted as they jolted along the uneven trail.

Chapter XXI
The Wilderness

Dusk was falling and the tired horses plodded slowly past the rows of shadowy trunks when the sound of running water came out of the gloom. Agatha ached from the jolting and felt cramped and sleepy, but she roused herself when a light began to flicker among the trees. The driver urged his team, the light got brighter as the rig lurched down a rough incline, and Agatha saw a man standing in the trail. His figure was indistinct and she could not see his face, but she no longer felt jaded and lonely, for she knew who he was.

"Tired?" he said in a sympathetic voice as he gave her his hand to get down when the rig stopped in an opening. "It's a long ride from the railroad, but after all it was better for you to make it in the day. Besides, we must pull out to-morrow."

Agatha said she was not excessively tired. She liked his matter-of-fact manner and thought he had struck the right note.

"Have you got the tent I recommended?" he asked.

"Yes," she said. "It's in the small box."

"Then as the poles are cut, the boys will soon put it up. In the meantime, supper's ready."

He took her across the narrow open space, and when near the fire she stopped and looked about. It was after ten o'clock, but a pale-green glow shone above the pines, whose ragged tops cut against it in a black saw-edge. Below, a river brawled among dark rocks, catching a reflection here and there, and then plunging into shadow. It was not dark; she could see the brush and the wild-berry vines that crawled between the trunks. Then she turned towards the fire that burned at the foot of a ledge. Two or three figures moved about the rocks behind it; sometimes picked out with hard distinctness so that she could see their brown faces and travel-stained overalls, and sometimes fading into gloom.

The smoke went nearly straight up and then spread slowly across the river; the flames leaped among the snapping branches and sank. Strong lights and puzzling shadows played about the camp; there was an aromatic smell, and the air was keen and bracing. The turmoil of the river rather emphasized than disturbed the quietness. It was different from the noisy city where the big arc-lights burned above the hurrying crowds, but Agatha did not find it strange. She felt as if she were revisiting a scene she had known before, and thought this was an inheritance from her father, who had loved the wilds. But perhaps she might go further back; it was, relatively, not long since all Ontario was a wilderness, and she sprang from pioneering stock.

Then Thirlwell indicated a folding chair and she sat down beside two logs, rolled close together to make a cooking hearth. A kettle and two frying-pans stood on the logs, supported by both, and the space between was filled with glowing embers, about which flickered little blue and orange flames. Thirlwell gave her a plate and a tin mug, and she found the fresh trout and hot bannocks appetizing. Then she liked the acid wild-berries he brought on a bark tray, and the strong, smoke-flavored tea. She smiled as she remembered that in Toronto she had been fastidious about her meals and sometimes could not eat food that was roughly-served.

When supper was over Thirlwell sat on one of the hearth-logs and lighted his pipe. Agatha was pleased that he did so. While they were in the bush their relations must be marked by an informal friendliness, as if she were a comrade and partner and not a girl. Anything that hinted at the difference in their sex must be avoided.

"You'll get used to camp-life in a few days," he remarked by and by. "At first I expect you'll find it a change from, the cities. Things are rudimentary in the bush."

"Nothing jars, except the mosquitoes," Agatha replied. "I have no sense of strangeness; in fact, I feel as if I had been here before and belonged to the woods."

"After, all, you do know something about them. I think you said you had camped in the timber."

"That was different. It was a summer camp, organized by the railroad, and supplied with modern comforts. You bought a ticket and a gasolene launch took you up the lake. Then the men wore smart flannels and the girls new summer clothes. In the evenings one sang and played a banjo, another a mandolin."

Thirlwell laughed. "You don't like music?"

"I love it; but not ragtime and modern coon songs in the bush. No doubt the people who went there had earned a holiday, but it would have been different had they gone to fish or hunt. They went to loaf, play noisy games, and flirt. Indeed, I used to think we jarred as much as the horrible dump of old fruit and meat cans among the willows."

"I think I know what you mean. Man makes ugly marks on the wilderness unless he goes to farm. A mine, for example, is remarkably unpicturesque."

"But it stands for endeavor, for something useful done."

"Not all mines. A number stand for wasted money."

"And vanished hopes," said Agatha. "Do you think I shall find the lode? I want you to be frank."

Thirlwell hesitated. "On the whole, I don't think so, but my judgment mayn't be sound and my employer, Scott, does not agree. Anyway, I'll help you all I can."

For a moment or two Agatha studied him. His face was brown and rather thin and had a hint of quiet force; his easy pose was graceful but virile. Somehow he did not clash with the austerity of the woods; nor did the other men, who now sat, smoking, round the larger fire. Agatha liked their quietness, their slow, drawling speech and tranquil movements. She knew she could trust Thirlwell, but remembering a remark of Mabel Farnam's, she asked herself why he had offered his help. She could find no satisfactory answer and thought it better to leave the puzzle alone.

"But you are doubtful," she said. "Confidence is a strong driving force."

"In a way, that's true," he agreed. "Still it sometimes drives you into mistakes, and when you get to work in the right way it doesn't matter much if you're confident or not. Your feelings can't alter Nature's laws. If you know how the vein dips, you can strike the ore; if you sink the shot-hole right, and use enough powder, you split the rock."

"It's obvious that you are a materialist."

"I'm a mining engineer," Thirlwell rejoined with a smile.

Agatha gave him a quiet, friendly look. "It's lucky I have you to help, because I could not have gone far alone. I've studied Nature's laws in the laboratory, but in the bush she works on another scale. There's a difference between a blow-pipe flame and the subterranean fires. Now if I don't find the ore, it will be some comfort to know that I have properly tried." She glanced at her wrist-watch and got up. "It is later than I thought!"

"Your tent is ready," Thirlwell replied.

She turned and saw a light shining through the V-shaped canvas on the edge of the trees, but although she was tired, felt reluctant to leave the fire. It had burned low between the logs, but it gave the lonely spot a comfortable home-like look, and the bush was dark. Thirlwell, sitting where the faint light touched him, somehow added to the charm by a hint of human fellowship. He looked as if he were resting by his hearth, and she had spent a happy hour with him in quiet, half-confidential talk.

"Thank you. Good-night," she said, and went away.

When she reached the tent she looked about with surprise. The earth floor was beaten smooth and sprinkled with pine-sprays that gave out an aromatic smell; a bed had been cleverly made of thin branches and packed twigs. Her blankets were neatly folded and the small canvas bucket was filled. All she was likely to need was ready, and the boxes that had held her outfit were arranged to make a seat and wash-stand. She felt grateful for this thought for her comfort, and putting out the miner's lamp, sat down on the twig-bed and hooked the canvas door back.

Although there was no moon, she could distinguish the black pine-trunks across the river, the lines of foam where the current broke upon the reefs, and the canoes drawn up on the bank. Thirlwell and his *Metis* packers had gone, and as hers was the only tent she wondered where they slept. The fires were nearly out, and except for the noise of the river a solemn quietness brooded over the camp.

She began to muse. She had liked Thirlwell when she met him at the summer hotel, but she liked him better in the bush. He harmonized with his surroundings; he was, so to speak, natural, but not at all uncouth. The woods had made him quiet, thoughtful, and vigilant. She had noted his quick, searching glance, and although there was nothing aggressive about him, he had force. Yet she did not think him clever; she had met men whose mental powers were much more obvious, but when she tried to contrast them with him, he came out best. After all, character took one further than intellectual subtlety.

Agatha blushed as she admitted that had she wanted a lover she might have been satisfied with a man of Thirlwell's type; but she did not want a lover. She had inherited a duty and must concentrate on finding the silver vein; the task in a manner set her apart from other women, who could follow their bent. Sometimes she envied them their freedom and gave way to bitterness, but her austere sense of duty returned. It was strong just now, but the picture of Thirlwell sitting opposite by the fire had a happy domestic touch that made her dissatisfied.

Then she remembered that if she found the vein she would be rich. So far, she had not dwelt much on this, because it was not a longing for money that animated her. All the same, she saw that success in the search would give her power and freedom to choose the life she would lead. Not long since, she had thought to find happiness in the pursuit of science; and with wealth at her command she could make costly experiments and build laboratories. The thought still pleased her, but it had lost something of its charm. Besides, it was too soon for such speculations and she must be practical.

Suppose she did find the ore? The claim must be recorded and developed as the mining laws required, and she would need a man who understood such matters to help her; but it must be a man she could trust. She could trust Thirlwell and admitted that she had half-consciously allotted him the supposititious post; for one thing, if he were manager, they would not be separated by her success. But this was going too far, and she resolutely pulled herself up. She had not found the vein and was perhaps thinking about Thirlwell oftener than she ought. Feeling for the hooks, she fastened the tent door and soon afterwards went to sleep.

They launched the canoes in the cool of the morning, while the mist drifted among the pines and the sun came up behind the forest. The stream ran fast and as they toiled up river a brawny half-breed waded through the shallows with the tracking line. Thirlwell stood in the stern, using the pole, and Agatha noted the smooth precision of his movements. He wasted no effort and did not seem to be working hard, but he did what he meant and the hint of force was plainer than when he talked. Two *Metis* were occupied with the canoe behind and as they poled and tracked they sang old songs made by the early French *voyageurs*. Although the river had shrunk far down the bank, there was water enough for the canoes, and Agatha remarked how skilfully the men avoided the rocks in the channel and drove the craft up angry rapids.

When they nooned upon a gravel bank near the end of a wide lake it was fiercely hot. The calm water, flashed like polished steel, and Agatha could hardly see the flames of the snapping fire; the smoke went up in thin gray wreaths that were almost invisible. A clump of juniper grew among the stones and she sat down in the shade and looked about with dazzled eyes. A line of driftwood, hammered by the ice and bleached white by the sun, marked the subsidence of the water from its high, spring level. Small islands broke the shining surface, some covered with stunted trees and some quite bare. The rocks about the beach were curiously worn, but Agatha knew they had been ground smooth by drifting floes. Behind the beach, the forest rolled back in waves of somber green to a bold ridge that faded into leaden thunder-clouds.

The landscape was wild, and although it had nothing of the savage grandeur Agatha expected, she thought it forbidding. Its influence was insidious; one was not daunted by a glance, but realized by degrees its grimness and desolation. The North was not dramatic, except perhaps when the ice broke up; the forces that molded the rugged land worked with a stern quietness. It looked as if they also molded the character of the men who braved the rigors of the frozen waste. The *Metis* were not vivacious like the French *habitants*; they were marked by a certain grave melancholy and their paddling songs had a plaintive undertone. Yet their vigor and stubbornness were obvious, and Agatha thought Thirlwell was like his packers, in a way. He was not melancholy, and indeed, often laughed, but one got a hint of reserve and unobtrusive strength. He did not display his qualities, as some of the professors and business men she knew had done, but she imagined they would be seen if there was need.

"In a sense, the North is disappointing," she remarked. "I expected to feel rather overwhelmed, but I'm not."

"Wait," said Thirlwell, smiling. "After a few hundred miles of lonely trail you'll know the country better. I don't want you to get to love it; but in the wilderness love often goes with fear."

"Once I thought that impossible," Agatha replied. "Now I don't know. I'm beginning to recognize that I'm not as modern as I thought. But have you ever been frankly afraid of the wilds?"

"Often. When you meet the snow on the frozen trail, a hundred miles from shelter, mind and body shrink. Perhaps it's worse when all that stands for warmth and life is loaded on the hand-sledge you haul across the rotten ice. Then it's significant that the *Metis* are sometimes more afraid than white men. They know the country better."

"They haven't the civilized man's intellect. Ignorance breeds superstition that makes men cowards."

"That's so, to some extent," Thirlwell agreed. "I suppose superstition is man's fear of dangers he can't understand and his wish to propitiate the unknown powers that rule such things. You and I call these powers natural forces, for which we have our weights and measures; but I must own that the measures are often found defective when applied to mining. I've met rock-borers who would sooner trust a mascot than a scientific rule."

"We are a curious people," Agatha remarked with a laugh. "But you passed a smooth beach with good shade where the river runs out. Why did you come on here?"

"The other's the regular camping spot. I remembered that you don't like old provision cans."

Agatha was pleased. He had thought about her and remembered her dislikes. While she wondered how she could tactfully thank him, he went on—

"Besides, I wanted to make another mile or two. A good day's journey is important."

"Would a mile or two make much difference?"

"You would have to take the distance off at the other end. The economy of travel in the North is sternly simple, and transport's the main difficulty. You can travel a fixed distance on a fixed quantity of food, and how much you take depends on the skill and number of your packers. Good men get good wages and money does not go far. I want to save up as many miles as possible for our prospecting."

"I see," said Agatha. "Yet you stated that you didn't think we would find the lode!" Then she gave him a shrewd glance. "Aren't you a little impatient to get on now?"

"I am," he admitted, turning to the south. "There's a threat of thunder and I'd like to cross the lake before the storm comes."

Agatha got up and in a few minutes they launched the canoes. The heat was overwhelming and Agatha felt no movement of the air, but the *Metis* sweated and panted as they labored at the paddles. The thud of the blades came back in measured echoes from the motionless pines and a fan-shaped wake trailed far across the glassy lake. In the meantime, the cloud bank rolled up the sky like a ragged arch and covered the sun. The glare faded and a thick, blue haze crept out upon the water, until it looked as if the horizon advanced to meet them, but the heat did not get less. At the edge of the haze, an island loomed indistinctly and by and by Thirlwell turned to Agatha.

"There's a good beach behind the point and shelter among the rocks," he said in a breathless voice. "Would you like to stop?"

"How long should we have to stop?"

He looked up at the moving cloud, which was fringed with ragged streamers.

"I imagine we wouldn't get off again to-day."

"Then we'll go on," said Agatha.

Thirlwell signed to the *Metis*, who had slackened their efforts, and the foam swirled up at the bows as they drove the paddles through the water.

Chapter XXII
Before The Wind

Soon after the island melted into the gloom, a flash of lightning leaped from the cloud and spread like a sheet of blue flame across the water. For a second, Agatha saw black rocks and trees stand out against an overwhelming glare, and then they vanished and she saw nothing at all. Lightning is common in Canada, but this had a terrifying brilliance unlike any that she had known. While her dazzled eyes recovered from the shock she was deafened by a crash that rolled among the cloud-banks in tremendous echoes, and before it died away another blaze leaped down. It was rather a continuous stream of light than a flash, because it did not break off but, beginning overhead, ran far across the lake. The next enveloped the canoes in an awful light and she felt her hair crackle before the thunder came.

She was too entranced to feel afraid, and glanced at Thirlwell with half-closed eyes. His face was set and his mouth shut tight, but he was paddling hard and she heard the others' labored breath as they kept time with him. The reason for their haste, however, was not plain; the storm was terribly violent, but they would be no safer in the woods than on the lake. Yet it was obvious that they wanted to reach land.

After a stunning crash, the thunder began to roll away, the lightning glimmered fitfully farther off, and a torrent of rain broke upon the canoes. Agatha was wet before she could put on her slicker, and when she sat, huddled together, with head bent to shield her face from the deluge, she could not see fifty yards in front. The water was pitted by the rain, which rebounded from its surface with angry splashes. It ran down the half-breeds' faces and soaked their gray shirts, but they did not stop paddling to put on their coats. Agatha wondered with some uneasiness what they thought was going to happen.

The rain got lighter suddenly and a cold draught touched her forehead. She saw Thirlwell glance astern, although he did not miss a stroke. His soaked hat drooped about his head and his thin overalls were dripping; she thought he saw she was looking at him, but he did not speak. Then the haze that had shut them in rolled back and a dark line advanced across the lake. It had a white edge and there was a curious humming, rippling noise that got louder. Thirlwell signed to one of the *Metis*, who stepped a mast in the hole through a beam and loosed a small sail. The sail blew out like a flag, snapping violently, and the man struggled hard to push up the pole that extended its peak. Then he hauled the sheet, and the canoe swayed down until her curving gunwale was in the water. The half-breed moved to the other side and Thirlwell beckoned Agatha.

"Come aft by me!"

She obeyed, although it was difficult to crawl over the cargo in the bottom of the sharply slanted craft. The humming noise had changed to a shriek, but it did not drown the turmoil of the water. Short waves with black furrows between them rolled up astern and although they were not high they looked angry. Agatha saw that Thirlwell wanted to trim the canoe. He held a long paddle with the handle jambed against the pointed stern, and the canoe's side rose out of the water as she paid off before the wind.

"We could do nothing with the paddles," he said. "A sail's no use in a river-canoe, but these heavy freighters run pretty well. Luckily it's a fair wind to the river mouth."

Agatha could scarcely hear him, but when she asked how far it was he nodded as if he understood.

"Three or four miles! Not much sweep for the wind, but it will raise a nasty sea before we get there."

Gazing at the driving clouds that blotted out the forest, she tried to ask if he could find the river, but just then the canoe rolled and the little spritsail swelled like a balloon. There was a hiss and a splash, and the top of a wave that split at the stern and rolled forward poured in at the waist. Thirlwell bent over the paddle and slackened the sheet, the canoe swung her bows out, and leaped ahead. Spray blew about in showers; the foam stood in a ridge amidships and boiled high about the stern. It seemed to Agatha that they were traveling like a toboggan, and she had an exhilarating sense of speed that banished the thought of danger.

"How fast are we going?" she shouted.

"I don't know. Five miles an hour, perhaps!"

It sounded ridiculous; Agatha had felt as if they were flying. Then she saw that skill was needed to keep the canoe before the wind and Thirlwell ran two risks. If he let the craft fall off too far, the sail would swing across and she might be capsized by the shock; if he let her swerve to windward, the following wave would break on board and she would be swamped. Thirlwell looked highly strung but very cool. A mistake would have disastrous consequences; if he gave way to the strain for a moment, the canoe would sink. But she knew he would not give way, and it was comforting to see that the half-breed shared her confidence. He was, no doubt, a *voyageur* from his boyhood, but it was plain that he did not want to take the steering paddle.

Sometimes, when a savage gust screamed about them and whipped up the spray in clouds, Thirlwell let the sheet run round a pin; sometimes he sank the paddle deep and she saw its handle bend and the blood flush his face. Drops of sweat ran down his forehead, but his glance was fixed and calm. The strain on brain and muscle braced without exciting him; he seemed to accept it as something to which he was used. He could be trusted in an emergency, and for some obscure reason she was glad to feel he was the man she had thought.

Then she watched the other canoe, which had dropped astern. The *Metis* had set their sail, but she was not running well. She swerved when she lifted with the waves and rolled until it looked as if she would capsize. Now and then a sea broke over the gunwale and a crouching half-breed desperately threw out the water. Another sat on a beam in the high stern and his pose was strangely tense. But for all Agatha's trust in Thirlwell, it was daunting to watch the laboring craft and the seas that threatened to swamp her. They looked worse when one saw their hollow fronts and raging crests, and Agatha fixed her eyes ahead.

The haze was thinning and now and then the blurred outline of trees broke through; but one belt of forest looked like another and she speculated with some uneasiness about the chance of Thirlwell's finding the river. If he did not find it, they would run some risk, because the men could not paddle to windward and the canoes might be smashed on a steep, rocky beach. They ran on, and sometimes the trees got plainer and sometimes vanished, but at length, when a savage gust rolled the haze away, Agatha saw an unbroken line of rocks and foam. It looked very forbidding and she wondered what Thirlwell would do.

"Sit as far as you can to windward," he shouted, and while she awkwardly obeyed the half-breed got up on the side of the canoe.

Agatha understood what this meant. Thirlwell had missed the river mouth and meant to skirt the coast, but when he tried to do so the wind would be abeam and its power to heel the canoe largely increased. So far, they had run before the gale, but to bring the craft's side to it was a different thing.

She set her lips as she watched Thirlwell haul the spritsail sheet. He was cautious and for a few moments brought the craft's head up with the paddle and kept the small sail fluttering. Then he let her go and she lurched down until her side amidships was in the water. To Agatha's surprise, not much came on board; it looked as if they were going too fast and the lee bow was the dangerous spot. In the plunges, the waves boiled up there, and one could feel the canoe tremble as she lurched over the tumbling foam. Then Agatha noted that Thirlwell was not steering with the gale quite abeam; he was edging the craft to windward as far as he could, but the beach got nearer and it was plain that they were drifting sideways while they forged ahead. Agatha began to doubt if he could keep them off the rocks.

He did not look disturbed. His glance was fixed to windward and his movements were strangely quick. Agatha saw that he kept the canoe from capsizing by the skilful use of paddle and sheet. When the craft could not stand the pressure he let the sail blow slack, and then hauled the sheet again, dipping his paddle to help her over a breaking wave. Sound judgment was plainly needed and the man must instantly carry out the decision he made. Handling a canoe in a breaking sea demanded higher qualities than Agatha had thought. She was getting anxious, for the rocks were nearer and one could see the angry surges sweep in tongues of foam far up their sides. It was surprising that such a sea could rise on a small lake. She could swim, but not much, and shrank from crawling out, half-drowned and draggled, from the surf; for one thing, Thirlwell would see her. She admitted that this was illogical and she ran worse risks, but it troubled her. A few moments afterwards, Thirlwell changed his course with a thrust of the paddle and slacked the sheet.

"All right now!" he shouted. "We'll find smooth water in a hundred yards."

A steep rock, washed by spouting foam, detached itself from the others and a narrow channel opened up between it and the beach. Agatha thought it looked horribly dangerous, but Thirlwell headed for the gap. They lurched through on the top of a curling wave, and she saw the mouth of the river behind the rock. The current rose in crested ridges where it met the wind, but the ridges were smaller than the waves on the lake and gradually sank to splashing ripples as the canoe ran up stream between dark walls of forest. The trees did not cut off the wind, which followed the channel, and by and by Thirlwell looked at Agatha.

"We have made a good run, but it isn't often one gets a fair wind like this, and poling against the stream is slow work. Still we'll stop and pitch camp when you like."

"Shall we save a day for our prospecting if we go on until dark?"

"Yes," said Thirlwell, "we'll certainly gain a day."

Agatha was cold and wet and cramped. She longed to stop, but it was important to save time and she wanted Thirlwell to see that she had pluck.

"Then go on as far as you can," she replied.

She had half expected the *Metis* to grumble, but they did not. It looked as if Thirlwell had carefully chosen his men, and she found out later that no fatigue she could bear troubled them. After a time, the wind dropped as they ran round a bend, and getting close to the high bank, they began to pole. At dusk they ran the canoe aground on a sheltered beach, and Agatha landed, feeling very tired and cold. When supper was over and they sat by the fire she did not want to talk, and, going to her tent, soon fell asleep.

Next day they poled against the current and paddled, in bright sunshine, across a lake. At noon they camped among short junipers, and the next morning carried the empty canoes, upside down, across a rocky point. It cost twelve hours' labor, relaying the loads, to make the portage, and then they launched upon another lake. After two more days they left the canoes, covered with fir-branches, on a beach, and pushed inland. A narrow trail led them across a high divide, seamed by deep gullies, where stunted pines and juniper grew among the rocks, and they portaged the loads by stages, carrying part for an hour or two, and then going back. Agatha was surprised to see how much a man could carry with the help of properly adjusted straps.

When the divide was crossed they found two canoes by the bank of a small creek, down which they drifted with the swift current. Then there was a chain of lakes, veiled in mist and rain, and after making a portage they reached a wider stream. They followed it down through tangled woods and when they camped late one evening, Agatha sat silent by the fire, trying to retrace their journey and speculating about what lay ahead. For the most part, her memory was blurred, and hazy pictures floated through her mind of lonely camps among the boulders and small pine-trunks, of breathless men dragging the canoes up angry rapids, and carrying heavy loads across slippery rocks. Their track across the wilderness was marked by little heaps of ashes and white chips scattered about fallen trees.

But some of the memories were sharp; there was the evening she found Thirlwell carrying her belongings a double stage in order that she might have all she needed when they camped. He panted as he leaned against a tree and his face and hair were wet; she felt moved but angry that he had exhausted himself for her. She did not want him to think she knew what her comfort cost and was willing to let him buy it at such a price. She remembered that she had begun to speculate rather often about what he thought.

Then there was the morning they saw a half-covered rock a few yards off in the foam of a furious rapid. She had tried to brace herself for the shock, expecting next moment to be thrown into the water, but Thirlwell with a sweep of the paddle ran the canoe past. So far, he had never failed in an emergency, and she felt that she could not have chosen a better guide and companion. He was resourceful and overcame difficulties; he seemed to know when she would sooner be quiet and when she liked to talk. They had talked much beside the camp-fires, and although he was not clever, she remembered what he said.

But she had something else to think about that gave her a sense of loss and a poignant melancholy. Indeed, she had forced her mind to dwell upon the other matters in order to find relief, and she was glad when Thirlwell broke the silence.

"We ought to make the Shadow by to-morrow noon, and the mine in the evening."

"I think we go down the Grand Rapid before we reach the mine?"

Thirlwell made a sign of agreement, and after a moment's hesitation she gave him a quick glance.

"I wonder if you know what day to-morrow is? I mean the associations it has for me?"

"Yes," he said in a sympathetic voice. "I thought you would sooner not talk about it; but I remember. In a way, it's curious you should be here now."

"Ah," she said, "I wanted to be in the North when the day came round, but I did not imagine I should go down the rapid in the evening. It was in the evening the canoe capsized!"

"Dusk was falling; the smoke of a bush fire blew across the river, and there was a moon."

"The moon will be out to-morrow," Agatha said quietly. "It is strange; I couldn't have arranged that things should happen like this!"

She paused for some moments and then resumed: "Perhaps it is ridiculous, but I imagine now I am going to find the lode. The doubts I started with have gone; I feel calmly confident."

Thirlwell noted the emotional tremble in her voice and thought he had better use some tact.

"I must see the load that got wet is properly put up," he said, and moved back into the shadow; but Agatha sat still, watching the smoke curl among the dark trunks.

She had not exaggerated, for a feeling of quiet confidence had been getting stronger all day. There was no obvious reason for it and the difficulties she must overcome were greater than she had thought; but she felt that she would succeed. After all, her father had loved her best, she was making the search for his sake, and when she reached the scene of his efforts she would find some help. The hope was, of course, illogical and she was a teacher of science; but it was unshakable and comforted her. Then she mused about her father's life in the wilds. Something had happened to him, for she had noted Thirlwell's reserve. Perhaps bitter disappointment had broken him down; she did not know and would not ask. It was enough that he had loved her; she was satisfied with this.

Chapter XXIII
Strange's Legacy

It was afternoon when the canoes slid out from the forest on to the broad expanse of the Shadow River. The day was calm and hot, although the sky was covered with soft gray clouds, that subdued the light. The river had shrunk, for the driftwood on the bank stood high above the water level, and Thirlwell had only known it sink so low during the summer when Strange was drowned. For all that, the current ran fast and the long rows of pines rolled swiftly back to meet the canoes as they floated down. The trees had lost their rigid outline and melted gently into the blue distance, while the savage landscape was softened by the play of tender light and shadow.

Agatha was glad that Thirlwell did not talk and thought he knew she wanted to be quiet. This was a day she set apart from other days when it came round, for it was in the evening her father's canoe capsized. Since they drifted out on the Shadow, she had followed the track of his last voyage, and wondered with poignant tenderness what he had thought and felt. Somehow she did not believe he had come back embittered by disappointment, and it was perhaps strange that she did not feel sad. Indeed, she felt nothing of the shrinking she had feared. Although her eyes filled now and then, her mood was calm, and sorrow had yielded to a gentle melancholy.

In the meantime, the current swept them on, past rippling eddies and rings of foam about half-covered rocks, and presently a gray trail of smoke stretched far along the bank. Thirlwell said the woods were burning; they often burned in summer, though nobody knew how the fires were lighted. By degrees the trees got dimmer, but the water shone with a pale gleam and presently the moon came out between drifting clouds. Then as they swept round a bend a throbbing Agatha had heard for some time got suddenly loud and she glanced at Thirlwell.

"The Grand Rapid," he said. "The water's very low; it's quite safe."

Agatha knew he did not think she was afraid; he had tactfully pretended to misunderstand her glance, and she fixed her eyes ahead. The shadows were deeper and the forest was indistinct, but it was not dark. Besides, the moon was getting bright and threw a glittering beam across the river. She could see for some distance and not far in front the water was furrowed and marked by lines of foam. The stream ran very fast and the throbbing swelled into a deep, sullen roar. There was a smell of burning, and now and then a trail of smoke drifted out from the bank, beyond which a red glow glimmered against the sky. It was like this, she thought, on that other evening when her father returned from his last journey, but the melancholy she had felt had given way to a strange emotional excitement. Somehow she knew the pilgrimage she had made for his sake would end as she had hoped.

For all that, she set her lips and grasped the side of the canoe when they came to the top of the rapid. Spray that looked like steam rolled across the water, blurring the tops of the crested waves that ran back as far as one could see, and here and there in the smooth black patches a wedge of foam boiled behind a rock. Outside the furious mid-stream rush of the current, dark eddies revolved in angry circles and their backwash weltered along the bank. Thirlwell seemed to be steering for this belt and Agatha thought he meant to run down through the slack. As they swerved towards the rocks she looked round sharply, for there was a shout from the canoe astern—

"*Voici qui ven!*"

An indistinct figure scrambled along the rough bank, turning and twisting among the driftwood and boulders. For the most part, the bank was in shadow, but in places where the trees were not so thick the moonlight pierced the gloom.

"But he run!" exclaimed the *Metis* in Thirlwell's canoe. "Lak' caribou, vent' a terre."

"*Pren' garde!*" said Thirlwell warningly, and thrust hard with his paddle as the canoe drove past a foam-lapped rock.

"It is the chase he make," the half-breed resumed, and another figure came out of the gloom, a short distance in front of the one they had seen.

The man moved feebly, stumbling now and then, but it was obvious that he meant to keep ahead of his pursuer. As he crossed a belt of moonlight one of the *Metis* recognized him, for he cried: "*Steve le sauage! Regardez moi l'ivrogne!*"

Agatha thought the man was drunk. This would account for his awkwardness, but as he turned and staggered down the bank she saw him plainer and he looked ill. He dragged himself along with an effort, his gait was uneven, as if one leg was weak, but he went on towards the water's edge. A moment later he pushed off a canoe, made a few strokes with the paddle, and then let her swing out with an eddy until she was caught by the mid-stream rush. After this he crouched in the stern and the craft began to drift down the rapid. The other man stopped and threw out his arms, as if he meant to protest that he could do nothing more.

"Father Lucien!" said Thirlwell. "Black Steve's risking a capsize."

They sped past the man upon the bank and Agatha watched the crouching figure in the canoe. The craft was a short distance in front of, but outside, theirs, and she could see the danger of her being smashed or swamped. It was plain that the only safe way down was through the slack along the bank, but the man made no effort to reach this smoother belt. He let the paddle trail in the water while the canoe rocked among the angry waves. His rashness fascinated Agatha and she could not look away, although she knew she might see him drown.

"Can't you do something?" she asked Thirlwell.

"No," he said sternly. "We're loaded and would be swamped. Steve's drunk and must take his chance."

A few moments later the canoe in front plunged down a furious rush of the current, lurched up on a white wave, rolled over, and vanished. Agatha trembled, and felt cold, and the *Metis* shouted: "*V'la! C'en est fait—*"

A black object that looked like a head rose from the racing foam and Agatha turned to Thirlwell imperiously—

"Go and help him."

He hesitated and she knew it was on her account. Then he lifted his paddle.

"*Au secour!*"

The canoe swerved, swung out from the slack, and plunged into the foam. She lifted her bows high out of the water while a white ridge rolled up astern, and for the next minute or two Agatha saw nothing clearly. Spray beat upon her, whipping her face; she had a confused sense of furious speed, but felt that the canoe was controlled. Water splashed on board; the *Metis* bent forward and his shoulders moved in savage jerks. Behind them, the other canoe plunged down the rapid, rather bounding than sliding from wave to wave. In front, the black shape of the overturned craft washed to and fro like a drifting log. Thirlwell shouted as they sped past a rock, the canoe was swung violently sideways, and they were out of the main rush. There was an eddy behind the rock and the water ran round in white-lined rings. The moonlight fell across the center and Agatha saw a man's dark head.

Thirlwell backed his paddle and as they swept round in a semi-circle the *Metis* stretched out his arm. They were very near the man in the water and when he spun round like a cork in the revolving backwash the moonlight touched his wet face. Agatha, leaning over the side, saw that he was the man who had broken into Farnam's house. The half-breed missed him and he looked up at her as the canoe shot past. He was so close that she could almost touch him, and she saw a look of fear in his staring eyes. Then, without making an effort to reach the canoe, he slipped under Thirlwell's hand and sank.

The canoe turned and an indistinct object broke the surface. It vanished, the canoe was swept back to the edge of the main rush, and for a minute or two Thirlwell and the half-breed struggled desperately. When they reached the slack again, there was nothing but angry water and racing foam. The man had gone and Agatha shivered and felt faint.

After that she had a hazy impression of streaming woods and flying belts of gloom as they swept down through the slack, until they drove out upon the tail-pool. For some minutes Thirlwell and the half-breeds battled with the eddies, and then they floated on smoothly and a light began to twinkle among the pines.

Thirlwell steered for the bank and Scott and some of the miners met them at the landing. Agatha was glad to leave the canoe, for her nerves were badly jarred.

Thirlwell presented Scott, who took them to the shack, which looked as if it had been recently cleaned. He said Agatha must make use of it for a day or two, and he and Thirlwell would find a berth in the store-shed. Then they began to talk about the accident and Scott said, "Driscoll came back from the bush, looking ill, a week since and shut himself up in his shack. One of the boys told Father Lucien, who went along to look after him and found him very sick. That's all I know."

Agatha asked a few questions and then told them about the burglary.

"I am sure he was the man who opened my trunk," she said.

"Ah!" said Scott. "Do you think he knew you?"

"I believe he did. It's curious, but I thought he was afraid."

"Perhaps he was afraid," Scott agreed, with a meaning look at Thirlwell, who got up.

"I had better go to meet Father Lucien. He'll come down to the landing after us."

He found the missionary hurrying along the bank, and stopping him, sat down.

"Driscoll's gone; we did our best to pick him up," he remarked and related what had happened. "We may find him in the tail-pool to-morrow, but I imagine he'll be washed away down river, like his victim."

"Then you think Strange was his victim?"

"I can't doubt it now. But how did Steve get out of the shack?"

"Perhaps that was my fault, but he had been delirious for a day and night; and in the afternoon, when he was calmer, I went to sleep. One is apt to sleep too long when one is tired. When I wakened he was not in bed and a whisky bottle I had taken from him was nearly empty. I think he must have disturbed me as he moved about, because when I went outside I saw him making for the river. I ran, but I came too late, and you know the rest."

"You are not to blame," said Thirlwell. "You have twice taken pity on a man who tried to starve you. He meant you to die of hunger the night he stole into your camp."

"He is dead. One must be charitable. What would he gain by leaving me to die?"

"Don't you know?" Thirlwell asked. "We can talk frankly now the matter has been taken out of our hands. When he got better after the first attack, the time I kept watch with you, he had probably some remembrance of his ravings. Anyhow, I expect he remembered he'd got a fright and may have talked. He thought you knew too much."

"It's possible," said Father Lucien, very quietly.

Thirlwell was silent for a few moments and then resumed: "I hesitated about going to his help. We were heavily loaded, the risk was great, and I thought Miss Strange's life worth more than his. She made me go and I believe I could have saved him, but he saw her and let himself sink. She declares he looked afraid!"

"It is very strange."

"I don't find it strange," said Thirlwell. "There's a touch of dramatic justice about the thing that appeals to me. I suppose you know what day it is? *Driscoll knew.*"

Father Lucien shook his head. "What is one day more than another, when all wrongs are put right and crimes punished in the end? Justice is not theatrical, but the obstinate offender cannot escape." He paused and then resumed: "Well, we shall never know all that happened, and as you have said, the matter is no longer in our hands. Perhaps for the girl's sake—"

"Yes," said Thirlwell, "she has borne enough. You can imagine the shock she'd get if we found out, and had to tell her. The thing's done with. It's some relief to feel that my responsibility has gone."

Father Lucien made a sign of agreement. "I will come to see her tomorrow," he said, but Thirlwell knew that Agatha would never learn from him that Strange's canoe had not been accidentally capsized.

Early next morning Thirlwell went to the tail-pool, but nothing except some driftwood washed about in the eddy. The latter had worn out a deep hollow and he scrambled over the rocks in order to look down into its revolving depths. There was nothing there, and when going back he made his way across some worn slabs that had been covered until the water sank to an unusually low level. By and by he stopped at the edge of a pool. A small round object that was not the color of the stones lay at the bottom.

Thirlwell knelt down and rolling up his sleeve got the object out. It was made of white metal that had tarnished but not corroded, and looked like an old-fashioned pocket tobacco-box. The thing was well made, for he could hardly find the joint of the lid and below the latter there was some engraving. He rubbed it with a little fine sand and then started as he read a name. It was Strange's tobacco-box and a light dawned on him.

He knew now why Driscoll had haunted the reefs when the water was low, and thought he knew what was inside the box. This was the thing Strange *had taken with him*. But Driscoll had looked in the wrong place. The box was heavy, but perhaps a flood had rolled it down the rapid, or it had fallen from Strange's pocket when the stream washed his rotting clothes away.

Thirlwell shook the box and something rattled inside, after which he noted a dark smear round the edge of the lid. He scraped this with his knife and thought the stuff was a waterproof gum the freighters used to caulk their canoes. It looked as if Strange had carefully made the joint watertight, and Thirlwell's curiosity was strongly excited, but the box was not his. It was too early to look for Agatha, and he waited with some impatience until she came out of the shack and sat down in the sunshine after breakfast.

"I think this was your father's," he said, putting the box in her hand, and told her how he had found it.

Agatha started. "Yes; I gave it him on his birthday long since. It was bright then; old English pewter, I think. I saw it in a little store where they sold curiosities, and had it engraved."

Somewhat to Thirlwell's annoyance, Scott came up with Father Lucien, whom he presented to Agatha, but she did not put the box away.

"Mr. Thirlwell found this in the river, but the lid is fast," she said. "Will somebody help me to open it?"

Scott took the box into the shack, where he had some tools, and brought it back with the lid just raised above its socket. He gave it to Agatha and was going away when she stopped him.

"I would like you and Father Lucien to wait. You knew my father, and I think there is something important in the box."

They came nearer and, pressing back the lid, she shook out a few small stones.

"Specimens!" she said in a strained voice, holding out two or three to Thirlwell. "Don't you think they're very like the piece I gave you?"

Thirlwell examined the stones and handed them to Scott, who nodded.

"This stuff and the specimen Thirlwell showed me came from the same vein."

"There's something else," Agatha resumed, taking out a folded paper. Her hand shook as she opened it and the tears gathered in her eyes. Then she gave Thirlwell the paper.

"Will you read it for me? I can't see very well."

The paper was spotted with mildew, torn at the bottom, and cut at the folds, but holding it carefully, he read—

"*The Agatha Mine*; frontage on the lode staked by Gordon Strange."

Compass bearings, calculated distances, and landmarks were given next, and then the writing stopped an inch or two from the bottom of the sheet.

"Your father found the lode," Thirlwell said, very quietly.

Agatha looked up with a curious smile. "Yes; I feel as if he had *sent* me this. I have come into my inheritance and it is easier than I thought!" She paused and added: "Once or twice I was afraid and nearly let it go."

Chapter XXIV
Agatha Resumes Her Journey

There was silence for a minute or two after Agatha had spoken, and then Father Lucien said, "Now we know what Driscoll looked for. Few secrets can be kept."

Thirlwell gave him a warning glance that Agatha did not note. She was gazing across the river, her face towards the North, as if she had forgotten the others, but she presently roused herself.

"Can we start to-morrow?" she asked.

"No," said Thirlwell firmly, "you must rest for two or three days, and there are a number of things to be got."

"I don't think I can rest until I have seen the lode."

"You will have to try. It may be some time yet before we find the spot. For one thing, the directions aren't complete. You see they stop—"

Agatha took the paper. "Yes; I hadn't noticed that. It begins very clearly and then breaks off. I wonder why."

Thirlwell said nothing. It looked as if Strange had been interrupted; the shakiness of the last few lines hinted that they had been written in haste. There was a space between the last and the bottom of the paper. Perhaps Driscoll had joined him and he had distrusted the man, who might have come into the camp while he was writing. Then, when he afterwards sealed the box, he had forgotten that he had not finished what he meant to say; but, if the supposition were correct, this was not remarkable. Strange might have taken some liquor with him. But Agatha must not suspect.

"The paper states the claim was staked," she resumed. "So far as that goes, it makes the ore mine. George must have a share, but I mean to work the lode."

"I'm afraid it doesn't go very far," Scott remarked. "The law requires that the discoverer stakes off the ground he is entitled to and then registers the claim at the nearest record office. After this he must do a certain amount of development work before he gets his patent and becomes the owner of the mine. The claim has not been recorded yet."

"No; it has lapsed," Agatha agreed. "This means that any adult British citizen may make a re-discovery record. Well, we must do so, as soon as we can."

"Developing a mine is rough work for a woman."

Agatha smiled. "There's something about the discoverer being allowed to appoint a deputy, and perhaps Mr. Thirlwell will look after my interests. But won't you see about getting us all that he thinks needful?"

"I'll see about it now," said Scott, who took Thirlwell away, but stopped when they were hidden by the pines.

"Strange has given you a useful clue, but that's all," he said. "You'll find the lode if you find the valley, but you may look for a long time."

Thirlwell made a sign of agreement. "Yes; there's something curiously elusive about this ore."

"All the same, it's certainly worth a proper search; but you'll need a large quantity of truck and one or two extra packers. I understand Miss Strange insists upon everything being done at her cost. Has she money enough?"

"I think not."

"You know she has not! Looks as if you had forgotten you showed me her letter when she stated the sum. It's hard to see how it covers expenses up to date."

Thirlwell looked embarrassed and Scott laughed. "You seem to have been generous, particularly as you didn't believe in the lode; but anything you have saved from your wages won't carry you far. Well, you can take the truck and tools you need, and I'll give you two of the boys. Miss Strange can pay me when she gets her patent, or, if she likes, I'll butt in on a partnership basis and run my risk. She can decide which line she'll take after she locates the ore."

"Thanks; I'll take the truck," said Thirlwell.

He knew Scott wanted to help him and not to gain something for himself, but it might be an advantage for Agatha to make an arrangement with him when she owned the mine.

"There's another thing," Scott went on. "Since the Clermont isn't paying, I might lend you to Miss Strange if you were anxious to undertake the development work, but the law doesn't require very much of this. What are you going to do when the patent's granted?"

Thirlwell made an abrupt movement. Until that morning he had doubted if Agatha would find the vein, but he was forced to admit the possibility of her doing so. When the vein was proved and she owned the claim she would no longer need him as she needed him now; nor would he be able to neglect his duties and follow her about as unpaid adviser.

"I don't know what I'm going to do. I haven't thought about it yet."

"Miss Strange must have a manager. If you're willing to undertake the job, I daresay I could let you go. Then, if she wouldn't sooner trust her judgment, I think I could give you a pretty good character."

"No," said Thirlwell sharply, and stopped. He suspected that Scott was amused, and it jarred him to think of becoming Agatha's hired servant.

"Well," said Scott, with a twinkle, "exploring the bush with a charming girl is no doubt very pleasant while the summer lasts, but it doesn't lead to much. In fact, so far as I know your views, it leads to nothing. Anyhow, I must see what we have in the store that would be useful."

He went away and Thirlwell, after sitting still for some minutes with a frown, got up and moodily followed the trail to the river bank. Scott had shown him that his friendship with Agatha could not continue on the lines it ran on now. In a way, he had for some time recognized this, but it was not until he found the tobacco-box the truth became overwhelmingly plain. Their pleasant relations must either come to an end very shortly or be built up again on a new foundation, and the first was unthinkable. He walked along the bank until he got calmer and then went back to examine a canoe he meant to caulk. After all, the lode was not found yet.

They stayed three days at the mine, while their outfit was got ready; and when Drummond was not at work he followed Agatha about. He said he liked the woods, spoke of his employers with frank appreciation, and declared that he was grateful because she had got him his post. Besides this, he made no secret of a humble devotion to herself that she sometimes found embarrassing and sometimes amusing. On the evening before they left the mine, he joined the group outside the shack.

"Well," said Scott, rather dryly, "what do you want?"

"Miss Strange pulls out for the North to-morrow, and if she'll take me I'm going along."

"Wait a moment," Scott said to Agatha, and then asked Drummond: "Why do you want to go?"

"I mean to get even with Stormont; and I want to put Miss Strange as wise as I can."

"Then we are to understand you expect nothing for the job?"

Drummond's black eyes sparkled. "You're my boss, so far, but I won't stand for being guyed. It's not *your* money I'm after."

"Perhaps the rejoinder's justifiable," Father Lucien remarked, smiling; and Drummond turned to Agatha with a touch of dignity.

"I meant to make my pile by selling the ore to somebody, but you treated me like a white man, and I guess the lode belongs to you. Well, if I help you get rich and you want to give me something, I won't refuse, but I'm not out for money. Say, you'll let me go?"

"Can you help?" Scott interrupted. "If you can, it looks as if you had kept something back when you made the other deal."

Drummond grinned. "I kept something back from Stormont; when I put him wise I put him off the track. But I'm playing straight with Miss Strange and Thirlwell. You can bet on me!"

"Then we'll take you," said Agatha, with a deprecatory glance at Thirlwell.

"You're not going to be sorry about it," Drummond declared, and when he went away Agatha turned to Father Lucien.

"It's your business to judge men's character: do you think I have done well?"

"I imagine the lad will make good. He has two incentives: he likes you, and hates your adversary."

"Ah," said Agatha, smiling, "I wonder which is the stronger!"

Father Lucien spread out his hands and his eyes twinkled. "I am a priest, Miss Strange, and must admit that I cannot tell. You have won the young man's confidence; but his is a primitive nature, and hate counts for much."

"You are an honest man," said Agatha. "After all, the truth is better than compliments."

The party broke up soon afterwards, and early next morning Agatha left the mine with Thirlwell, Drummond, and a white rock-borer as well as the half-breed packers. They poled up the Shadow for some distance, and then followed a small creek, tracking the canoes, which were heavily loaded. Indeed, when they carried the freight by relays across the portages, Agatha was surprised to note the quantity of tools and stores. Since the cost of transport made such things dear, it looked as if Thirlwell had made her money go a long way.

As they pushed on the country got wilder. The rocks were more numerous, the trees smaller, and in places they crossed wide belts where fires had raged. The flames had burned off the branches, but left the trunks, and the long rows of rampikes sprang from the new brush, shining a curious silver-gray where they caught the light. The mode of travel, however, did not change. Sometimes they paddled up sparkling lakes, and sometimes dragged the canoes over ledges and gravel-beds in shallow creeks until the water shrunk and they made a laborious portage across a rocky height.

The journey was made as much by land as water, and at first Agatha wondered that the men were capable of such toil, but by degrees she found that she could carry more than she had thought, and laughing at Thirlwell's protests, often struggled through the brush with a heavy load. The hot sunshine that lasted so long, and the freshness that followed when the shadows deepened, calmed and strengthened her. She felt braced in mind and body; her doubts and impatience had gone. She was quietly confident that they would find the ore.

But they did not find it, and at length the time Agatha had allowed herself came to an end. It was possible that she had already lost her post at the school, but if not and she wanted to keep it, she must return at once.

She did not, however, mean to give up the search while their food held out and there was no shortage yet, perhaps because the half-breeds often went fishing and gathered wild berries. Then one hot day, when they nooned beside a shining lake and she sat in the shade of a boulder, she heard the men talking.

"The summer she is good," a *Metis* remarked. "Me, I lak' better make the prospect than the freight. *Chercher l'argent, c'est le bo' jeu!*"

"We haven't struck much argent yet," said the white miner. "I wonder what the boss thinks and guess he's up against something. Walked past at an awkward piece on the last portage as if he didn't see me, with his forehead wrinkled up. Seen him look like that when he reckoned the roof was coming down on us."

Agatha's curiosity was excited, because she thought she had noted a subtle difference in Thirlwell's manner. There was a hint of reserve, and sometimes he looked disturbed. Then Drummond interrupted his companion.

"You can't tell what the boss thinks when he doesn't want, and we're certainly going to find the lode."

"I'd like to see you strike it all right, because if you don't, you're going to be some dollars out," the miner replied. "Don't know who's paying for this outfit, but I'd put it pretty high."

"What d'you reckon it cost?" Drummond asked.

The miner made a calculation and Agatha listened with strained interest as he enumerated the different items.

"Well," said Drummond, "I can't value the tools and powder, but allowing for transport, you've got the stores nearly right. Anyhow, I'm going swimming. If Pierre will give me ten yards, I'll race him to the island."

They went away and Agatha sat still with a hot face. She had trusted Thirlwell and he had deceived her; her money had soon been exhausted and the journey was now being made at his expense. She felt as if she had been robbed of something to which she had a sacred right; she had let a stranger undertake the task that was peculiarly hers. Then she had been cheated so easily. Thirlwell must think her a fool, or perhaps that she was willing to be deceived.

Getting calmer, she admitted that his object was good. He wanted to help, but it was unthinkable that she should trade upon his generosity. She resolved to talk to him about it, but he had gone into the bush to look for the best line across the neck between them and another lake. When he came back the men were unloading the canoes and he occupied himself with making up the packs.

They had camped and eaten supper before her opportunity came, and then as they sat by the water's edge she told him what she had heard. He listened quietly until she asked: "Was the man's calculation correct?"

"Nearly so. He was rather above the mark."

"Then I am in your debt?"

"Does that hurt?"

"Yes," said Agatha, with some hesitation, "in a way, it hurts very much. I don't mean that it's embarrassing to take your help, though it *is* embarrassing. You see, I felt I must find the lode myself; it's my duty, and you have taken away the satisfaction I might have felt. Besides, you cheated me."

Thirlwell was silent for a few moments, and then said: "I'm sorry you find it hard to let me help, but unless I had done so you couldn't have gone far."

"You should have been frank and let me wait."

"For another year? The North is no place for a white woman after the rivers freeze."

Agatha said nothing. She had not thought about this, and it would have been very hard to wait until summer came again.

"Well," he resumed, "I cheated you, because I could see no other plan. I think you have waited too long. If you had gone on thinking about nothing but the lode, it would have done you harm."

"Did it harm my father?"

"Yes," said Thirlwell quietly, and Agatha dared ask nothing more. Besides she knew that he would not tell her much.

"Now," he went on, "I have owned my fault; but you're rather taking it for granted that my object was altogether unselfish. After all, the law only gives you so much frontage on the vein, and there's nothing to prevent my staking off a claim on the rest."

"That is so," said Agatha. "But the paper states that my father claimed the edge of the cliff, where, for a time, the ore could be easily worked. As your block would lie farther back, you would have to sink a shaft and drive a tunnel. This would cost you much."

"The cost wouldn't matter if the ore was rich. I could get all the capital I wanted."

Agatha gave him a quiet ironical smile. "Then you really came with me because you meant to stake a claim? That's curious, Mr. Thirlwell, because I think you never believed my father found the lode at all."

He colored and hesitated. "We'll let it go; there's something else. If you turn back now, can you reach Toronto before the school reopens?"

"No," said Agatha, with a soft, excited laugh. "I did not mean to turn back until I was forced. When I reached Toronto I should find somebody else had got my post."

Thirlwell noted her courage, although he thought she was rash. "Wouldn't it be awkward? But I suppose your brother—"

"I should not go to George. He is kind, but believes I have inherited my father's illusion. He always hated to hear him talk about the lode, and would think I was properly punished for my folly. But I needn't go on. You must understand—"

"I don't understand. The only thing I see is that you're not logical. It's obvious now that you must, if possible, find the ore; and yet you object to letting me help. If you give up the search and return to Toronto, it may be a very long time before you can make another trip."

"No, I suppose I'm not logical," Agatha admitted, with a mocking smile. "Logic is perhaps a useful guide for a *man*, but it doesn't always take him far. However, I oughtn't to have expected you to understand, and you're getting impatient—"

"Let's try to be practical," Thirlwell rejoined. "If we turn back at once, some of the truck we haven't used might be sold, and we would save the wages I promised the boys, but all we have spent would be thrown away. Well, I'd hate to feel that either of us must bear a loss like that."

"I have heard George say that a good business man cuts his losses."

"It's sometimes a better plan to hold on and get your money back."

"But how can we get our money back if we can't find the lode? You don't think we'll do so."

Thirlwell frowned. "There's a chance of finding it; a fighting chance. Now we're near the spot and have the truck, let's play the chance for all it's worth. You can pay me when you get your patent, or make any plan you like. Then Scott really supplied the stores and made some suggestions that I didn't mean to talk about unless our search succeeded."

He related what Scott had said, and added: "Anyhow, let's go on for a fortnight. Then if you insist, we'll take the back trail."

Agatha gave him a quick glance and he thought her eyes had softened, but she got up.

"Very well," she said, and went to her tent.

Chapter XXV
The Broken Range

The fortnight Agatha agreed to had nearly gone when, early one morning, Thirlwell and Drummond climbed a hill behind the camp and stood on the summit, looking about. Thin mist drifted across the low ground in front, but some miles off a forest-covered ridge rose against the sky. It was hardly a range of hills, but rather what prospectors call a height of land; a moderately elevated watershed marking off two river basins. Running roughly east and west as far as he could see, it limited Thirlwell's view and had puzzled him for some days.

Since the rivers that drained the country flowed northeast to Hudson Bay, it was obvious that there must be an opening in the ridge, but he had been unable to find one. Moreover, as Strange's creek ran south before it turned east, he imagined it was on his side of the heighth of land, but he had seen no stream flowing in either direction. Strange's notes were incomplete; and although Thirlwell calculated that he was about thirty miles from the spot where the ore outcropped, he had found none of the landmarks. The creek was not behind him, but a radius of thirty miles would cover a wide belt of country, and he doubted if he could persuade Agatha to extend the fortnight. Her obstinacy was ridiculous, but must be reckoned on.

By and by a faint breeze sprang up and the mist rolled back. Here and there a lake sparkled in the light of the rising sun and dark pines rose out of the streaming vapor. But there was no glistening thread to indicate a creek, and Thirlwell turned to Drummond with an impatient frown.

"Do you see anything that you think you ought to recognize?"

"No," said Drummond, rather sulkily, "I don't."

"You haven't been of much use to us yet! I think you stated that when you got here you'd recollect all your father told you about Strange's talk. Seeing the places would bring things back!"

"I haven't seen the places, and the old man was very sick when he told me. Anyhow, I've tracked your blamed canoes, and packed your stores across the divides. Guess I'd have hit the back trail long since if it wasn't for Miss Strange."

"Then we had better get down," said Thirlwell. "The boys don't seem to have started to cook breakfast, and I want to pull out soon."

He was turning away when Drummond stopped him, stretching out his arm. "Hold on! What's that yonder?"

"Mist," said Thirlwell, impatiently.

"No; it's too dark. Look again!"

Thirlwell started. The mist was drifting past the detached clump of pines his companion indicated, but its color was silvery, and he now noted a faint blue streak. This was something of a shock, for he had thought there was nobody but his party in the neighborhood.

"Smoke!" he exclaimed. "Go down as fast as you can and tell the boys not to make a fire."

When Drummond went off Thirlwell sat down and watched the smoke. It got plainer, and rose in a thick blue cloud when the mist rolled away. Somebody was cooking breakfast and the volume of smoke indicated a large fire. It looked as if there were a number of men to be fed, and Thirlwell had not expected to find Indians near the spot just then. After a time, the smoke died away and he went back to camp, but told Agatha nothing about what he had seen. When breakfast was over he took one of the *Metis* and plunged into the bush. There was not much need for caution, because the party would, no doubt, set off when they had finished their meal, and if they were Indians, it did not matter if he met them. But he did not think they were Indians.

When he had gone a mile or two, he stopped at the edge of a muskeg and sent the *Metis* on to a clump of pines on the other side. The man, keeping in the shadow, stole round the swamp, and vanished noiselessly in the underbrush. After a time, he reappeared, beckoning, and Thirlwell knitted his brows when he joined him.

The ashes of a fire smoldered between two hearth-logs; white chips and broken branches were scattered about. Near his feet were six small round holes, spaced in a regular pattern, and a cotton flour-bag and some empty cans lay beneath a bush.

"A white man's camp; they had a tent," he said.

"Sure," agreed the *Metis*. "Teepee poles they not mak' hole lak' dat."

"Well, I reckon a sour-dough prospector wouldn't have bothered about a tent. Looks as if one of them was a tenderfoot. *Qu'en pense-tu?*"

The *Metis'* keen eyes had wandered round the camp and he nodded. "But, yes! Dat man *sait vivre*; he lak' it comfortable."

"A city man!" Thirlwell remarked, with a frown. How many packers?"

"*Quat*," said the *Metis*.

"*Voyageurs?*"

The *Metis* laughed scornfully as he indicated the trampled brush, broken branches, greasy papers, and scraps of food. "Me, I think no! Railroad outfit. *Voyageur* not muss up camp lak' dat."

Thirlwell agreed. A half-breed *voyageur* does not waste food, and with inherited caution seldom disturbs the bush. It looked as if the city man had engaged a gang of track-layers, who are used to pioneering and sometimes carry surveyors' stores through the wilds.

"Well," he said, "we'll follow their trail."

The party had obviously left the water for a time, because their track led away from the creek in the valley and the bush was too thick to permit the portaging of canoes. Thirlwell followed the trail until he satisfied himself that they were going east, and then went back to his camp. Finding Agatha at the water's edge he sat down opposite.

"I'm afraid you didn't get much breakfast, but I didn't want the fire lighted," he said, and told her what he had seen.

"Ah!" she cried. "Do you think Stormont is looking for the ore?"

"I think so; I'm not certain."

"But he failed to find it once and nearly starved."

Thirlwell smiled. "I understand the fellow's obstinate. He may have got a fresh clue or found out something we don't know."

"Do you think he has been following us?"

"I don't. If he'd known we were in the neighborhood, he would not have lighted a fire."

"After all," said Agatha thoughtfully, "my father stated that he had staked the claim."

"I'm afraid that doesn't count for much. You're not recognized as prospective owner until your record's filed. I imagine your father's statement would carry some weight, but going to law about a mine is generally an expensive job, and it's hard to put up a good fight against a man with capital."

"Then what are you going to do about it?" Agatha asked anxiously.

"Get away from here at once, and as far as possible keep to the lakes; water carries no trail. Then Stormont has decided a point that has been bothering me—since he's gone east, we must go north or west."

"Yes. Unless it's possible that his clue is better than ours."

"I thought about that," Thirlwell replied. "We don't know if he has a clue, but we'll stick to ours and take the risk. Your father's directions are plain enough if we can find the first of his landmarks."

"Then go west," said Agatha. "I imagine the creek is on this side of the range."

Thirlwell got up and went to see the canoes launched, but he wondered whether Agatha remembered that there were only two or three days of the fortnight left. He thought she did remember, but he resolved that they would not turn back.

Soon after they started, a fresh breeze sprang up from the north-west and the shadows of flying clouds sped across the lake. The sky between the clouds was a curious vivid blue, the light was strong, and the woods along the bank flashed into bright color and faded to somber green as the gleams of sunshine passed. For a few minutes, trunks and branches stood out, sharply distinct, and then melted suddenly into their background. By degrees the ripples that lined the lake got larger; there was an angry splashing at the bows of the canoes, and little showers of spray began to fly.

"This clearness means the wind will hold and it's right ahead," Thirlwell said to Agatha, "We haven't had much luck of late!"

"The luck will change," she answered, smiling. "I am confident."

"Confidence doesn't cost you much effort," Thirlwell rejoined. "You were persuaded from the beginning that you would find the ore. It looks as if you were naturally optimistic."

"Oh, no! I had my weak moments when I wanted to shirk. I hated to feel I wasn't free like other people, and was willing to throw away my chance of getting rich. But that wouldn't have helped much; I couldn't get rid of the duty."

"You have pluck. For all that, I think you're indulging a rather exaggerated sentiment. Anyhow, it's hard to imagine you have had many doubts since we left the mine."

"I've had none. When you found the tobacco-box I knew I would succeed. There was something strangely significant about your finding it."

"I happened to look in the right place," said Thirlwell, dryly.

Agatha laughed. "You take a very matter-of-fact view."

"Perhaps so," Thirlwell agreed. "If I were steeped in sentiment, it wouldn't help me drive the canoe faster against a head-wind or carry a heavier load across a portage. That's a purely mechanical proposition. In the meantime, we're slowing up and will soon begin to drift astern."

"Then paddle," said Agatha, smiling. "After all, you're much more of a sentimentalist than I think you know."

Thirlwell bent over his paddle and the canoe forged ahead, but the breeze freshened, and the ripples changed to crested waves. Agatha's face was wet, her slicker dripped, and the men breathed hard between the strokes. They labored on, and at noon ran the canoes aground in the lee of a rocky island. Thirlwell ordered the *Metis* to use nothing but dry driftwood, which makes little smoke, for the fire, and when they rested after a meal found Drummond sitting alone outside the camp. He looked moody and his eyes were fixed on the height of land.

"Feeling bothered about something?" Thirlwell asked.

"Yes," said Drummond. "I'm trying to get back all the old man told me about Strange's tale. He only talked about it once, when he was sick. Looks as if he hadn't thought the lode a business proposition, and I didn't *then*. Besides, I was anxious and didn't listen much. Part of it came back afterwards, but not all. There's something I can't get."

"That's unlucky," Thirlwell remarked in a dry tone. "We need a hint."

"I reckoned I'd get it when I saw the country," Drummond went on. "I allow we're not far enough yet."

Thirlwell made a sign of disagreement. "Strange said the creek ran south and then turned east. I imagine there isn't another neighborhood where that's likely to happen. If we cross the divide, I expect we'll find the water running north."

"Well," said Drummond moodily, "you'd better leave me alone. There's something—if I'm quiet, I may get what I'm feeling for." He knitted his brows and a curious fixed look came into his eyes. "I know it's not far off, but I miss it when I'm just getting on the track."

Thirlwell left him and smiled half impatiently as he went back across the rocks. He had sometimes been puzzled, and sometimes amused, by Agatha's confidence, and now Drummond, who had given him no help so far, talked about an elusive clue. It looked as if both allowed their imagination too much rein, and trusted to vague feelings instead of their reasoning powers. Give him a compass bearing, or a definite base-line to calculate an angle from, and he would engage to take the party to the required spot; but he had frankly no use for the other thing. Yet he sometimes wondered—there was a calm assurance in Agatha's eyes. If this was not founded on superstition, from what did it spring?

They launched again in the afternoon, and reached the head of the lake wet and tired. Thirlwell did not talk much after supper, but sat by the fire, smoking, for some time after Agatha went to her tent. He had, in fact, been rather silent for the last few days. Now they were near the end of their journey he did not know if he wanted Agatha to find the lode or not. When they started he had imagined that the search would lead to nothing, and had gone because her society had a charm and he wanted to free her mind of a dangerous illusion. But he could no longer think the lode an illusion. The silver was there, and if one searched long enough, could, no doubt, be found.

This was somehow disturbing, but with a half-conscious wish to shirk the truth he would not inquire bluntly why it disturbed him. He wanted the girl to be happy, and had thought it best for her that she should give up the attempt to find the lode. Now he must readjust his views, and it was hard to see what place there would be for him in her affairs if she became the owner of a rich mining claim.

Next morning they made a difficult portage to another lake, and launching the canoes at noon found the wind blowing fresh. The lake was wide, and when by and by an angry sea got up Thirlwell reluctantly steered for the shelter of a rocky point. They had covered very little ground since they started, and there was only another day of the fortnight left. After supper some of the men went fishing, and Drummond set off alone along the beach, while Agatha and Thirlwell sat among the rocks where the pungent wood-smoke drifted past and kept the mosquitoes off. The sun had set and the air was very clear; they could see the ragged pines across the lake, but the trees on the point behind them cut off their view to the north.

Presently Drummond came back, running fast, and stopped in front of Agatha. His eyes sparkled and the sweat ran down his face.

"What's the matter?" Thirlwell asked. "Have the timber wolves got after you?"

"The *broken range!*" Drummond gasped. "Get up, Miss Strange, and come right along!"

Agatha looked at Thirlwell, who smiled. "I don't know what he means, but perhaps we had better go."

They followed the lad for some distance, though the shingle was large and rough. Now and then he turned and looked back impatiently, as if they were not coming fast enough; but at length he stopped and indicated the high ground to the north. Its bold line, colored a soft blue, stood out against the yellow sky, and in one place there was a sharply defined gap.

"There!" he exclaimed breathlessly. "I guess that's the *broken range!*"

"I see the break," said Thirlwell. "What about it?"

"Don't embarrass him," Agatha interrupted. "It's something he remembers. Perhaps his father talked about the gap."

"He did," said Drummond. "The thing's been kind of floating in my mind all day, but I couldn't get it fixed. Then I saw that gap and knew I'd got what I'd been feeling for."

"What did your father say?"

"The Indian camp he sent Strange to was in thin bush, close under the broken range, on the north side."

Thirlwell turned to Agatha. "Then we oughtn't to have much trouble in locating the ore. We know where the factory stood, and if we can find the thin bush, I can follow the line your father took."

Agatha's eyes shone and her color came and went, but with an effort she preserved her calm.

"After all, the bush may have grown."

"I think not," said Thirlwell. "It's probably rocky ground where the trees are small."

"But how was it my father did not see the gap?"

"That is easily accounted for. The gap's not large, and I expect you can only see it when you're directly opposite, at a right angle to the line of the high ground. If you moved back a mile or two, the rocks and trees would shut it in. Drummond didn't see it as we came up the lake."

"I suppose we must wait until to-morrow?"

"Yes," said Thirlwell. "We must leave the water, and can't get through the bush in the dark."

Agatha made a sign of agreement. "Very well; I am glad the nights are very short. But I would like to start at daybreak."

Then they turned and went back silently to camp. Thirlwell was conscious of a keen disturbance that he would not analyze and saw that Agatha did not want to talk. As a matter of fact, Agatha could not talk. She felt a curious exaltation: her heart was full.

Chapter XXVI
The Lode

At daybreak next morning Thirlwell sent the *Metis* up the lake to make a *cache* of the provisions he did not need, and hide the canoes in the brush. In the meantime, he scattered the ashes of the fire and buried the empty cans and all the chips he could find. There was another party in the neighborhood, and he wanted to leave nothing to indicate that the spot had been recently occupied by a camp. When the men returned the party set off along the beach, loaded with food and tools. Walking across the stones and ledges was laborious, but he did not mean to leave a trail, and kept to the water's edge for some distance before he plunged into the bush.

After this, their progress was very slow. The small trees grew close together and in places the ground was covered with rotting trunks and branches. Moreover the line he took led steadily upwards towards the break in the range. It did not look very far off when they started, but dusk was falling and the packers were nearly exhausted when they threw down their loads at the bottom of the gap. Thirlwell's back ached and the straps had galled his shoulders, but he noted with some surprise that Agatha did not look tired. She dropped behind as they toiled up the last rough stony slope, but she helped to pitch camp. Her movements were not languid and her eyes were bright.

By and by she took out the worn paper from the tobacco-box and asked Thirlwell a few questions. He answered rather moodily, and as soon as he could picked up his blanket and went off to the bed he had made of twigs. The hollow he had found was sheltered and the twigs were soft, but it was long before he slept. They were near the spot where Strange claimed to have seen the ore, and he was now persuaded that they would find the vein. If the ore carried as much silver as the specimens indicated, Agatha would be rich. She would go back to the cities, and if her riches were not to separate them altogether, he must enter her employment. Somehow he shrank from this.

But the ore might prove poorer than one thought and the mine cost much to work. He would not admit that he hoped so, since he wanted

Agatha to enjoy all the happiness that wealth could give. Indeed, he did not know what he hoped; he was physically tired and although he felt strangely restless his brain was dull. At length his eyes closed and for some hours he slept brokenly.

Getting up at daybreak, he scrambled along the bottom of the gap until he could look down on the other side, and presently turned with a start as he heard a rattle of stones. Agatha, whom he had thought asleep, advanced with a smile. She looked very fresh, and although he imagined she was highly strung, her face was calm. For a few moments she said nothing, but stood close by, gazing fixedly in front.

There was some mist on the low ground, but, for the most part, the tops of the pines rose above the haze. The sky in the east was getting red, and here and there one saw gleams of water and the gray backs of rocks. That was all, for the landscape was blurred to the north, where a vague gray line hinted at another range.

"The haze is tantalizing," she remarked by and by. "One could not see when we got here and I have been waiting for the dawn."

"I hoped you slept. We made a long march yesterday."

"Did you sleep?"

"No," said Thirlwell. "Anyhow, not very much."

Agatha smiled. "Yet you haven't been thinking about the lode as I have—thinking of nothing else for ever so long! Can't you imagine what it means to feel I am near the place at last?"

"I can imagine it to some extent. If the ore carries as much silver as we think, you can do what you like when you get your patent; build laboratories, travel, make friends with clever people. In fact, your money will buy you anything you want."

"Do you really believe that?" Agatha asked, with a hint of mockery in her voice. "Do you imagine I have been thinking about the money?"

"I have thought about it," Thirlwell said, and stopped when she gave him a curious glance. "Of course," he resumed, "there's some satisfaction in feeling you have finished a difficult job."

"Now you're nearer the mark! But you don't feel in the mood for philosophizing?"

"I'm often dull before breakfast," Thirlwell replied. "All the same, I'm glad you're happy. In fact, I'm trying to be sympathetic."

"And you find it hard!"

Thirlwell colored, but looked at her steadily.

"Anyhow, if the thing's possible, I'm going to find the lode for you."

"Yes," she said, without moving her eyes from his face, "I know you'll try to find it. You're trustworthy; you play a straight game!"

"I cheated once."

"That was when you thought the advantage would be mine. But how far do you think we will have to go?"

"Perhaps I can tell you when the sun gets up. We may have to search for three or four days; we may strike the creek to-night."

"Ah," she said, "I hope it will not be three or four days. Now we are very near, the suspense is keen." Then she smiled. "However, we will go back and get breakfast, because you must set your brain to work."

It was next morning when they saw the first of Strange's landmarks; and Thirlwell, taking its bearing with the compass, changed their line of march. In the evening they climbed a low hill, and when they reached its top, which rose like an island from a waste of short pine-scrub, Drummond stopped and, touching Agatha, indicated the ridge across the valley.

"Look!" he said. "The *hollow rock!*"

A small gray object, dwarfed by the distance, stood out against a smear of dark green on the crest of the high ground. After studying it for a few moments Thirlwell nodded.

"Yes; I think he's right."

Drummond turned to Agatha with a sparkle in his eyes. "I quit now, Miss Strange. You've got there ahead of Stormont; I guess I've made good!"

"You made good when you found the broken range," Agatha replied, giving him a grateful look, and Drummond's dark face flushed with color as he turned away.

They lost the rock as they went down hill, but when they made camp the roar of falling water came faintly across the woods.

"*The creek that runs south!*" said Thirlwell as he lighted the fire.

They started early next morning, but the ground was rough and the sun was getting low when they came down a rocky hill into a small round hollow, through which shining water flowed. The opposite slope was in shadow, but the slanting sunbeams touched a belt of fresh growth that glowed a vivid green against the somber color of the surrounding trees.

"That," said Thirlwell, "is, no doubt, where the rampikes stood. They've gone, and young willows have sprung up. Yonder's the low cliff. It looks as if we had arrived!"

Agatha stopped for a few moments and felt her heart beat. The dream she had first dreamed long since had come true, but she knew it might not have done so had she not had Thirlwell's help. In the meantime, the scene impressed itself upon her brain, so that she could long afterwards recall it when she wished—the nearly level sunbeams falling across the trees and turning their bark fiery red, the gleam of water, and the figures of the men plodding slowly downhill with their loads. Their faces glowed like polished copper in the searching light, their overalls were ragged and stained, and one stumbled and lurched wildly down a slope with a rattle of rolling stones. Then she glanced at Thirlwell, who stood close by, watching her with a sympathetic smile, though his pose was rather strained.

"Ah," she said, "you have brought me here! Just now I cannot thank you as I ought."

"We'll go on," he answered quietly. "I'd like to fire a shot or two before it's dark, and we'll need some time to drill the holes."

Agatha gave him a quick look. "You are nothing if you're not practical, but perhaps that's fortunate. One trusts practical people when there are things that must be done."

The sunshine had faded when they reached the bottom of the hill and the hollow was shadowy and cool. Thirlwell ordered the men to make camp and then went with Agatha to the foot of the cliff. The creek that flowed past the rock ran clear and low, and he got across by jumping from ledge to ledge. Then, as he scrambled among the boulders towards a spot he had marked he heard a splash, and looking round saw that Agatha had slipped into the stream. She waded across, with the water rippling round her long boots, and when she joined him trembled with suspense.

"You needn't have come over," he said, smiling as he indicated a band of darker color that seamed the ragged face of the gray stone. "That's all there is to see! Hardly looks as if it was worth your coming so far to find it? It was a lucky accident the color caught your father's eye; the vein's only distinct for a few yards where the frost has brought down the cliff. I think we'll find it dips."

Agatha noted that his tone was very matter-of-fact, although his face was set, and thought she had better follow his lead.

"Then the ore must once have outcropped. It's a good example of denudation."

"Yes; it probably ran out some distance back. You can see how the creek has cut down the rock, but frost and snow have helped. One can't tell yet whether the best or worst has been lost; but to begin with, we'll look for the discovery post."

They found it driven among the gravel; then, climbing a gully, reached the crest of the rock. Thirlwell led Agatha through the bush by his compass until he traced a rough oblong, marked by other posts. She followed him with confused emotions and once or twice her eyes filled with tears. Her father had driven these stakes; she could imagine the thrill it gave him to feel that at length his faith and labor were justified. His confidence had never wavered, although he had borne mockery and contempt and the gentle ridicule of his anxious wife. Then, when the prize he toiled for was won and he went back to enjoy it, the river had swept him away. But after all, love had conquered the angry flood, for he had left a clue that the rapid could not destroy.

Agatha thought Thirlwell understood something of her feelings, because he did not talk except when he showed her the posts. When they reached the last he said, "On the whole, I imagine your father's judgment was good. In fact, he picked his ground like a mining engineer."

"He had twenty years to brood about the vein at home," Agatha replied. "Are you surprised that he studied all the books on mining he could get?"

Thirlwell made an apologetic gesture. "I oughtn't to be surprised: he was your father, and it's obvious that you have prepared yourself to carry on his work. Well, I think he has staked off the best of the vein; at least, his claim covers the part that can best be reached. But you'll have trouble with the water; it may mean driving a drainage heading and putting up expensive pumps. The ore may be rich enough to stand the extra cost, but I can tell you more when I have fired a shot."

They went back to the camp, where the *Metis* had cooked supper, but Thirlwell did not eat much and soon returned to the cliff. He took the white rock-borer, but Agatha did not go with him. She felt chilled by his quietness. It was now plain that, since her father had marked off the exposed edge of the inclined lode, Thirlwell must sink a deep shaft if he wished to reach it farther back. This, however, did not account for his moodiness; for one thing, he had not expected that they would find the ore. Besides, he was generous and would want her to have the best. It would have been a comfort to give him half the claim, but he would refuse the gift. She had meant to enjoy her triumph with him, but this satisfaction had gone. It hurt, her to see him disturbed, but she colored as she resolved that her success should not separate them. If he was obstinate, something must be risked.

In the meantime, Thirlwell struck the drill his companion held. His face was damp with sweat and the hammer slipped in his hands, but he did not miss a stroke. He had promised the girl his help, and when the hole was sunk he chose the best spot for the next with fastidious care. He meant to play a straight game, although it would cost him much to let her win. By and by the miner picked up some of the bits of stone.

"Weight's all right; guess the stuff's carrying heavy metal," he remarked. "Still, I've seen a lode pinch out. It may be a pocket and the dirt run poor when you get farther in."

"It's possible," Thirlwell agreed in a dull voice.

The miner gave him a sharp glance. "Looks as if you wouldn't be much disappointed! Don't you *want* the dirt to go rich?"

"Let's get on," said Thirlwell. "I want to fire the shot before it's dark."

"Then watch out for my fingers," the miner rejoined. "When you pound her as you've been doing I like to see you keep your eye on the drill."

They worked for some time and then Thirlwell sent for Agatha, and helping her across the creek, held up the ends of two or three fuses and a match-box.

"It's proper that you should fire the first shot. I've put in a heavy charge and we'll know something about the ore when we see the stuff the blast brings down."

Agatha lighted the fuses and they hurried back to the shelter of the trees, where she stood with her heart beating fast. It was proper that she should be first to undertake her father's work; Thirlwell's thought was graceful. She glanced at him, but his brown face was inscrutable, although his mouth was firm. His quietness jarred; she felt angry and disappointed, as if she had been robbed of something.

For all that, she thrilled as she watched the faint sparkle of the fuse. She had won the first battle more easily than she had thought, and had now begun the next stage of the struggle. She sprang from a pioneering stock and knew that the shot she fired would break the daunting silence of the woods for good. If she failed to develop the mine somebody else would succeed. The lonely hollow would soon be covered with tents and shacks; men's voices and the rattle of machines would drown the soft splash of the creek. She was blasting a way for civilization into the wilderness.

A flash, springing from different spots, leaped across the foot of the cliff; gray smoke rolled up, and there was a roar that rolled in confused echoes across the woods. The front of the rock seemed to totter behind the smoke, great stones splashed in the water, and flying pieces rattled among the trunks. When the vapor began to clear and she wanted to run forward Thirlwell put his hand on her arm.

"It won't be safe for some time; you're not used to the fumes," he said. "If you went there now, you wouldn't be able to get up to-morrow."

She followed him back to the camp, where Drummond and the miner joined them.

"In the morning I'll go with you to see where we ought to stake the other claims," he said to the men. "You can, of course, locate where you like, but this job will need some capital and you want to get the best frontage you can. That will help us later."

They agreed without much enthusiasm. Now they had reached their object, a reaction had begun, and Agatha was sensible of a curious flatness. She knew that Drummond and the rock-borer could do nothing with their claims except sell them to somebody who could supply the money to develop the mines; but before they started Thirlwell had outlined a plan by which the holdings might be consolidated and worked together. The men had approved and promised to give her what Thirlwell called an option, if it seemed worth while to do the work required before the patents would be granted.

When the fumes had cleared they went with him to the cliff and he came back with a heavy bag. It was dark, but the firelight shone about him as he poured out the stones he had brought and gave her one or two.

"The stuff looks as good as the specimens we have," he said quietly.

Agatha agreed as she weighed the pieces, but her eyes were fixed on his face. He looked stern, but forced a smile—

"Your father was not deceived, and what he left unfinished you can make good. I think you are going to be rich."

"If so, I owe it all to you."

He shook his head. "You might have found the lode without me, but I expect you're tired and you ought to sleep well to-night. I must begin at daybreak. The sooner we start back to record the ground we claim, the better."

"Then good-night," she said quietly, but when she moved away through the shadow her face was resolute.

Chapter XXVII
THIRLWELL'S DULLNESS

Soon after daybreak, Thirlwell, Drummond, and the rock-borer pushed their way through the woods behind the cliff. The vein dipped and in consequence the farther one went back from the creek, the greater would be the cost of reaching the ore. Besides, it was possible that the ore pinched out and the uncovered part was an unusually rich pocket. His companions had agreed that he should have the next best location after Agatha's, and followed his advice about staking their claims. The half-breeds had, however, declined to exercise their rights; they were trappers and *voyageurs*, and stated that they had no use for mines.

Thirlwell thought there was no more ground worth recording, and doubted, for that matter, if his and the others' claims were worth much, but it was prudent to keep intruders out. Disputes often rose about the application of the mining laws, and it might be dangerous to have a rich and unscrupulous antagonist. His companions went away feeling puzzled by his coolness. On the journey he had encouraged the party with humorous banter, and made a joke of their difficulties; now he was quiet and reserved.

When they had gone Thirlwell sat down and lighted his pipe, for he knew he must grapple with his trouble before it mastered him. Looking back, he saw that he had been strangely pleased by Agatha's letters, and when he met her had at once felt her charm. This, however, was all; he frankly enjoyed her society and thought she liked his, but he was not romantic and was satisfied that they should drift into a close and confidential friendship. It was obvious now that he had been remarkably dull; Scott had seen how things were going.

Then he had taken it for granted that Agatha would not find the vein, and had helped her because he thought it better she should convince herself that Strange had been the victim of his imagination. He had honestly thought this when they started, but now recognized that he had unconsciously had another object: he wanted her society and to earn her gratitude.

A light began to dawn on him when he found Strange's tobacco-box, but he had, so to speak, evaded full illumination until it became obvious that they were near the vein. Then the truth could no longer be denied. He was in love with the girl, and had unconsciously loved her from the first. In a sense, this looked ridiculous; but there it was and he must face it. If she had been poor, he would have urged her to marry him, although it might have exposed her to some risk of hardship. But she was rich, and the best he could hope for was a post at a mine like the Clermont.

He had no ground for imagining that Agatha would be willing to marry him; but if she were, it would look as if he meant to share her riches when he offered his help. In fact, it would look as if he meant to take advantage of her ignorance about mining matters and her trust. It would not disturb him if outsiders thought this, but she might come to think so.

Besides, he was not going to be supported by his wife's money. In view of their characters, the situation would be humiliating for both. Agatha might learn to despise him, which would be intolerable.

Then he felt a touch on his shoulder and got up with a start. Agatha stood close by and he thought there was more color in her face than usual, although her eyes were calm.

"Brooding over our good luck?" she said with a smile. "Isn't that a curious attitude?"

"The good luck is yours."

"If you insist on the difference, but I don't know that it's kind! Besides, I wanted to give you half my frontage on the vein."

"That's quite impossible," said Thirlwell firmly.

"Why is it impossible?"

"It would look as if I'd meant to take advantage of your generosity."

"Does it matter how the thing would look?"

"Yes," said Thirlwell, who hesitated. "I want to keep your good opinion—if I have it."

Agatha smiled, but her glance was soft. "I won't flatter you, because I think you ought to know. But why are you moody? I'd expected you to be sympathetic to rejoice with me."

"For your sake, I am glad."

"But not for yours?"

"I haven't quite got used to the situation yet," Thirlwell answered awkwardly. "You see, I never expected to find the ore."

"That was rather obvious," Agatha rejoined with some dryness. "But if you thought we would be disappointed, why did you come?"

Thirlwell was silent. He did not mean to admit that he had thought a sharp disappointment would be good for her and might save her worse pain. It was difficult to state this properly. Then if he owned that he had come for the pleasure of her society, she might misunderstand him and he might say too much. Agatha was half amused by his embarrassment, but was moved all the same, for she understood more than he knew.

"We'll let it go," she resumed. "Still, I don't see why you should be disturbed by my success."

"One often feels sorry when one finishes a big job. It means one has come to the end of things one has got used to and likes."

"But this is rather the beginning than the end."

"No," he said moodily. "We have had a glorious trip, but it's done with. You will go back to the cities; there are only two or three months when a civilized girl can live in the woods. The trail we have broken stops here."

"But what do you mean to do?"

"Help Scott at the Clermont, until he's forced to give up."

"Sit down and light your pipe," said Agatha. "We must talk about this."

He obeyed and picked up his pipe. Although he did not light it, its touch was soothing and he wanted to keep cool. Agatha sat down opposite on a fallen trunk and presently went on: "To begin with, the mine must be worked, not sold, and I need help."

"You can get a good manager for the wages you'll be able to pay."

Agatha's color was higher, but she gave him a steady look. "I want a man I know and trust. There are many ways in which I shall need advice, because I cannot take this fortune without its responsibility. The mine must be worked to the best advantage and the people I employ treated well. I mean to build good houses for them, not rude shacks, make it possible for them to lead happy lives, and see they get the best, not the worst, that our cities can send them when a settlement springs up."

"It's a fine ambition," Thirlwell remarked. "However, it will cost you something, and you'll find some resistance from the people you want to help; but if the ore's as good as we think, you'll be able to carry out your plans."

"Do you think I could trust this work to a stranger? A man hired for wages, who might have no sympathy with my aims?" Agatha asked. "Then, if when I've done all I mean, I'm rich, somebody must help me to use the money well." She turned her head for a moment, and then resumed: "Can't you see that it's daunting to feel I may have to struggle alone with a task I'm hardly fit for—to know I'll make mistakes?"

"There is your brother."

Agatha smiled.

"George would see I made prudent investments, and think I ought to be satisfied with getting ten per cent." She gave Thirlwell a look that made his heart beat. "I need help George cannot give, and know nobody but you."

She stopped, for she could go no farther. It was for him to meet her now, if he wanted, but for a moment or two he was silent and knitted his brows. His brown face was resolute, but something in his eyes indicated that resolution cost him much. Then he said, "You offer me the post of manager?"

She turned her head, for it was difficult to preserve her calm. He was dull in some respects, but it was scarcely possible that he was as dull as he now pretended. Looking up with a forced smile, she said: "Yes, of course. I want a manager, and if you would sooner be businesslike—"

"I'm afraid I'm very unbusinesslike," he replied with some grimness. "However, if Scott is willing, I'll help you to develop the mine and get your patent; but I think it would be prudent to let him join us. You may have some trouble to get the money we will need; then he's straight and a very good sort."

"But what will you do when the patent's granted?"

"We can talk about that later. It will be some time before the mine is yours, and I'm not certain that we have heard the last of Stormont."

"Very well," said Agatha. "I like Mr. Scott and feel I can trust him because he is your friend. Do what you think best; I leave it all to you."

She went away with very mixed feelings, and was glad to reach the shelter of the woods. Her face was hot and her nerves were jarred, but when she got calmer she laughed—a rather strained laugh. It was a lover she wanted, not a manager, and unless Thirlwell was strangely dull she had been firmly repulsed. She hoped he was dull, but it seemed impossible that he had not understood. Then it was significant that he had shown some strain and she found comfort in this. After all, the line he took had cost him much and his obstinacy might break down.

Besides, when one looked at it dispassionately, the situation was humorous. She had engaged Thirlwell for her manager, but nothing had been said about his wages, which she could not pay; for that matter, she was in his debt. Although she was the prospective owner of a valuable mine, she had only a few dollars left of the money George had given her; hardly enough, in fact, to pay for a week's board when she reached Toronto. Her post there had, no doubt, been filled.

The ore was rich, but might get poor, and she knew enough about mining to realize the difficulties that must yet be overcome. Getting the money she would need for the preliminary work was perhaps the worst; and if the money could be raised, it would be a long time before she could look for much return. Still she was not alone; Thirlwell had promised to help and she knew he would not fail her. She meant to let him help, not because she wanted to get rich, but because she really knew what had influenced him, and suspected that he was not as strong as he thought.

For all that, she kept out of his way as much as possible while they camped by the creek, although she was careful to talk with easy friendliness when they met at meals. Thirlwell, however, was generally occupied, and when he had made a rough survey of the claims they started south. The loads were light now and he forced the pace because he was anxious, and felt responsible. There was another prospecting party, with an unscrupulous leader, not far off, and one's title to a mineral claim is open to dispute until the record is filed. Although Agatha's prosperity would be his loss, he meant to run no risk. He was her manager and must justify her trust.

When they reached the lake he found there would be some delay. They had covered the canoes with branches, but the pine-needles had withered off and the hot sun had opened the seams. Some of the thin planks were badly split, one had sprung away from its fastenings, and it would take a few days to repair the damage without proper tools. The caulking composition he had brought would not go round, and he had to send the *Metis* into the bush to look for gum to make the Indian pitch. Then it cost him a day's hard labor to rough out new plans with an ax and saw, and he afterwards found he must make a steaming-box to soften the wood so that it would bend into place.

On the second night he was tired and disturbed, but his sleep was light and he wakened shortly before daybreak. It was not dark; he could see the trunks behind the camp and Agatha's white tent. The ripples broke upon the beach with a gentle splash, and there was a faint sighing in the pine-tops. Except for all this all was very quiet, and he wondered whether he had heard a canoe paddle in his dreams. Then, not far off, a stone rattled as if it had been trodden on.

Thirlwell got up quietly and glanced about the camp. The men were asleep. He counted their indistinct figures, wrapped in blankets; nobody was missing. Still somebody had disturbed a loose stone and he moved cautiously into the gloom. One could not creep up to an Indian, but Thirlwell imagined there were none about, and if an Indian had meant to steal something, he would not have crossed the slanting bank strewn with large gravel, from which the noise had come. Thirlwell, himself, would not have done so, for he had learned to be silent, when hunting in the bush. He suspected a clumsy white man, from the cities. When he got near the bank he stopped behind a tree. There was a narrow opening, but he saw nobody and heard nothing except the wind in the pine-tops.

He tried to creep round the opening, but fell among a clump of wild-berry canes. They were green and did not rustle much, but he knew that after this it would be useless to go on with the search. Besides, he was not certain that a man had disturbed the stone. The camp-fire had gone out and an animal might have come down to drink. He grumbled at his awkwardness and going back to camp, went to sleep again.

In the morning he returned to the bank, but found no tracks. He could account for the stone falling in two or three natural ways, but the splash of the paddle was a different thing. Still he had not actually heard the noise, but, so to speak, wakened with its echo in his ears, and sitting down, he pondered the matter. Supposing that somebody from Stormont's gang had prowled about the camp, it was difficult to see the fellow's object. Thirlwell did not doubt that Stormont knew he was the leader of Agatha's party and she could do nothing without his help. If Driscoll had been with his former confederate, one could have understood the thing. Black Steve had an Indian's cunning and the instincts of a savage animal, but he was dead and Stormont was a rascal of another kind. Steve's primitive methods would not appeal to him. Thirlwell gave up the puzzle and got about his work.

Chapter XXVIII
Stormont Tries A Bribe

When the light began to fade Thirlwell put W down his tools and went off to try to catch a trout. He had noted that Drummond was not about the camp and when he got near the mouth of a creek where he meant to fish thought he saw an indistinct figure some distance in front. It vanished, but he felt he had not been deceived and stopped for a minute or two.

Although he had no grounds for distrusting Drummond, he had marked certain weaknesses in his character. The lad might have gone to fish, but Thirlwell had not seen him make a rod, and remembering the falling stone resolved to find out. The wood was thin, but the light was dim, and the turmoil of the creek would drown any noise he made. After walking obliquely inland for some distance he stopped to listen. He heard nothing, but Drummond was now between him and the lake, and Thirlwell thought he could not get across the creek. He came down to the mouth of the latter cautiously, and when he was close to the lake stopped behind a trunk. The water glimmered between the trees, and he saw two dark figures outlined against the pale reflection.

There was some risk of his being seen, but he thought if Drummond was afraid he might be followed, he would watch the bush along the edge of the lake, and he advanced cautiously, moving from trunk to trunk. A thicket of wild-berries grew near the water, and stealing up behind it, he stopped and crouched down. Drummond was perhaps a dozen yards off, and stood, holding a fishing-rod, while Stormont sat on a fallen log opposite. Thirlwell clenched his fist and listened. He could hear them talk.

"How'd you know you'd find me here?" Drummond asked.

"I didn't know," said Stormont; "it was good luck. I wanted to find out if Thirlwell had finished the canoes. One can see into your camp from the top of the high ground, and I've brought good glasses."

It was plain that Drummond had not gone to meet the fellow, and Thirlwell saw that he had, to some extent, misjudged the lad. For all that, Drummond had reached the spot a few minutes before he did, and something had obviously been said in the meantime. If possible, he must find out what they had talked about.

"Take a smoke; this is a pretty good cigar," Stormont resumed. "You'll let a soft snap go if you don't do what I want."

"You put me on to a soft snap before," Drummond remarked with a touch of scorn.

"I think you got fifty dollars—for nothing. Anyhow, I want you and I'm willing to pay in advance."

"With a cheque that can be stopped!"

Stormont laughed. "No. I don't pay for this kind of job by cheque. You can have it in bills; I've got a wad in my pocket. Better take your money now than trust Thirlwell to let you in when he makes good his claim; but if you like, I'll give you some stock when we float our company."

"I'll take the bills," said Drummond in a meaning tone. "But you want to put it high."

Thirlwell found it hard to control his anger. Drummond had professed some liking for him and had made no secret of his devotion to Agatha, but now he was coolly bargaining with her antagonist. It looked as if he was willing to betray her if he could get a good price. For all that, Thirlwell saw that he must find out the plot and lay still behind the thicket, watching the lad. Drummond's pose was easy and his voice was calm. He had not lighted the cigar Stormont gave him, and now and then twisted it round carelessly.

"Very well," Stormont resumed. "As I've got to bid against Thirlwell, I'll risk five hundred dollars: two hundred and fifty now. Then, as soon as we make a good start, you can have a job in the company's office."

"Oh, shucks!" said Drummond. "Five hundred dollars for a silver mine? You can't find the lode unless I put you wise."

"That's not going to bother us. Thirlwell has left a trail we can follow without your help. Well, you've heard my offer. What do you say?"

"I'm thinking some. I get two hundred and fifty dollars now, but what about the rest? Suppose I have to wait until you put the job over? How are you going to put it over when Thirlwell holds the claims?"

"They won't be worth much after I get to work. Going to law's expensive and Thirlwell can't stand up to the men who are backing me. He'll be glad to sell out at our price when we put the screw to him."

This was illuminating to Thirlwell, since it justified his fears. The mining regulations were complicated, and it was not unusual for unscrupulous speculators to dispute a poor man's claim. He knew of instances where grave injustice had been done. Moreover, he noted that Stormont said nothing about Agatha, but thought him the prospective owner of the minerals. People obviously took it for granted that he meant to marry the girl.

"Your job is to stop Thirlwell," Stormont went on. "The thing must be done cleverly and look like an accident. The best plan would be to get at the canoes. They're hauled up side by side and you might perhaps set them on fire when he makes his caulking gum. Or you might knock loose a plank or two in the bottom. Anyhow, you'll have to hold him up long enough for me to pull out his stakes."

Thirlwell, burning with indignation, found it hard to keep still. It was a cunning plot, because a few days' delay might enable Stormont to re-stake the ground and file his record first. If this were done, Agatha would have to bear the disadvantage of challenging his claim and, if the law expenses were heavy, might be forced to compromise. Still, he controlled his rage.

"The thing's not as easy as it looks," Drummond replied. "Thirlwell's not a fool. If you, want me to put it over, you'll have to come up."

"A good job in our office and six hundred dollars: three hundred now. If Thirlwell finds out and gets after you, come along to my camp."

"Where is your camp?"

"Behind some rocks, about two miles up the lake. Follow the creek and you'll come to a log that has fallen across."

"Very well; I'll take the money."

Stormont pulled out his wallet, and then Thirlwell came near to betraying himself, because the dramatic surprise was almost too much for his self-control. Drummond snatched the bills from the other's hand and laughed, a savage, scornful laugh.

"You thieving hog; you blasted *fool!*" he cried.

"What d'you mean?" Stormont shouted, springing to his feet.

"Did you think you could play me for a sucker *twice?*" Drummond rejoined. "Three hundred dollars, for my claim on the lode? That's what it comes to, and I reckon that's all I'd get!" He flung out his hand, scattering the crumpled bills. "There's your dirty money. I've got you corralled!"

Stormont was quiet; dangerously quiet Thirlwell thought, because it was obvious that Drummond had led him on until he learned his plans. He stooped and began to pick up the bills, moving about, for the bits of paper were scattered and indistinct. One had fallen by a heavy stone, and

Thirlwell felt his nerves tingle as Stormont got nearer. Drummond did not seem to be suspicious; his pose was careless, and Thirlwell imagined the lad was enjoying his triumph. Both thought they were alone and they stood on a ledge that ran out into deep water.

Then Stormont clutched the stone and Thirlwell sprang to his feet. The fellow's caution had given way; mocked and cheated by the lad he meant to use, he had suddenly become primitive in his disappointed greed and rage. It looked as if Drummond did not know his danger; but as Thirlwell ran forward Stormont lifted the stone and the lad leaped upon him like a wild cat.

Thirlwell stopped. For the moment he did not see how he could interfere without doing harm, and thought Drummond did not need his help. The men were locked in a savage grapple at the edge of the ledge and the ripples splashed upon the rocks four or five feet below. Stormont had been deceived to the end. It is hard for a white man to match the instinctive cunning that goes with a strain of Indian blood, and Drummond had suspected that the other meant to pick up the stone.

Neither saw Thirlwell. They swayed and panted, striking when they got an arm loose, and then pressing body against body while each strained for a grip to lift his antagonist from his feet. Stormont, indeed, made a better fight than Thirlwell had expected, but after a time his knees bent, his head went back, and Drummond threw him heavily. When he struck the ground he felt for his pocket, but Drummond fell upon him with a cry that was like a wild beast's howl.

Thirlwell saw it was time to interfere. An Indian never forgets an injury, and Drummond had inherited his father's grim Scottish stubbornness. He rolled over with Stormont, and then getting uppermost, savagely bumped his head against the rock. This gave Thirlwell his opportunity, and seizing the lad's shoulders, he pressed his knee against the small of his back.

"Stop!" he shouted. "Do you mean to kill the man?"

"Sure!" gasped Drummond. "Lemme go!"

"You'd better quit. I've got you tight."

Drummond struggled furiously, but since he could not turn round found it impossible to break loose. His hands, however, were free and he gave Stormont's head another violent bump. Then Thirlwell, using his knee as a fulcrum, pulled the lad's shoulders back until he cried out with pain and let go. Thirlwell threw him off and stepped between the two before they could get up.

"This has got to stop and I'm fresh and able to see it does stop. If you try to start again, Drummond, I'll throw you into the lake," he said, and turned to Stormont, who did not move. "Get up."

Stormont did so, shakily. "I suppose you had this thing fixed with him!"

"I had not. I came along by accident and it might have been better if I'd left you to Drummond and gone off again. It was rather for his sake than yours I butted in. Can you walk?"

Stormont said he thought he could, and Thirlwell indicated the bush. "Then get off and take the hint that it's prudent to leave the Agatha Mine alone."

When Stormont had gone, Thirlwell turned to Drummond, who was now standing up. "Are you hurt?"

"Not much. I don't mind if I am hurt, so long as Stormont is. But why in thunder did you come just then?"

"It's lucky I did," said Thirlwell dryly. "I think you saw he wanted to get that stone?"

"Sure; I meant to let him. Wanted him to fire the rock and begin the circus. Then, when he'd made me mad enough, I'd have finished it."

"It would have been awkward if he'd brought a pistol."

Drummond smiled. "He thought he had, but he'd forgot the thing. I'd been studying his clothes; blue shirt and thin overalls. There wasn't a bulge." Then he stooped and picked up a crumpled bill. "Five dollars; don't see much use in leaving money lying round."

He hesitated, and then putting the bill in his pocket, remarked: "Anyhow, he gave me the wad. Let's see if I can find another."

Thirlwell laughed and told him to rest for a few minutes, because he wanted to think. Stormont had obviously returned to what he imagined was a good center to work from in his search for the vein, and had seen the smoke of Thirlwell's fire. He could now follow back the latter's trail and then make for the Record Office after altering the stakes. If he did so, the probability was that he would arrive too late, but accidents often happen in the bush and Thirlwell meant to leave nothing to luck. Moreover, Stormont had given him a hint when he tried to bribe Drummond to damage the canoes. In the wilds, travel depends upon the means of transport, since one cannot go far without food, and Thirlwell did not see why he should not carry on the game Stormont had meant to play. He told Drummond his plan.

"Well," said the latter thoughtfully, "I guess his packers will be asleep in camp, but we want to get there before he does and he's gone off first."

"He'll go round by the log he talked about and I don't think he's able to walk very fast. Then we'll save some time by going through the creek."

"That's so," Drummond agreed. "We'd better hustle."

They crossed the mouth of the creek, wading among the boulders and swimming a few yards, and then followed the edge of the lake. They could see for some distance across the water, but the woods were dark and Stormont would have some trouble in making his way through the brush. He would be behind them if he came down to the lake, but it was obvious that they must carry out their plans before he arrived.

When Thirlwell thought they were near the camp they left the beach and crept cautiously into the darkness among the trees that grew upon a rocky point. Now and then the underbrush rustled and a low branch cracked, but they heard nothing when they stopped and listened. After a few minutes they reached the other side of the point and lay down among the stones. In front, a narrow bay opened, with the shadowy bush running round. Two canoes lay on the beach, and although they were black and indistinct, Thirlwell imagined they had only been pulled up a few feet.

Farther back, the glow of a fire flickered among the trunks, but it was a small fire and burned low and red. Stormont had, no doubt, given orders that no smoke must be made. A tent, half seen in the gloom, stood at the edge of the bush, but Thirlwell could not see the packers. It looked as if they were asleep, because all was quiet except for the wind in the trees and the distant splash of the creek. The breeze was light but blew off the shore. This would suit Thirlwell's plan, but it would be difficult not to make some noise and he must not be caught. The packers were rough men and he rather thought he had taken a risk he ought not to have run.

Touching Drummond's arm, he slid down a slab of rock and crouched in the gloom on the ledge below. His boots had scratched the stone, and he listened when Drummond came down, but there was no movement in the camp. Dropping from the ledge, he reached the shingle, which rattled sharply, and for a moment or two he stopped and held his breath. He heard nothing, and making Drummond a sign to be cautious, went on again. They were now confronted by perhaps the most dangerous part of their task, for one cannot cross a stony beach in silence and men used to the wilds are easily wakened by a suspicious noise. Besides, the water glimmered, and Thirlwell would have liked a darker background.

Still he meant to reach the canoes, and moved on, leaning forward to shorten his height and stepping as gently as he could. When the stones rattled he and Drummond sank down and waited, but heard nothing to alarm them, and at length stopped and lay down beside the canoes. They could not be seen now, but what they must do next was risky, and Thirlwell wanted to get his breath. Although he had not used much muscular exertion, his nerves tingled and his face was wet with sweat.

After a few moments, he got on his knees and felt inside the canoe. It had not been unloaded and this was the craft to launch, although the weight would make a difference. Lying down again, he felt along the keel and found that the gravel was small and mixed with sand. Then he touched something round and knew that a roller had been put under the canoe in order that she might be pulled up without disturbing the cargo. This was a stroke of luck, because it would help him to run her down.

He touched Drummond, and getting up seized the gunwale. They strained their muscles, but for a moment or two could not move the craft; then the roller jarred across a stone, there was a crunch of gravel, and she stopped, a foot lower down. Thirlwell gasped and moved his hands to get another grip. He thought they had made an alarming noise, but it was too late to be cautious. They must finish the job.

"Lift her as you shove!" he said.

She went a yard, with the roller jolting in the sand, and there was a splash as her after-end took the water. He could not understand why the packers had not wakened, but there was no movement in the camp, and the next effort would be easier, since the stern was nearly afloat.

"Again!" he gasped. "Quietly, but with all your strength!"

The roller ran smoothly and they followed the canoe down. When their feet were in the water they gave her a last push and small ripples splashed about them as she slid out on the lake. The impetus would carry her some distance and the off-shore breeze would do the rest.

"I guess we'll light out now," Drummond remarked.

They regained the point and the camp was quiet. The canoe was distinguishable, but Thirlwell thought he would not have seen her had he not known where to look; it was plain that she was drifting across the lake. Five minutes later they heard somebody coming through the bush, and dropped behind a boulder. They could not see the man, but heard him push through a thicket and then stumble among some stones. He passed, and when they went on again Drummond laughed.

"Looks as if he was pretty savage, but he's hitting up a smarter clip than I thought he could make. Guess he'll feel worse in the morning."

Thirlwell agreed. The canoe would be out of sight when Stormont reached the camp, and it was unlikely that he would miss her until next day. She was, no doubt, loaded with food and prospecting tools, and Thirlwell had gained an important advantage by setting her adrift, since Stormont would not venture farther north without supplies. He had probably some stores in camp and would find the canoe, but if she stranded on a beach far up the lake, the search might cost some time. The delay would give Thirlwell a longer start.

He had fitted the new planks in his canoes and when he got back wakened the *Metis* and melted the caulking gum. By daybreak the seams were hard and after a hurried breakfast the party paddled across the lake. He would sooner have waited to see if Stormont would try to retaliate, but this would be rash. If the canoes were damaged or he were injured, it might prevent him from getting back to record the claims.

Chapter XXIX
GEORGE REPROACHES HIMSELF

The days were getting shorter fast, but the evening was warm when George Strange leaned against the rails of Farnam's veranda. He had arrived, looking anxious, as supper was served, but did not state why he felt disturbed and Mrs. Farnam waited. She knew he had come to consult her, and thought she knew what about. Now he gazed moodily across the orchard, where red and yellow apples gleamed on the bent branches. The slanting sunbeams struck across the trees, which melted, farther off, into the blue shadow of the bush.

"That's a great show of fruit," he remarked.

"Pretty good," Farnam agreed. "Reports indicate that packers won't find much surplus for shipping in the United States, and prices will be high. In fact, I rather think my speculation is justified. Although clearing new ground and buying young trees made a drain on my capital—"

"Don't tell him he's enterprising! He's too adventurous," interrupted Mrs. Farnam, who wanted to give George a lead. "It's exciting to take chances, but they don't always turn out as one hopes. But how's your business? I understand trade is dull."

"I have known it better, but that's not bothering me."

"Still as you don't look serene, I imagine something is bothering you."

"I don't feel serene, and that's why I came. You know Agatha better than anybody else. Have you heard from her recently?"

"Not since the letter she sent me when she reached the mine, and you saw that. I'm getting anxious. She has stopped some time and the school has reopened."

"She has stopped too long," said George, whose face got red. "It looks as if you didn't know they had filled her post."

"I was afraid they might do so, but it's a shock all the same. But perhaps you can do something. You persuaded the principal and managers when Agatha was ill."

"I've come from Toronto and I saw the principal," George replied. "Couldn't get at anybody else and imagine they didn't want to see me."

"Well?" said Mrs. Farnam when he stopped with some embarrassment.

"She was very polite, with the kind of politeness that freezes you. Didn't say much—nothing that I could get hold of and deny. But she implied a lot."

"You can be frank. I believe I'm Agatha's oldest friend and I trust my husband with all I know."

"Very well; I've got to talk. Miss Southern began by supposing I had come to explain my sister's neglect of her duty, which had made things awkward at the school. I said I had not; I didn't know why Agatha had not come back, but had no doubt it was because she found it impossible. She'd gone off on an excursion into the northern bush, and accidents happened. One lost one's canoes and provisions ran out.

"Miss Southern said it was plain that as Agatha had important duties she ought not to run such a risk, and asked what was the object of the excursion.

"I said it was a prospecting trip. Agatha had gone to find some silver ore; and Miss Southern gave me a look that made me mad. It hinted that she thought my statement much too thin! Then she remarked that the managers felt that their teachers must concentrate on their work and divided interests made for slackness. In short, as Agatha had not come back, they had got somebody else to take her post.

"That was a knock, but I said I supposed they'd give her a first-rate testimonial if she applied for another job.

"She looked as if she didn't want to hurt me, but admitted that they would be willing to state that Agatha had ability and taught science well. Then she stopped and I asked if she could go no farther. Ability wasn't all a teacher needed.

"She said she must agree, and hinted that she had expected much from Agatha, but felt badly disappointed now. She remarked that managers made searching inquiries when they engaged a teacher for young girls and thought I could understand that she felt responsible—

"Well, I'd had enough. I said my sister was fit for a better job than the best they'd got and wouldn't bother them for a recommendation. Then I left; thought I'd better quit before I let myself go." George paused and wiped his hot face. "You see how I was fixed? I could have bluffed a man into making a plain statement and then have knocked him out; but that cool, polite lady made me hate my helplessness."

"You were at a disadvantage," Mrs. Farnam agreed with a smile that was half amused and half sympathetic. "But I wonder who told her! Do you think that fellow Stormont—"

"I'm going to find out," George said grimly. "In the meantime, it's not important. I reckon you understand what this thing implies? If these people won't support Agatha's application, she can't get another post. She'd have made her mark teaching, but now all that's gone; she's turned down, and I'm responsible!"

"You are not to blame. I wonder whether she really knew the risk?"

"She knew she'd lose her job, but it wouldn't stop her; Agatha's like that! Anyhow, I am to blame," George rejoined. "I'm the head of the family and ought to have made her cut out the blamed foolish notion. I knew what the lode meant to my mother and how she hated to hear the old man talk about it. It took him—and now it's got my sister—"

He stopped, struggling with emotion, and Mrs. Farnam said:

"Perhaps I ought to have given Agatha a plainer hint; but, except for school managers, we're not very conventional people in this country. Then I liked her pluck. It's weak to give way to the prejudices of censorious folks. Besides, in a sense, she really wasn't rash."

"That's not the trouble," George replied with heat. "I know my sister; so do you! But she's got to start business since she can't teach school, and I hate to think of her clerking in a store. She has talent and ambition."

"Talent will make its way anywhere," Farnam remarked consolingly.

"I don't know! Agatha's proud and has no use for the cheap tricks that help you get ahead of the other man. She won't advertise her smartness and she's too dignified to snatch at chances among the scrambling crowd. I've pushed through; but it has put some marks on me, and I'm most afraid my sister's going to be hurt."

"You're taking it for granted she won't find the lode," Farnam resumed.

"Shucks!" said George with scorn. "All the comfort I've got is knowing she won't have the money to waste on looking for the ore again—"

He stopped and listened to a rattle of wheels. "Some of your friends coming? Don't mean to be rude, but I hope they're not. I'm not in a mood to talk to strangers."

"We expect nobody," Farnam replied. "I ordered some goods from Kingston, and Gordon's man promised to bring them from the depot if they came."

The rattle got louder, but the trees hid the rig, which was approaching the back of the house. It stopped, there were steps in the hall, and Mrs. Farnam turned with an exclamation. Farnam pushed his chair back and George sprang upright as Agatha came out on the veranda.

She was very brown and thin; her clothes were new, but obviously cheap and the fit was bad. As she glanced at the group she smiled and there was nothing in her tranquil manner to indicate the repentant prodigal. She kissed Mrs. Farnam and gave George her hand.

"It really looks as if you were rather surprised than pleased," she remarked.

"We're both," said Mrs. Farnam. "But how did you come? It's some time since the Toronto train got in. George has been here nearly an hour."

"Your neighbor's hired man drove me from the station. I came by Amprior and Prescott; there was a wash-out on the Sudbury track. But what was George doing at Toronto?"

"Looking after your business," George replied. "I'm afraid you've got to brace up. They told me you were fired!"

Agatha laughed. "I expected something like that! It really doesn't matter."

"It doesn't matter!" George exclaimed, and gasped with indignation. "Anyhow, it matters to me. I've been fuming and fretting since I saw your principal." He turned to the others, as if for support. "What can you do with a girl who talks in this way? How'm I to make her understand?"

"I think you had better wait a little," Mrs. Farnam said and glanced at Agatha. "But did you travel in those clothes, my dear? Where did you buy them?"

"At a bush store," said Agatha, smiling. "They were not as cheap as they look, and my others had worn to rags. Besides, I hadn't much time, and it wasn't worth while to bother about my dress."

"You don't seem to bother about much," George remarked. "In fact, you've come back with a lordly calm that's as exasperating as it's unjustifiable."

Agatha gave him a thoughtful look. "Is Florence well?"

"Quite well. She's disturbed about you."

"Then it's probably business! I suppose trade is bad?"

George lost his self-control. He was glad to see her back, but remembered what he had suffered for her sake.

"My business doesn't occupy all my thoughts and you have made a blamed poor joke! Here am I and your friends, trying to grapple with an awkward situation and puzzling how we're to help you out, and you *laugh*. So far as I can see, there's nothing humorous—"

"Don't be cross," Agatha interrupted. "I don't need helping out. If business isn't very good, I can offer you a post."

George made an abrupt movement and looked hard at her. Farnam laughed softly, and his wife leaned forward.

"You see, I've found the lode. It's richer than I thought," Agatha resumed.

There was silence for a few moments, and then George said: "I want time to get hold of this. You found the ore the old man talked about! It's not another stupid joke?"

"Not at all. Father located the vein on his last journey and left a paper with directions. Mr. Thirlwell found it in his tobacco-box. The directions were not complete and we had some trouble—but we'll talk about this later. The claim is recorded and Mr. Thirlwell has gone back to begin the development. Mr. Scott, his employer, is coming to see you."

"Well," said George dully, "I'll own I've got a knock. I reckoned if there was a lode, it would never be found. Looks as if I didn't know as much as I thought. But that's not all. Since I was old enough to guess my mother's fears I did the old man wrong. He's made good. I doubted, but you knew him best and you believed."

"Agatha's tired," Mrs. Farnam broke in. "She needs a rest and I'm going to get her some food. You can ask her what you like when I bring her back."

"I suppose you want to satisfy your curiosity first," Farnam suggested.

"We're not going to talk about *mining*," Mrs. Farnam rejoined. "However, I must do you justice; you took Agatha's side from the first. After all, your judgment's good now and then."

She took Agatha away and when they had gone George remarked: "I can't grip the thing yet. It's hard to get rid of a fixed idea you've had from boyhood. Still I ought to have known that Agatha wouldn't undertake a job she couldn't put over."

It was getting dark when Mrs. Farnam and the girl came back, and George said, "Now I want to know all about your trip. Begin where you left the cars and go right on."

"That will take some time," Mrs. Farnam interposed. "Shall I light the lamp in the room?"

"I think not," said Agatha, and smiled. "My story goes best with the twilight in the open. We had no lamps and pretty furniture in the bush."

She was silent for a few moments, looking across the orchard. The fruit trees were blurred and dim and the pines were black, but the sky shone softly red and green above their ragged tops. Then she began to talk; disjointedly at first, but the scenes she recalled got clearer as she went on, and she forgot her audience. It was her business to make things plain; she had studied this part of her vocation and unconsciously used her power to seize and hold the other's interest, but she did not know that she was drawing a lifelike portrait of her guide. Mrs. Farnam knew, and with a tactful question here and there led the girl forward.

It was, however, impossible to relate her journey and leave Thirlwell out. He took the leading part that belonged to him, and his character was firmly outlined by her memory of the things he had said and done. With something besides artistic talent Agatha unconsciously developed the sketch, dwelling upon his cheerfulness, courage, and resource. She told the others how he had nerved her to resolute effort when they had difficulties to overcome, sympathized when she was tired, and held the confidence of his men. Moreover, she made it obvious that there had been no romantic philandering. He had given her an unselfish, brotherly protection.

The narrative lost something of its force after she came to the finding of the broken range. She saw she had been franker than she thought, and the change in Thirlwell could not be talked about. It was dark now, the red and green had faded above the trees, and she was grateful for the gloom. She was not afraid of George and Farnam, but did not want Mabel to study her. Only the latter noted that she paused awkwardly now and then and added a rather involved explanation. The men were engrossed by Thirlwell's efforts to find the ore. When she stopped they were quiet for a few moments.

Then George said: "You would never have struck the lode without that man." He turned to the others. "Some story of a prospecting trip! What do you think?"

"I think Agatha was very lucky," Mrs. Farnam said with meaning. "Perhaps luckier than she deserved."

"Thirlwell's all right," George bluntly agreed, and then addressed Agatha: "You have often got after me about being a business man, and I'll own I don't let many chances of making a dollar pass. But this thing goes back of business. Thirlwell's entitled to half of all you get."

Agatha was moved. She had found out some time since that she had not always understood George.

"I offered him half," she said and paused. "He wouldn't accept."

Mrs. Farnam, seeing the girl was embarrassed, got up. "I'm cold. We had better go in."

When she had lighted the lamp, Farnam went out and came back with a tray of bottles and glasses.

"It's not often we celebrate an event like this," he said as he opened a bottle. "We have no wine, but this is some of our own hard cider that I meant to send to the Fruit-Growers' Exhibition. There's nothing else good enough."

He filled the glasses and with a few happy words wished Agatha success. She thanked him and afterwards stood up, very straight but silent, and with her eyes shining softly lifted her glass above her head. The others lifted theirs, in grave quietness, for they knew what she meant. The pioneers touch the ridge-pole of the tent, or the roof-tree of the shack, when they drink to the memory of comrades who have gone out on the last lone trail. But George's look was troubled and his hand shook.

"He made good," he said, and added, when they had drunk and Farnam refilled the glasses: "Here's to the man who helped you prove it; the man who did my job!"

Mrs. Farnam studied Agatha and noted the softness of her look. Then she took the girl away and some time afterwards, when they were talking in her room, remarked: "There's an obvious end to your romance, my dear. I suppose you're going to marry Thirlwell?"

Agatha blushed, but gave her a steady glance. "He has not asked me."

Mrs. Farnam pondered this and then made a sign of understanding. "I think I see; the man is white, although perhaps he's foolishly proud. In fact, I imagine he's worth one's taking some trouble about—"

She stopped, seeing Agatha's frown, and then resumed with a smile: "No; I'm not going to meddle! It's better to wait. He's a man, after all; you really have some charm, and human nature's strong."

Chapter XXX
A Change Of Luck

Scott met George at Montreal, and after spending some days there left for New York. When he stated the time of his return, George sent for Agatha and in the evening they went to meet him at the Grand Trunk Station. As they walked down the hill and by the Cathedral, Agatha felt excited. She had soon discovered that it was one thing to find a silver vein and another to raise the capital one required to open up the mine and refine the ore. The cost of these operations, as calculated by Scott, seemed enormous, and people rich enough to help either wanted the largest share of the profit or were frankly skeptical. George had got promises of some support, but much depended on the result of Scott's visit to his wealthy friends.

It was dark when they walked up and down outside the platform gates; the train was late, and Agatha tried to control her nervous impatience. She could trust George's judgment about money matters and she liked Scott, but she had got a habit of looking to Thirlwell when difficulties must be met, and he could not help her now. He was in the North, where winter would soon begin, doing her work with drill and giant powder. It was good work that demanded strength and courage and knowledge of Nature's laws; she would have liked to have been there with him, instead of in the city where one must grapple with commercial subtleties.

By and by a bell tolled, there was a harsh rattle as the cars rolled in, and a few moments later Scott pushed through the crowd at the gate. Agatha went to meet him under a big lamp and saw by his look that he had been successful.

"I have fixed things and imagine you'll approve," he said, as she gave him her hand.

"That's a relief," George remarked. "We'll talk about it when we've got some supper."

Scott laughed. "I think we'll call it dinner to-night. I'm suffering from a natural reaction after our Spartan habits at the mine, and believe the occasion indicates the Place Viger. In fact, I telegraphed about a table and rooms."

They drove across the city, and Agatha looked about with some amusement and curiosity as she ate her dinner among wealthy English and American tourists in the big dining-room. George had taken her to a hotel of another kind that catered for small business men, but she hoped Scott's fastidious choice of the wines and the late flowers he had ordered were justified. As she studied some of the other women's clothes and contrasted them with hers, he looked up with a twinkle.

"It's obvious that Toronto can hold its own with London, Paris, and New York," he said. "However, if you're fond of diamonds and such ornaments, there's no reason you should exercise much self-denial."

"I don't know if I'm fond of diamonds or not. I have never had any," Agatha replied.

"Well, they're quite unnecessary, but you'll soon be able to have them if you like. Your brother is plainly cautious; it will be your privilege to enlarge his views."

George smiled rather grimly. "Agatha and I were brought up in a shabby frame house behind a store and learned to think of cents instead of dollars. Our father made some sacrifice to start us well; I know what it cost him now."

"Perhaps we had better tell Miss Strange what we have done. When they have brought us our coffee we'll find a quiet place where we can talk."

Some minutes later they sat down at a small table: behind a pillar in a spacious room, and Scott took out a bundle of documents.

"This is the first meeting of the *Agatha Mine Company*, and it's proper that Miss Strange should be our chairman. To begin with, we must appoint executive officials and the president comes first. I think the place belongs to Mr. Strange."

"No," said George, "the treasurer's my job. You want a business man to keep a tight hand on the money."

They looked at Agatha, who made a sign of agreement. "Mr. Scott will be president."

"Very well. The next is the general manager. Thirlwell's the best man I know."

"I appointed him some time since," Agatha replied. "It's his post as long as he likes, and he ought to be paid better than anybody else."

George glanced humorously at Scott. Agatha's manner was imperious and her voice resolute. It looked is if she meant to use her new authority. Scott nodded and gave her a document.

The Lure of the North | 193

"The shareholders may have something to say about these appointments later. In the meantime, this is a draft of our constitution. I must state that we could have kept all the profit if we had borrowed the money we need, but we should have had to pay high interest. On the whole, it seemed better to float a small company; just large enough, in fact, to get the protection the law allows a registered joint-stock body. We find we can get the money easier in this way, and it divides the risk. You will see that a large block of shares is reserved for yourself and your brother; I take some in payment for the men and supplies I am sending Thirlwell; and a number will be allotted at about ninety, to the people who find the cash."

Agatha studied the document and gave it to George. "What does issuing the stock at ninety mean?"

"Ninety cents for the dollar's worth of stock," George explained. "That's a ten per cent. margin when it touches face value and it will soon go higher."

"I see," said Agatha. "But the mine is ours, and by parting with these shares we lose control."

"Not altogether," Scott replied. "Every share carries a vote. You and your brother hold a large block, and the friends I've persuaded to join us will vote with me. Of course, if anybody bought up the most part of the other shares, he could give us trouble, but that's not likely. When it's obvious that we're making a good profit none of the holders will be willing to sell. In the meantime, some of the people are sending up a mining expert, and if they're satisfied with his opinion they'll give us the money."

"I suppose it's a good arrangement," said Agatha. "But before I agree you must send the draft to Thirlwell."

"It might mean some delay. However, I expect he'll come down from the mine to meet the expert, and if you insist—"

"I do insist," said Agatha. "I can do nothing until I know what my manager thinks."

Scott promised to mail the document, and Agatha remarked: "When the people have taken up the shares there will be some left."

"That is so," said George. "It may be convenient later; I dare say we will want more money when we begin the smelting, but we'll probably be able to issue the stock at a dollar then. In fact, I reckon we'll presently have to ask for power to extend our capital."

"You must only sell this reserve block to people you can trust," said Agatha, who began to ask questions about the mine.

Scott was surprised to find how much she knew, but he told her all he could and it was late in the evening when the party broke up.

The engineer whom the subscribers sent North returned with a satisfactory report, and Thirlwell got to work. He had much to do, and although he was undecided about the future, resolved to stay until he had opened up the vein. From the beginning he had to grapple with numerous obstacles, for when he drove his adit the water broke in and the rock was treacherous. Still he had tunneled far enough to escape the frost when winter began, and the snow that stopped all surface work made transport easier. One could travel straight across divides and frozen lakes, and the sledges ran smoothly on the ice. When the trail south was broken he built shacks at the camping places and kept a gang of half-breeds felling trees and improving the road.

After some months, he found it necessary to visit the railroad settlement, and reaching it one evening, tired and numbed by cold, followed his sledge to the hotel in a thoughtful mood. For one thing, he must write to Strange, whose last letter had hinted that he was anxious, and it would be hard to send an encouraging report. The ore was good, but the vein was thin and expensive to work. In fact, the working cost was much higher than he had thought. When he entered the hotel he was dazzled by the light, and the sudden change of temperature made him dizzy. He stopped, wondering whether his eyes had deceived him, as a man dressed in clothes that were obviously English came forward.

"Hallo, Jim!" said the latter.

"Allott!" exclaimed Thirlwell. "What are you doing here?"

The other laughed. "I left Helen at New York. She's going to Florida for the winter with her American friends and I thought I'd look you up before I followed. I've news, but it will keep until you have had some food."

Had Thirlwell not been an important man, he would probably have had to wait until next morning for a meal, but the landlord's wife bustled about and supper was soon on the table. There were no other guests, and when Thirlwell's appetite was satisfied he and Allott pulled their chairs to the stove. The floor was not covered, the rough board walls were cracked, and a tarry liquid dripped from the bend where the stovepipe pierced the ceiling.

"The hotel is not luxurious and they have very crude ideas about cookery, but they tried to suit my fastidious taste when I told them I was a friend of yours," Allott remarked. "However, I don't suppose you are remarkably comfortable at the mine, and you can change all this when you like."

Thirlwell looked puzzled and Allott resumed: "You haven't opened your mail yet and I didn't suggest it, because I wanted to talk to you first. I wonder whether it will be a shock to hear that Sir James is dead?"

"I'm sorry," Thirlwell answered. "I think he'd have been kinder if I'd let him. Perhaps I ought to have indulged him more than I did; but I was obstinate, and—well, you know, he was harsh to my father—"

Allott made a sign of comprehension. "He died six weeks since and left Helen most of his money; but he didn't cut you out."

Thirlwell moved abruptly.

"I expected nothing!"

"That was obvious," Allott remarked with some dryness. "Sir James was very sore when you refused to come back, but he came round after a time. When he was ill he told Helen it was refreshing to find a man who could not be bought, and you were probably better fitted for roughing it in Canada than the career he had planned for you. He added that he doubted if there were many like you in that country. Still I think if you had married Evelyn, you'd have got a larger share."

"Ah," said Thirlwell, "I had forgotten Evelyn! Is she with Helen?"

"Your admission's significant. Evelyn married Campbell—you remember him? However, you don't seem very curious about your legacy."

"I was thinking about my quarrel with Sir James," Thirlwell replied. "But I am curious."

Allott told him about the will and Thirlwell mused for some minutes. His share was not very large, but he had expected nothing, and since he had known Agatha he had felt the strain of poverty. He was not rich now, but his handicap was lighter and he began to see a ray of hope. Then he opened a letter from the English lawyers and asked Allott some questions.

After a time Allott said, "Helen rather felt she was robbing you when she heard the will and she was excited when you told us about the mine. I hope the ore is as good as you thought."

"The ore is good, but difficult to work. Then I'm only manager; I hold no shares."

"If you wished, you could buy enough to give you some control."

"Yes; I shall do so, now I'm able."

"Well," said Allott, "Helen sent me to look you up and gave me a message. This money was something of a surprise, and after building a vinery and buying a new car, she doesn't know what to do with it. I pointed out that it could be invested on good security at three or four per cent., but she declares this is not enough. In short, she's resolved that you are to use the money to develop your mine, but she ordered me to mention that she expects a handsome profit."

Thirlwell smiled, although he was moved. He knew Mrs. Allott had tried to help him before, and it was plain that she had not resented his refusing her aid.

"I think I see," he answered. "Helen's very kind. We ought to make a profit, but there's a risk."

"Helen likes a risk. She's something of a gambler; for that matter, so am I. Besides, although you disappointed her once, she has a rather remarkable confidence in you. Now have you, so to speak, a sporting chance?"

"The situation's much like this," said Thirlwell thoughtfully; "the ore's rich, but I expect we'll spend all our money before we get results that would encourage the subscribers and warrant our asking for more capital."

"Then if you and Helen invested, it would enable your friends to carry on, and perhaps qualify you for a director's post?"

"Yes. I shall invest, but don't know that I'd be justified in using Helen's money yet. However, suppose you come up and look at the mine. The journey's not so rough now we have broken the trail and put up rest-shacks at the camps."

"Thanks," said Allott. "I hoped you were going to ask me."

They started in a few days and Allott spent a week at the mine. On the evening before he left, he sat talking with Thirlwell in the shack. The frost was arctic outside, but the night was calm, and the corner they occupied by the red-hot stove was comfortable.

"What about Helen's money?" Allott asked. "I'm not a miner, but the assay reports look remarkably good, and I imagine you'll get over your engineering troubles."

"The financial troubles are the worst," Thirlwell rejoined.

"Then why not take the money?"

Thirlwell pondered. It was his duty to help Agatha, and Mrs. Allott's offer, by making this easier, would enable him to earn the girl's gratitude. He meant to invest his share of the legacy, but felt that he ought not to risk his relative's capital for his private gain.

"I'll know better how we stand when we get the new machines to work. Then, if I think it's pretty safe, I'll buy some shares for Helen."

"Very well," said Allott. "I'll open an account for you at the Bank of Montreal, and Helen will give you legal power to act for her. This will enable you to command her proxy if you want to vote at a shareholders' meeting. If you don't use the money, she will get better interest than in England."

Thirlwell thanked him and Allott began to talk about something else.

The latter left the mine next morning and when he had gone Thirlwell occupied himself in strenuous and often dangerous work. He felt he had to some extent misled Agatha and Strange. Expenses had outrun his calculations and he had encountered obstacles he had not foreseen. More money would soon be needed, and he must get results that would encourage its subscription and warrant his using Mrs. Allott's capital.

Sometimes the adit roof came down and sometimes the sides crushed in; the inclination of the vein was irregular and the dip was often awkwardly steep. Then the pines about the mine were small and damaged by wind and forest-fires. It was difficult to find timber that would bear a heavy strain, and Thirlwell walked long distances in the stinging frost to look for proper logs, and now and then camped with his choppers behind a snowbank. For all that, he made progress, and as he pushed on the adit his confidence in the vein grew stronger. Expenses were heavy, but the ore would pay for all.

He grew thin and rather haggard. Sleeping in the snow one night with half-dried moccasins, he found his foot frozen when he awoke, and the dead part galled. He limped as he went about the mine, and soon afterwards his hand was nipped by a machine and the wound would not heal. He held on, however; meeting his troubles cheerfully and encouraging his men, and the ore-dump began to grow.

His party was not alone, for soon after he got to work three men drove in their stakes behind his block of claims. They went south to file their records, and returning with several more, began the development the law required. Others followed, and the neighborhood was soon dotted with tents and discovery posts; but, for the most part, the men were satisfied with blasting a few holes in the surface of their claims. One or two experienced miners talked to Thirlwell, and agreeing that the ore could only be reached from the ground owned by Agatha's Company, abandoned their holdings and went back; the others waited for a time, and then returned, disappointed, when their food was exhausted.

The first arrivals, however, stayed and had opened two or three rude shafts before the frost began. Then, instead of leaving, as Thirlwell expected, they brought up provisions and built a log shack. It was plain that they meant to hold the claims and Thirlwell was puzzled, because he saw the men were miners and thought they knew their labor was thrown away. He imagined that Stormont had sent them, but could not see the latter's object. The fellow could hardly expect to reach the inclined vein except at a depth that would make it extremely expensive to work, and Thirlwell had improved his own and the adjoining claims enough to protect them legally from encroachment. Still Stormont was unscrupulous and it was possible he had some cunning plan for embarrassing the company. Thirlwell felt disturbed, but he had no grounds for interfering with the men, and although their relations were rather strained when they met, he left them alone.

Chapter XXXI
Thirlwell's Reward

Winter was nearly over when, one evening, George and Scott arrived at the Farnam homestead where Agatha was a guest. The house was centrally heated, and when the party gathered in Mrs. Farnam's pretty, warm room, Agatha wondered what Thirlwell was doing in the frozen North. Farnam had invested some money in the mine, and Agatha knew George had come to talk about the company's business.

"Things are not going well with us," he said presently. "Our money's nearly spent and Thirlwell has not been able to get out much ore. I think I told you he suspected Stormont sent the men who staked the claims behind our block, and the fellow's now getting on our track. He's been to see Gardner, Leeson, and one or two others."

"It would be awkward if they turned us down," Farnam remarked.

Agatha waited. She knew Gardner and Leeson held a number of the shares, but she did not understand the matter yet.

"Very awkward," George agreed. "I went to Leeson, and although he didn't say much, I reckon Stormont wants to buy his stock. He allowed that he and Gardner were not satisfied about our prospects, and I couldn't give him much ground for holding on. Then I went to Hill, who said he'd got an offer for his stock and meant to sell, but wouldn't name the buyer. I suspected Stormont again, but we won't know until we get the transfer form."

"One could head him off by bidding higher for the shares," Farnam suggested. "Still I suppose it's impossible. Anyhow, I have no more money."

"That applies to all of us," George said dryly.

Agatha smiled, for the situation had a touch of ironical humor. In a sense, she was rich, but she was forced to practise stern economy and had not the means to defend her wealth.

"But what is Stormont's plan?" she asked.

"I don't know," said George. "That's the worst, because it's a sure thing he has a plan. When he's ready he'll get after us."

"For revenge?"

"Not altogether, I think," Scott replied. "He has a pick on you and Thirlwell, but it's money he wants. If he could let you down when he got the money, it would, no doubt, add to his satisfaction."

"If he bought up a large number of the shares, it would give him a dangerous power," Agatha said thoughtfully. "Besides, he might persuade some of the other people to vote with him. It's unlucky we issued so many shares, although, of course, we needed the capital."

Scott made a sign of agreement. "We kept a block large enough to give us control unless nearly all the other holders voted against us, which we could not expect. The trouble is, that our difficulties at the mine have made them anxious. Stormont has probably worked on this, but it's hard to see how he means to use the people."

For some time they puzzled about Stormont's object, but could not find a clue, and by and by Agatha said, "You must write to Mr. Thirlwell."

"Thirlwell's job is to get out the ore, and we're up against things now because he hasn't done as much as we expected," George replied.

Agatha's eyes sparkled. "He has done all that was possible. You must write to him."

"Very well," said George, and began to talk about something else.

A week or two later Stormont bought a large number of shares, but this was all, and the snow was beginning to melt when George got an ominous hint that the other's plans had matured. Stormont telephoned asking if he would meet him and a few of the shareholders at Montreal to talk about an important matter, and George fixed a day a week ahead. Then he went to see Agatha.

"It's lucky Mr. Thirlwell is coming down," she said. "Telegraph for somebody to meet him and tell him to be quick. He must get to Montreal for the meeting."

"I doubt if he can get through in time and don't see what he can do if he comes," George objected.

"Don't argue, but send the telegram. He has always been able to do something when there was a difficulty to be met," Agatha rejoined; and George did as she ordered.

On the day of the meeting she joined George and Scott at Montreal and felt a pang of disappointment when she found Thirlwell had not arrived.

"Your messenger couldn't have gone far, and a number of things may have delayed Thirlwell, but I know he'll come," she said to George, who smiled.

"He'll come if it's possible; he's an obstinate fellow," Scott agreed. "There's a train just before the meeting. Will you go to the station?"

"Yes," said Agatha. "I feel he will be there."

"Then you'll hold us up; that train is often late," George grumbled.

"Have you got a hint about what Stormont wants?" Agatha asked Scott.

"Not yet, but we'll know soon. I expect George told you Stormont has floated a company to work the claims his men staked behind our block."

They had some hours to wait because the meeting was in the afternoon, and Agatha found the shops strangely unattractive; moreover, she did not know if it would be prudent to buy the things she wanted. In the afternoon she went to the Canadian-Pacific Station, and being told the train had left Ottawa late, she sat down in the neighboring square by the Cathedral. She was surprised to find that she was nervous, but this was not altogether because of the money at stake. Thirlwell had not failed her yet and it would be a painful shock if he did so now. She had a half-superstitious feeling that it was important he should come. If he arrived, all would go well; if not—but she refused to follow the thought, and looked at her watch. Only a few minutes had gone since her last glance and she tried to conquer her impatience.

Her heart beat when she stood beside the platform gate as the long train rolled in. The cars were crowded, but she thrilled when Thirlwell jumped down from a vestibule. He looked thin and tired, but smiled when she gave him her hand.

"I'm here," he said. "A little late, but the train was held up by a broken trestle."

"You are always where you are wanted," Agatha replied, with a touch of color in her face. "One trusts people like that."

Thirlwell said he would get a hack in the square, and Agatha studied him as they drove across the city. Sometimes his face was stern, but for the most part, it wore a look of quiet satisfaction, and once or twice his eyes twinkled, as if he were amused by something.

"It's too bad to hurry you off to an important meeting when you're tired," she said.

Thirlwell laughed. "I expect to hold out until the business is finished. In fact, I'm looking forward to meeting Mr. Stormont."

He had made a long and risky journey over a rough trail and across rotten ice, and after George's messenger found him had pushed on as fast as possible through deep, melting snow, but he did not mean to talk about this. By and by he gave Agatha a humorous account of a small accident at the mine, and she followed his lead. She had felt disturbed and anxious, but now he had come she could smile. For all that she was silent when they drove up a shabby street where the company's office was situated at the top of an old building.

The office had two rooms; one very small, where a wheat-broker had a desk and combined the secretary's duties with his regular business. The other was larger, and when George and Scott went in was occupied by Stormont, Gardner, and two or three other gentlemen. George imagined they had come early to arrange their program.

"You are punctual, but I'm sorry I must ask you to wait," he said. "Miss Strange will not be long and wishes to be present when we begin. She holds the largest block of shares."

"Then I suppose Miss Strange must be indulged; but I don't know that her holding is larger than these gentlemen's and mine," Stormont replied with a meaning smile.

George saw he had been given a hint, but he and the others began to talk good-humoredly. All knew that a struggle was coming, but polite amenities were dignified and marked one's confidence. By and by the door opened and Stormont frowned as Thirlwell came in with Agatha.

"We are glad to see Miss Strange, but Mr. Thirlwell owns none of the company's stock," he said.

Thirlwell smiled, in a rather curious way, but said nothing and Agatha replied: "Mr. Thirlwell is the manager; I asked him to come."

"Then I take back my objection," Stormont said with a bow. "I asked you and Mr. Strange to meet us so that we could talk informally about some business. Although we must call a shareholders' meeting if my suggestions are approved, we hold enough stock between us to force through any decision at which we arrive."

"To begin with, you had better state whose votes you command," said George.

When Stormont gave the names the secretary opened the register and then nodded. "If all who are present and the others Mr. Stormont mentions agree, it would give a larger majority than our constitution requires."

"We'll take it for granted that the gentlemen would vote as Mr. Stormont directs," said George, who looked disturbed. "We wait his proposition."

"My friends and I are dissatisfied with the way things are going. No ore has been smelted; and, so far as we can learn, the quantity in the dump is small. We are working on an unprofitable scale, and need more labor and better and more expensive machines. In short, we need more money. I have no doubt Mr. Thirlwell will admit this."

"A larger capital would be an advantage," Thirlwell assented dryly.

"We can't extend our capital," George objected. "It was hard work to get the stock we have issued taken up."

"I can show you how the difficulty can be got over," Stormont resumed. "You know I floated the Adventurers Company to work the back blocks, and as the claims haven't come up to our expectations, we have more money than we can use, while the Agatha Company has not enough. Well, I propose that you combine with us on the terms I've drafted. If you don't approve them all, we'll meet you where we can."

He gave George a paper, but Agatha interposed: "You can take it for granted that we will not make the combine."

Stormont smiled, deprecatingly. "I'm afraid you cannot help yourselves, Miss Strange."

Agatha looked at George, whose face got red.

"I can understand the Adventurers being anxious to take us in. Your property is worthless, Mr. Stormont, and ours is rich."

"We're willing to pay."

George studied the paper and then threw it down. "You're willing to pay about a quarter of what the mine is worth! After reading that document, it's obvious that you mean to put the screw to us; but we'll fight."

Scott, who glanced at the draft of agreement, nodded, but Stormont said: "You might make some trouble, but must be beaten."

"Why?" Agatha asked.

"I think your brother knows. Each share in your company carries a vote; I hold a large block, and the gentlemen who have promised to support me hold more. If you force us to call a meeting, we will count you out."

"There are some shares in reserve," said Agatha, whose eyes sparkled defiantly.

Stormont smiled. "If you have some rich friends, you might, of course, persuade them to buy the shares and vote for you; but you can't sell them in the ordinary way. I imagine Mr. Strange has tried!"

Agatha saw that George had tried when she glanced at his disturbed face. Then she turned to Thirlwell and noted, with surprise, that he looked amused. She could see nothing in the way matters were going that warranted his humorous twinkle. It looked as if Stormont would win, and she felt that she was being robbed to satisfy his greed; but the mine meant more to her than the money she had expected to get. She had resolved to make it famous as a monument to her father; its success was to prove that his life had not Been wasted in empty dreams.

"Investors are a suspicious lot," Stormont went on. "They don't like to lose their money, and you must admit that there's not much to encourage buyers of your shares to run the risk. The ore is rich, but we are up against obstacles that your manager is obviously unable to remove. In fact, my scheme ought to work out for your benefit."

The sneer at Thirlwell roused Agatha. "The obstacles will not vanish if you get control, and you cannot find a manager who will do as well. Then the scheme will not benefit me; it is meant to benefit nobody but you. If your friends are foolish enough to support it, you will find a way of overreaching them."

George frowned. Agatha's indignation was warranted, but this was not the line to take at a business meeting. Then Gardner looked up, rather sharply, as if the girl's remarks had excited some suspicion that was already in his mind.

"I think you must see that any advantage Mr. Stormont gains will be shared by the rest."

"If you believe this, you are very dull," Agatha replied.

"Anyhow, you'll admit that we are short of money and don't know where to get it, while to combine with the Adventurers would supply the needed capital."

"Yes," said Agatha. "But Mr. Stormont wants to take your shares for much less than they are worth. You can let him have yours, if you like; he shall not get mine!"

"Then you must try to sell them, and you'll find it difficult," Leeson interposed. "If you force us to call a meeting, we can carry our scheme."

"You are all against me!" Agatha exclaimed, looking at the others. "You have let Mr. Stormont cajole you!"

"I don't know that we have been *cajoled*," Leeson answered with a doubtful smile. "In a sense, however, we are against you. We are business men and must protect our interests in the best way we can."

"Trusting Mr. Stormont is not the best way," Agatha rejoined, without regarding Scott's amusement and George's frown.

"I'm afraid we must call the meeting," Gardner broke in. "We hoped you would have met us, Miss Strange, because you are bound to lose when we take a formal vote."

Agatha felt desperate and glanced at Thirlwell; if he could do nothing else, he could sympathize. He gave her an encouraging smile as he got up, for he knew his time had come and had been silent because he wanted to let Stormont reveal his plans. The latter, however, obviously meant to leave the argument to his dupes. Agatha, noting his confidence, remembered that when they reached the office he had asked her to wait a few minutes while he talked to the secretary.

"Mr. Stormont made two rash statements," he said. "He told us the reserved shares could not be sold, and that he could count upon a majority."

"I object to Mr. Thirlwell's speaking," Stormont said with some alarm. "We allowed him to stay at Miss Strange's request, but the manager has no vote."

"I imagine Mr. Stormont doesn't know I am a shareholder. Perhaps the secretary will enlighten him."

Stormont started, Scott smiled, and George looked surprised. The others waited anxiously.

"Mr. Thirlwell holds a quantity of our stock."

"How much?" Stormont asked, and when the secretary told him, struggled to preserve his calm.

"The reserved block is sold," Thirlwell resumed. "I bought the shares half an hour since for myself and a friend of mine." He paused and put a stamped document on the table. "Here's my authority to use the proxy votes."

He sat down and Scott remarked: "I think Mr. Stormont will admit that the majority has, so to speak, changed sides!"

Stormont examined the register, and then stood by his chair with his fist clenched. He said nothing, his supporters looked embarrassed, and Agatha saw that Thirlwell had saved the situation. Her heart beat with confused emotion; she had known he would not fail her.

"Well," said George, rather dryly, "do you still demand a meeting?"

"Certainly not," said Gardner with frank relief, and the others murmured agreement. Then he turned to Agatha: "I'd like you to understand that we took the line we did because it seemed the only plan. Now, however, there's no necessity for making the combine."

Stormont gave him a savage look. "This means that you and the others turn me down?"

"It means that we want to save our money," Gardner replied, and Stormont, who said nothing, walked out of the room.

His friends seemed relieved when he left and began to talk to Agatha and George in apologetic tones. One or two, however, looked thoughtful, and presently Gardner said: "Mr. Thirlwell has removed the obstacle that bothered us most and I mean to keep my stock, although I expect it will be some time before I get a dividend."

"Not as long as you think!" Thirlwell remarked.

"Then you have something to tell us?" said another.

"Not yet; I'll make a full report at the shareholders' meeting. In the meantime, do you think Stormont will sell out?"

"It's possible," said Gardner. "He wanted control. We knew that, but backed him because it seemed the safest plan. I guess he knows he's beaten."

"Then if he offers you his stock, you had better buy," said Thirlwell, smiling.

Gardner looked hard at him, and nodded. "I can take a hint. What you say goes."

After this the party broke up and Scott gently pushed George out when he saw that Agatha was waiting while Thirlwell picked up some papers he had got from the secretary. When the others had gone, she gave him her hand and her face flushed.

"I wonder whether you know how much you have helped?"

Thirlwell kept her hand. "I got some satisfaction from beating your antagonist."

"But you wanted to help me?"

"I did," said Thirlwell, with a steady look. "I was anxious to do something that would make you happy."

Agatha turned her head. "Yet you once refused; the morning after we found the lode—"

"Ah," said Thirlwell, "I fought a pretty hard battle then! But, you see, I was a poor engineer, and you—"

She looked up with a smile and blushed. "Do you think I didn't *know*? But you were foolish; ridiculously stupid!"

Thirlwell took her other hand. "Perhaps I was, but I thought I was right. Things, however, are different now—"

He drew her to him, but she resisted. "Wait! If things had not been different, would your resolution have held out?"

"No," said Thirlwell, "I'm afraid not; I'm not as strong as I imagined."

"Oh!" she said, "perhaps that's the nicest thing I have heard you say! But you really didn't often try to be very nice."

"I was afraid I might say too much if I began."

"No!" she protested, as his grasp got firmer. "There's something else! How long have you really—"

"How long have I wanted you? Well, I think I began to feel the need a day or two after I met you at the summer hotel."

Agatha blushed, but smiled with shining eyes.

"Then if the need hasn't gone, you can take me."

Thirlwell said nothing, but took her in his arms.